The Vultures
and the
Vulnerable

By

Zents Kunle Sowunmi

Books by   ZENTS KUNLE SOWUNMI

- President Obama: Hero or villain of Capitalism?
  - Ogun State Policy of Manipulation.
  - Before the Journey Became Home
    - 100 ways to Laugh
    - Cien Maneras de Reir
  - What happened to Our Democracy?
    - Not a stranger Anymore

Coming soon!!!

- The Loopholes
- The Price of Arab Revolution
  - Unequally Yoking
  - The Covenant Breakers
  - The Beautiful Widow

The Vultures and the Vulnerable

ZENTS KUNLE SOWUNMI

The Political History of Nigeria since 1945
Copyright © 2014 Zents Kunle Sowunmi

Korloki Publishers Inc. is a division of Allzents Group Inc.

Cover Design: Lisa Bracken
Front Cover Images: Yoram Shipere 2008 images Book Front
Cover Picture: Griffon Vulture and
                     Jackal, By Yoram
ShpirerWebsite: shpirery.com/Used with Permission
Interior Design: Korloki Publishers Inc.
Photographs: Courtesy of Google images and friends
Book Reviewer: Professor Ade Oyedijo LASU Nigeria

Sowunmi, Zents
    The Political history of Nigeria since *1945* is probably a
novel coined out of the political history of Nigeria. A
provocative new political history of the most populous black
nation in the South of Sahara and probably the most
interesting political history book since 1945.

ISBN-13   978-1936739172
ISBN-10   1936739178

Printed in the United States of America

Dedicated

To

The victims of the June 12, 1993
Presidential elections in Nigeria.

If any man speaks, let him speak as the oracles of God; if any man ministers, let him do it as of the ability which God giveth: that God in all things may be glorified through Jesus Christ, to who be praised and dominion for ever and ever. Amen.1 Peter 4:11

The vultures and the Vulnerable *have several functions—it can be read for political inspiration and history of Africa's largest democracy, when and how it all started in 1945. It is the history of almost everything that became the problems to the growth of Africa's largest concentration of Black race in the south of Sahara. It is also for readers to develop critical thinking on those accidents of history. Possibly, the country called Nigeria could have done it better; maybe it could have taken a different route than the one we took for almost 54 years as a nation.*

The vultures and the Vulnerable *is an ongoing project book; we encourage readers to send their comments and observations as to the historical contents of this book by email to* <u>kpcbooks@yahoo.com</u> or call 017189510538

CONTENTS

What people said about "The Oracle?"

Appreciation

Foreword, by Dr. Michael "Dr. Biggie" Adeyemi

PART FOUR

PART FIVE

What people said about the Oracle?

The Oracle Zents Sowunmi extended the words of the Bible from speaking to writing for God as the Oracle.

Pastor Tunde Bakare. Latter Rain Church of Assembly Lagos Nigeria

"Every book is a creation which surpasses the life time of the writer; and this is one of them from the Oracle, as an academic, I judge publications by their contents. The proficiency of the author in the literature and social engineering is manifested yet again in this book. Zents is a world-class writer and a pride to our generation. Versatility is his forte I am happy that the journey is gradually returning home."

**Dr. Gbemi Onakoya
Tai Solarin University of Education,
Ijebu Ode, Nigeria**

"Zents Kunle Sowunmi is a master political analyst who knows the heart of Nigerian politics with an experience on how its arteries function. Oracle Zents confidently with the mastery of a genius weaves Nigerian politics like a bird building its nest and compare it to happenings around the globe."

**George Onmonya Daniel Abuja FCT Nigeria
Editor-at-Large, NEW ISSUES magazine,
Abuja, Nigeria**

"When the Oracle speaks from his heart you will know it. But to know how He speaks from within requires knowledge and discernment. The Oracle has spoken. And, His words are poignant for this critical stage in Nigeria history."

Olu' Olaoye, Nigeria

"This piece is indeed very, very interesting. May the Lord enrich you physically, morally and spiritually?"

Lanke Afo, United Kingdom

*"The Oracle discusses issues with the best intentions, especially for our country, Nigeria. This book, **The Political history of Nigeria**, delves into the past political issues with a view to creating sound future political decisions, resulting in alleviating economic conditions of our people regardless of ethnicity."*

Chief Dauda Shokeye Bronx NY USA

*"In the book **The Political history of Nigeria** the Oracle in a lucid but highly intellectual approach delineates the concepts and dynamics of the Nigerian economy and posits that we can still move this nation forward."*

Emmanuel Nwogbo, Lagos, Nigeria

"The Oracle is a writer that will put a smile on you with his sense of humor."

**Prince (Col) Ahmed Zubair,
Abuja Nigeria**

"Going through his books, you cannot but agree that Zents is a prolific writer and a chronicler of social, economic and political events of his time."

**Adebisi Bada,
Abeokuta, Nigeria**

"Oracle is an amazingly talented writer with well thought out opinions on global issues and the knowledge to back them up."

**Moses *Oduntan*
*Dallas, Texas USA***

Well researched, intriguing, it offers much to think about on Nigeria and Africa generally.

Dr. Imoru Igoyega El Paso, Texas

Zents is a prolific writer whose understanding of the Nigerian political development and experience with the U.S. political environment has given him a sound base to interpret events with accuracy. I believe his new book will add value to the political discuss in our country and enrich the knowledge of those that lay their hands on it.

Ibrahim Dan-Halilu Abuja Nigeria

Zents books are provocative with new societal ideas.

Alhaji Ayinde Soaga

General Manager, *OGTV Abeokuta*

APPRECIATION

I would like to acknowledge the contributions of those who faithfully read this publication when it first came out as series of fifteen articles on social media online news media. Your feedback prompted me to research more into areas I originally omitted and some of your concerns made it possible to develop the publication into a chronicle for the coming generation to keep abreast the complicated aspect of our political history.

I will also want to thank Ms. Dee in El Paso, Texas who first read the manuscript and my Editor, Kathleen Tracy in the State of California, Engr. Fola Soboyejo in Canada who also read the edited part of the book with useful suggestions, and Mrs. Adeola Sowunmi for her contributions.

This book has been published seven months earlier to mark the fifty-fourth anniversary of Nigeria's independence from Great Britain in 1960, with the hope; it will give a better understanding of the political details of Africa's largest democracy in the south of the Sahara.

I have to confess, this is the most emotional book I have ever written. It took three years to write it and I am sure you will enjoy reading it, with the hope it will lead to further challenges from readers and those with interest in political history of countries in Africa. **The Vultures and Vulnerable** is an unusual way of reporting the political history of a nation like Nigeria.

This book started more like a story book to the youths in diaspora to enlarge the readership and inculcate the love of Nigeria in all readers with the hope that one day a Messiah will come to straighten up the system. It is not the panacea but a road map towards an egalitarian society, particularly on the recommended five articles in the last few pages of the book. Thank you.

Zents Kunle Sowunmi February, 2014

FOREWORD

Most people rightly say Nigeria is a complex country. Not just because Nigeria is the most populous black country in the world or just because she is a secular multi-ethnic, deeply religious multi religious country, but because of the mutual suspicion and rivalry that exists between the various ethnic, religious, social, and political groups. Attempting to write details of part or all of Nigeria's political history is like attempting to navigate a complex labyrinth filled with many landmines. Just few have been successful with this as many authors have failed in this respect and have been consumed in the quagmire, leaving readers even more confused. It takes a genius to write just a part of Nigeria's political history seamlessly.

This author has not only prevailed where others failed, he has seamlessly rendered almost all of Nigeria's complicated political history from the period of Hubert Macaulay down to the era of the pioneer Premiers - Awolowo, Azikiwe, Balewa and Ahmadu Bello, down through all past leaders to the civilian regime of Olusegun Obasanjo. This versatile and gifted author has written all of that in this book, explaining the peculiarities of each leader and era, as all these too are inter-related.

You need a good knowledge of one to accurately explain the other. He did extensive research, explaining deeply the role of each leader, and telling us the complexities involved, even giving us many details that was hidden to many citizens without attempting to unnecessarily blame or vilify any leader, but explaining the roles each played, even giving the available versions of some accounts, where there are versions, leaving the reader to make up his final judgment. He has done excellently in this area.

I have known this author for over 2 years now and have extensively read his works and articles and I see his passion as a writer who does extensive research on a topic of interest, bringing out the facts and truth forthrightly, without any fear or favor, not caring whose ox is gored, in an attempt to make the reader make his final judgment based on unbiased facts. It just appears as if he is foretelling the future, no wonder he is nicknamed *The Oracle* on social media.

It is a known fact that politicians try to distort history to suit their selfish agenda. By reading this book, one would know the history of Nigerian politics. And as the popular saying goes, *"if you don't know where you are going you should at least know where you are coming from."* As Bob Marley put it in one of his songs, when you know your history, you then know where you are coming from. I'll end it thus. By reading this book, we'll know where we are coming from and if we decide to repeat mistakes, we will know where we are going and reach there no sooner than later.

Dr. Michael "Dr. Biggie" Adeyemi,
A Lagos based Medical doctor,
Writer, author, social affairs analyst &
commentator

Politics is like cholera bacteria that thrives in warm waters and causes diarrhea so severe that it can kill someone within a week.

-David Biella

Part One

The shift of population from subjects to citizens was an index of the shift from a passive society to an active role. A nation is always presented as an active force, as a generative form of social and political relations. In most cases, a nation is often experienced as a collective imagination, an active creation of the community of citizens.

-Benedict Anderson

Meet the Oracle

In the month of January 2009 in Dallas Texas, John was elected the President of the Association of Nigerians in the United States of America, one of his goals was to keep the unity of those in diaspora and bond them with those in his home country. It was a philosophy based on the words of Nigeria's former national anthem: *"Though tribes and tongues may differ in brotherhood we stand."* No matter the politics at home, in a foreign country outside Nigeria they are and will always be brothers and sisters, a bigger family outside the home.

July 28, 2011, was an eventful day for John. It was a very bright morning in Dallas, Texas, in the heart of America, the brightness of the sunshine was promising, the weather was warm and friendly, the traffic was flowing on the beautiful sixteen-lane Highway 635.

What a beautiful day, John thought.

He was approaching U.S. Route 75 and the High Five, an imposing complex five-level interchange and impressive display of technology, in his 2011 black Honda Ridgeline. He loved his truck. Like the slogan said, everything was big in Texas.

He drove pass the imposing Texas Instruments company on the far left, one of the largest corporations in the State. Its computer chips were the breakthrough into twenty-first century computer industry for the whole world.

What a feat, he thought.

Glancing at the magnificent Texas Instruments Corporate Head office, to the users of Highway 635, the gigantic road leading to Dallas-Fort Worth Airport, everything seems to be fine but it was not.

Something was missing, yet John could not lay his hand on it. John was thinking about his eighteen years in America. He was worried about the future of the children his generation brought out of Nigeria to the United States.

At first, it was a relief to escape from the home country and the stress the military government imposed on Nigeria like bad gas in the 1990s by the dictator Gen. Sanni Abacha. But the joy had since been replaced with despair. Most of the children of his peers from Africa did not want to think or know how the history of Nigeria, the birth place of their parents, could affect their future. It was the same problem for all Africans of his generation after several decades in the United States.

Apart from video games and computers or IPods or texting each other, nothing matters to these children. What will be the future of African history to this generation? They called it the period of no eye contact; as long as their radial nerve effectively controlled their thumbs and a working index finger so they could text and play with their phones, they couldn't care less. He wondered. He had to see his friend Femi on what to do, but Femi lived in Houston, about a four-hour drive from Dallas. The last time he visited Femi was about four years ago. Everything had been reduced to telephone and texting now; it saved money but the personal touch was gradually reducing social connections of the society.

The only major road to Houston was through InterState-45. However, the police had been too tough on him. The last time he traveled to Houston, and he was slammed with almost $300 fine for a mere traffic offense. It took him a good payment plan to get over it and his insurance premium went up because he could not attend the defensive driver's class, which his lawyer recommended.

John and Femi had been friends since High school back in the days in Ibadan. As fate would have it, they went to the University of Ibadan together, and both did the National Youth Service program in Kano State in the 1980s. And when they were lucky to win the immigration lottery to travel out of the country in 1992 to the United States, both concluded they were tied together by fate.

They sold everything they had to bring their families to the United States of America; however, it was difficult for them to sell away the love of the country they left behind in their hearts. They were disturbed over what Professor Fashola went through after twenty-six years in America. He was so excited about his heritage when he took his three sons, who were in their twenties to Ado Ekiti in Nigeria, he was almost to the point of tears when he narrated his story to the, *"The Association,"* in the last meeting.

The Professor showed his boys all his ancestry and heritage from a generation spanning over 250 years and his position as the head of the Fashola family, the first warrior from Ado, with all the glories and conquests of years preceding the colonization of Nigeria. He got the shock of his life when with a wave of hand, his boys dismissed his ancestry as nothing but primitive exuberance; they told him all they wanted was to just be Americans, nothing more. He knew he had lost everything to a country with just fifty years of freedom to the African Americans, if his boys would not return to the land of his ancestors, they never mentioned it again.

What would he tell his forefathers in the world beyond? He could not imagine the look of disgust and the letdown his late father would give him in the midst of all his other ancestors, maybe the great Fashola will spank him on the head for failing Oduduwa, the progenitor of his Yoruba tribe. Something must be done.

John got home after a ten-hour shift at a local hospital as a pharmacist. He worked so hard to support his family. His wife Bola, a registered nurse, also put in her efforts and the couple's income gave them a very good middle class life in the United States. He discussed details of his concern with Bola, who was not totally excited about the family returning to Africa.

Furthermore, several years in America had exposed her to the extended freedom women have there, the years of subservience to the extended family issues back home was history for her. She could not be compelled to respect her brother in-laws in the way African culture prescribed by history and tradition.

However, with all cleverness and calculated purposes, Bola had selected the friends and families she wanted her husband to associate with. It was the politics of marital life she had learnt from her mother. But she could do nothing to influence the executives of the Association of Nigerians in the United States of America, which had elected her husband as President. All contenders stepped down for him and there was nothing she could do as he got deeper and deeper into his job as President of the association and Bola's fear of relocating back to the motherland in Africa was becoming real.

Initially, Bola did not comment on the anxieties of her husband over Nigerian issues; her joy would always be where her children were, not the primitive location in the heart of Mokoloki village in Owode local government of Ogun State in Nigeria, which her husband talked about every day. She had enjoyed his company alone excluding the interference of any African tradition. He was a perfect husband, and he helped with the cleaning and some kitchen jobs in the last twenty-four years, all of which were alien to their culture in Africa. She was still beautiful and John had always been careful to keep the fragrance of their romance alive and fresh, every other week he gave her flowers and dinners in Dallas' finest restaurants.

She had asked him to include swimming in their activities but he had refused.

"Black men don't swim," he informed her.

She wished she could wear her bikini like most African Americans and Caucasian ladies in Lewisville, Texas, by the lake in hot summer time. She also watched everything about women on television, from Oprah Winfrey to Jerry Springer and every day she convinced herself going back to Africa was not going to be in her future.

At fifty-five years of age, her husband was still a handsome man with lots of drive. Bola noticed women still looked at him when they were out together. But his hair was turning grey and like an unwanted visitor, she could see age was no longer on his side, both of them were graciously aging, and she dreaded the relocation to Nigeria John talked about.

Bola hoped John would lose interest in his relocation to Africa dreams after the death of his mother but her mother-in-law never stopped taking her supplements and still looked strong and healthy to the surprise of everyone.

I wish she could die, Bola thought, but then she quickly dismissed the ugly thought. She remembered how the old lady stood with them like the Rock of Gibraltar, when things were rough early in their married life. The rest of the family thought she brought bad legs into the family but the old lady assured them her son had made the right choice of a life partner. That was twenty-four years ago.

Bola rolled to the right side on the bed and felt a sharp pain in her shoulder, which the doctor said was as a result of her posture tilting to the right side most of the time. She watched John breathe heavily away into the nights; she was still looking at him with a hanging smile on her lips when she slept off peacefully herself. She dreamt of social parties in Africa right in the heart of Mokoloki village in Ogun State and her in-laws telling her it was time to send food to the neighbors and John was smiling mischievously because he knew how she felt.

Dan Mohammed was a Fulani from Nigeria; he was six feet tall with a lean look, and the rugged determination of a bull. He was a board certified medical doctor in the State of Kansas and the General Secretary of the Association of Nigerians in America. Despite his distance from Nigeria, he loved to read the history of his country and the might of the defunct Sokoto Caliphate led by Othman Dan Fodio in 1865 who left Gobir after Yunfa asked him to leave his Kingdom. Mohammed never stopped wondering what his heritage would have been if the Caliphate had not been destroyed in 1903 by the British.

Maybe the culture of his people would have been better preserved if the British had not cleverly brought in their so-called western civilization to his people, and sometimes he wondered if the future would be fine for the generation yet to come. He never stopped thinking of how the values of his people were gradually being wiped away by the events around him. The new generation had no respect for elders anymore. He was determined to redirect the lives of his own children to reflect the culture and tradition of his people. He could still remember when he became a United States citizen in Dallas, Texas, and they were told never to allow the values of American society to take away their culture.

Dan had read one of the articles of the Oracle in a local Library titled *"The Clash of Civilizations vs. West African Values."* He had lots of questions to ask the writer. He was pleased the writer was also a Nigerian and was surprised his friend John in Dallas' had read the same article. They planned to invite the Oracle to tell their children the history of Nigeria from 1945.

Surprisingly, it was also the decision of the Association at the last meeting that Oracle would be invited to tell the Nigerian children in the United States the true story of Nigeria; to allow the Oracle tell it as it was to the children in diaspora, how the country had performed politically in the last sixty-eight years.

Interestingly, the Oracle wrote back with instructions. Before the seminar, all participants were to read the printed history of the five noticeable players and founding fathers who were the event movers and shakers of the years before the independence of the country in 1960: Herbert Macaulay, Dr. Nnamdi Azikiwe, Chief Obafemi Awolowo, Sir Ahmadu Bello who was the Sardauna of Sokoto, and Alhaji Tafawa Balewa the first Prime Minister of Nigeria among few others.

Furthermore, the Oracle sent copies of the various articles on these players with references from Wikipedia, journals and books on various topics, and Association members were wondering if he had anything else to teach the children, but they were wrong!

Surprisingly, the children of all the members had been excited; they also invited their friends from other nations and the African Americans yearning to know more on African history. They read voraciously the stories about Herbert Macaulay and the politics that ensued after his death in 1946, and they were surprised at the turn of events on the roles played by the three emerging founding fathers of the country: Dr. Nnamdi Azikiwe, who later became Nigeria's first President from a parliamentary type of government in 1960; Chief Obafemi Awolowo who founded the Action Group (AG) Party and later became the Leader of Opposition despite his political party's active role in asking the British for a date on the independence of the country; and Ahmadu Bello, the Sardauna of Sokoto who had the opportunity of being the first Prime Minister of Nigeria but he allowed one of his surrogates Alhaji Tafawa Balewa to take his place.

They were astonished with the role of the British before the Independence in 1960 and could not wait for the Oracle to tell it as it was for them and answer various questions bothering them. They prepared their notes and the date was set for long term vacation in the month of July.

Founding Leaders / Fathers of Nigeria
1914-1960

- ❖   Frederick Lord Luggard

- ❖   Herbert Macaulay

- ❖   Dr. Nnamdi Azikiwe

- ❖   Chief Obafemi Awolowo

- ❖   Abubarkar Bello Sardauna of Sokoto

- ❖   Chief Samuel Ladoke Akintola

- ❖   Chief Anthony Enahoro

- ❖   Joseph Tarka

- ❖   Mallam Aminu Kano

Fredrick Lord Luggard
1858-1946

First Governor General of a British Colonized Nigeria in 1914-1918. Known as Sir Frederick Luggard between 1901 and 1928 was a British soldier, mercenary, explorer of Africa and colonial administrator, who was Governor of Hong Kong (1907–1912) and Governor-General of Nigeria (1914–1919).

Fred Luggard later in life believed in all he stood against on education and Banking. He said Colonization was to spread Christianity and to end Barbarism in Africa. The founder of West African Frontier force that later became Nigeria Army. His achievement in Colonization was more than Nigeria, but all over Africa and Asia.

His wife Flora Shaw was a writer and a journalist for the "Times" who wrote untruthful stories that led to many problems including South Africa. In 1897 her article led to the name of Nigeria as a people around River Niger area, which was formerly called Royal Niger Company Territories

The marriage produced no children. She died in 1928.

Ref. Wikipedia.org

Herbert Macaulay
November 14, 1864 - May 7, 1946

Herbert Samuel Heelas Macaulay was a Nigerian nationalist, politician, engineer, journalist, and musician and considered by many Nigerians as the founder of Nigerian nationalism. He was a grandson of Bishop Ajai Crowder, a creole and Saaro in West Africa.

Dr. Nnamdi Azikiwe

The first post-independence President of Nigeria 1960-1966 and Leader of NCNC after Herbert Macaulay, his tenure as a parliamentary Ceremonial President had no serious control of the power around imposing Sardauna of Sokoto. He escaped the 1966 Coup on what analyst thought was a planned action of the coup plotters because of his tribe. He died in May 1996.

Chief Obafemi Awolowo
Died 1987

Awolowo was the first Premier of Western Region, and first leader of Opposition of the Federal Parliament, a man whose political party AG demanded for the independence of Nigeria from the British Government later in life, his ideas and policies would be the foundation for Nigeria progressive democratic values of the centuries to come.

Awolowo's imprisonment on charges of treasonable felony saved him from the 1966 bloody military coup unlike his very unfortunate colleagues.

Ahmadu Bello Sardauna of Sokoto

A descendant of Othman Dan Fodio of defunct Sokoto Caliphate, his surrogate Tafawa Balewa became the first Prime Minster of Nigeria, in reality the Prime Minister reported to him, thereby making him the Head of Nigeria Government by default. Sardauna of Sokoto was killed in 1966 in a coup led by Major Kaduna Nzeogu.

Tafawa Balewa

A surrogate of the Sardauna of Sokoto and a man with the golden voice, he was the Prime Minister from 1960 to 1966. Balewa was killed in 1966 first military coup led by Majors Kaduna Nzeogu, Emmanuel Ifeajuna, and Adewale Ademoyega.

Samuel Ladoke Akintola
2nd Premier of Western Region 1959-1966
Nigeria first and the last Prime Minister
Killed in 1966

As a representative of Action Group Party in National Assembly, he moved the first motion for the independence of Nigeria. The motion was shot down for various political reasons most likely for the unpreparedness of the North for the independence of Nigeria. Ladoke Akintola was the second Premier of Western Region. SLA was voted out of office but refused to vacate office. He was killed in 1966 military coup led by Major Nzeogu.

Hon. Joseph Tarka

He was the acclaimed leader of the Middle Belt for many decades, with active cooperation with the values of the Action group from the West of Nigeria.

He later became the Federal Commissioner of Communication in the General Gowon Regime in the seventies. Joseph Tarka was cleared of corruption by General Gowon on what became a national scandal led by Godwin Daboh.

Mallam Aminu Kano

A Muslim progressive political leader of the Talakawa or the poor from the Ancient City of Kano, he was the leader of PRP in the seventies and UMK in the sixties. A very honest politician, he died in April 1983. He organized established purposeful koranic schools in the North of Nigeria.

A popular and honest progressive icon called Seriki Tsusu (Leader of the flocks)

Zik, Sardauna and Awolowo

The three acknowledged founding fathers of Federal Republic of Nigeria

Part Two

Post First Republic players
1966-2014

Major General Aguiyi Ironsi

General Yakubu Gowon

General Muritala Mohamed

General Olusegun Obasanjo

President Sheu Shagari

General Mohamadu Buhari

Gen. Ibrahim Babangida

Chief Ernest Shonekan

General Sanni Abacha

General Abdul Salam

President Olusegun Obasanjo

President Yar'Adua

President Goodluck Ebele Azikiwe Jonathan

Some are gifted to see and write about the future but most people are not gifted to listen even when they read or hear, and until we can reconcile the two, the world will still not be at peace.

~ ORACLE

Until the era of the three great bourgeois revolutions (the English, the Americans, and the French) there was no political alternative that could successfully oppose this model of the absolutists and patrimonial model, which survived only with the language of force.

~**Empire by Michael**

Major Kaduna Nzeogu   *Major Emmanuel Ifejuana*

NO PICTURE AVAILABLE
For
Major Adewale Ademoyega

The three leaders of the first coup that changed the dreams of Nigeria as a peaceful nation they killed leaders of the first Republic, a mission that changed the political history of Nigeria and which then led to a twenty-seven month civil war in which almost two million Nigerians died. Nzeogu died serving with the Biafra Army in a secession effort against the Federal Republic of Nigeria.

Major Gen. Aguiyi Ironsi

First Military Head of State
2ⁿᵈ Head of Government of Nigeria
Jan 1966 - August 1966

As the most senior officer, he became the Head of State from a coup he had nothing to do with. He was a victim of the failure of the executioners of the plot that favored his Igbo tribe. He was killed in 1966 by Major Theophilus Yakubu Danjuma and Lt. Jeremiah Usenni in Ibadan in the present Oyo State along with his host Lt. Col Adekunle Fajuyi which could be classified as a revenged coup by the North of Nigeria.

Gen. Yakubu Gowon
Military Head of State
3rd Head of Government 1966-1975

Yakubu Gowon at the age of 32 was the Chief of Staff Army of Nigeria Army, who took over after Gen. Ironsi was killed. He fought a twenty-seven months civil war to keep Nigeria united from the insurgence led by Col. Odumegwu Emeka Ojukwu. Gen. Gowon was removed in 1975 and in 1997 he tried to come back and lost in the primaries of his ward. Gen. Gowon was a minority from the Middle Belt of the North of Nigeria.

Major Gen. Jeremiah Usenni

Lt. Gen Danjuma

Major Gen. Sheu Yar Adua

Chief of Staff

Supreme Headquarters

The trio above saw the second coup more of a revenge coup by the North against the East of Nigeria.

Gen. Muritala Mohammed
4th Head of State 1975-1976

A veteran of Nigeria Civil war, and Federal Commissioner for Communication, he became the Head of State in 1975. Mohammed hailed from the City of Kano. His foreign and domestic policies reshaped Nigeria. He introduced executive presidency into the body politic of Nigeria. He was killed in an abortive military coup de tat led by Col. Buka Suka Dimka in 1976.

Gen. Olusegun Obasanjo
5th Head of State 1976-1979

A veteran of wars in Congo in Central Africa, Obasanjo led the third Marine Commando of Nigeria Army; the Biafra he successfully battled surrendered to him in 1970, which ended the twenty-seven month civil war. He handed over government to President Shagari in a controversial election in 1979. He carried out faithfully all the domestic and foreign policies of General Muritala Mohamed. General Obasanjo hailed from Abeokuta in Ogun State.

Alhaji Sheu Shagari
First Executive President of Nigeria 1979-1983
6th Head of Government in Nigeria

President Sheu Shagari was perhaps the laziest President ever to preside over a large and complex country like Nigeria. His government was corrupt. Critics like General Gowon, his former boss said, the only thing Shagari could do without help was to light his cigarette. Surprisingly, in his third year in office it was the assignment he gave to his political adviser, Dr. Chuba Okadigbo. When Shagari was asked by General Buhari's probe panel, which investigated his government after he was toppled, on what he was doing when criminals were sharing money in his office, Shagari said he was praying.

Gen. Mohamadu Buhari
7th Head of State 1983-1985

Gen. Buhari toppled the civilian government of President Sheu Shagari in 1983 and his military government suspended the 1979 constitution. Most of the politicians were jailed for corruption and abuse of office. He was noted for his war against indiscipline.

Gen. Buhari was probably the most untainted Nigerian leader since 1960, except for looking the other way when the 52 suitcases of Nigeria currency notes were caught in illegal possession of the Emir of Gwandu who smuggled the from overseas.

Gen. Tunde Idiagbon
Chief of Staff Supreme Headquarters 1942-1999

Gen. Tunde Idiagbon was the favorite of those who believed Nigeria should be ruled with iron hands, with no respect for human rights, a crusader, he vigorously waged the war against In disciple (WAI) He was however, caught in his double standard; he took his underage son on a pilgrimage to Mecca after it was banned by the Federal Military government.

He made the infamous Statement of any government against Press freedom: "If the truth will embarrass the government it must not be published" General Idiagbon died of food poisoning on March 24th 1999.

Fela Afro beat King was jailed by Gen. Buhari's government for money laundering because he failed to declare his money at Lagos Airport. He never believed in banking. He kept all his money in his pocket most of the time, he had a bitter history of confrontations with almost all the military governments of Nigeria. He however, refused to participate in 1977 FESTAC, his music was revolutionary. He was a defender of the poor and black race. Like his mother, Fela was the darling of those against the military government in Nigeria. Some of his popular LP's *included Zombie, Mr. Follow Follow, Gentleman, Shakara, and Casket for the Government, VIP, Sorrow Tears and Blood* among others. Fela hailed from Abeokuta in Ogun State.

President Gen. Ibrahim Babangida
8th Head of Government

Self-proclaimed Military President and fondly called evil genius or IBB, he claimed to have been involved in most of the military coups in and out of Nigeria. He annulled the freest election in Nigeria and left a baggage of unending political problems for the nation. He was forced to step aside after 1993 Presidential election. General Babangida hailed from Minna in Niger State of Nigeria.

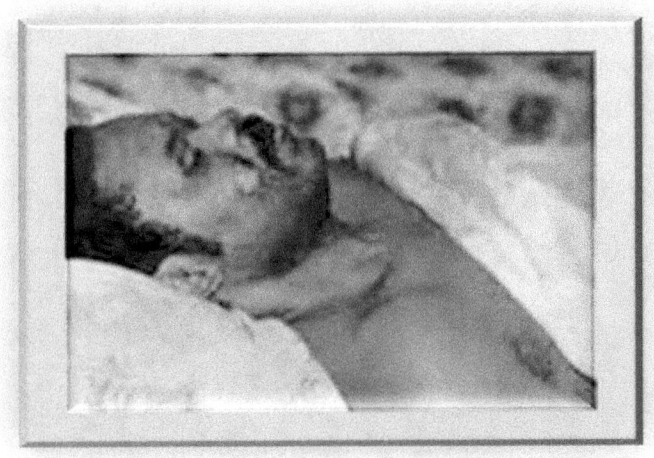

Late Dele Giwa
Pioneer Editor-in-Chief Newswatch Magazine

Probably Nigeria most celebrated investigative journalist. He was parcel-bombed in 1986 at the time General Ibrahim Babangida was military President of Nigeria. Every effort to prosecute those security agents was impeded by the government, which placed a question mark on the activity and involvement of the government on his death. Giwa was the pioneer Editor–in-Chief of Newswatch Lagos.

Late Chief Gani Fawehinmi SAN
1945-2009

Gani was one of the most respected lawyers in Nigeria. He was Dele Giwa's attorney but was prevented by the government from prosecuting the killers of his client. Gani was probably one of the Lawyers that kept the courts busy with so many human rights and abuse of power litigations. He ran for the office of President of Nigeria but gathered insignificant votes unable to match his popularity.

Gani died of cancer September 5, 2009.

Prof. Humphrey Nwosu

Prof. Nwosu oversaw the June 12, 1993, election, considered the freest and fairest election to date, in which Chief Moshood Abiola was presumed to have won. The Electoral body on his watch introduced the novel Option A4 voting system and the Open Ballot System. Nwosu had released the result from 14 States before he was ordered to stop further announcement by the military regime led by evil genius General Ibrahim Babangida.

Chief Ernest Shonekan
9th Interim Head of State of Nigeria (84 days)

Head of Interim Government for eighty-four days before the Abacha military coup. He was the first Head of State to be sworn into Office in Abuja. To most Nigerians, his government was illegitimate and was never respected. Chief Ernest Shonekan was a respectable former Chief Executive of UAC. He hailed from Abeokuta in Ogun State.

Late Chief Moshood Abiola
1937-2008 (60 yrs.)
Winner of 1993 Presidential election in Nigeria

The winner of the 1993 Presidential election in Nigeria, Abiola was jailed by Gen. Sanni Abacha for treason when he declared himself President. MKO Abiola died mysteriously in 1998 in the presence of American representatives Susan Rice and Ambassador Thomas R. Pickering while drinking tea; at the time President Clinton was in office. His death came like thunderbolt to all.

MKO Abiola was believed to have been killed to appease the military, and the North of Nigeria, for a President from the South they could trust, June 12, the day of the election for 1993 has since been adopted as Democracy Day in Southwest of Nigeria.

Alhaja Kudirat Abiola
Killed June 1996

The wife of MKO Abiola the winner of June 12, 1993 Presidential election in Nigeria, she was murdered in Lagos by a government-sponsored killing squad to destroy the actualization of the June 12, 1993 election. A radio station was established in her honor and a street in front of Nigerian Consulate office in New York, USA was named after her.

In retaliation, Gen. Sanni Abacha named Eleke Crescent, where the United States Consulate is situated in Lagos, Louis Farrakhan Street, to taunt the American government.

Gen. Sanni Abacha
10th Military Head of State 1993-1997

General Sanni Abacha, a professional coup plotter, a ruthless General, and a dictator of the worst order in the history of Nigeria Army, he destroyed the myth around the Sokoto Caliphate. He partitioned the country into six zones for administrative purposes and to weaken the oppositions and his administration. His government executed Ken Saaro Wiwa of the Ogonis tribe a playwright, professor and environment activist and a critic of military government.

Abacha jailed MKO Abiola, the winner of 1993 Presidential election and other critics of his government. He siphoned the treasury for his Swiss banks accounts. Many Nigerians went on exile. However, his five years in office reduced an inflation rate of 54% inherited from Ibrahim Badamosi Babangida to 8.5% between 1993 and 1998. To all Nigerians his period was a nightmare.

Gen. Abdul-Salam Abubarkar
11th Head of State 1998-1999

General Abdul-Salam Abubarkar handed over to a civilian government led by his former boss in the Army General Obasanjo. MKO Abiola the winner of June 12, 1993 elections died under his watch in a mischievous manner in the presence of United States Representatives Susan Rice and Ambassador Thomas R. Pickering. At the time, MKO Abiola security personnel were strangely and suspiciously changed. Surprisingly, when he left office, the foreign reserve disappeared in a very suspicious way. It was during Abubakar's leadership that Nigeria adopted its new constitution on May 5, 1999, which provided for multiparty elections. Abubakar transferred power to president-elect Olusegun Obasanjo on May 29, 1999.

President Olusegun Aremu Obasanjo
Nigeria 12th Head of Government
1999-2007

President Obasanjo met an empty treasury in his second coming to the office as the President of Nigeria. He also met a politicized Army, a very corrupt society, and a nation no country wanted to trust for anything in and out of Africa. General Obasanjo reorganized the Army, and created EFCC to fight corruption. His government made use of season technocrats, which made his government one of the best in the 54 years history of the country. He wiped away the national debt. His third term ambition was rejected by the National Assembly. Perhaps Gen. Obasanjo in future would probably be known as the Mandela of Nigeria or Africa for his contributions to freedom of former colonies in African like Congo, Zimbabwe, Namibia, Cape Verde,

Genuine Bissau South Africa and Mozambique and world, the Oracle says perhaps

Late President Sheu Yar'Adua
Nigeria 13th Head of Government
2007-2009

President Yar'Adua solved the Niger Delta crises with amnesty. His removal of the EFCC Chairman destroyed the fight against corruption. He was sick for a long time; he refused to hand over to his Deputy as required by the Constitution. Far away in a foreign land on hospital bed, he was assumed to have fraudulently signed the Supplementary Budget. He died in office of cardiac related disease, in 2009, which became a political problem for his political base to accept the reality of power transfer to his Vice President. It was an embarrassment to the country on how to convince the North of Nigeria of the simple letters of the Constitution on succession.

President Goodluck Jonathan
Nigeria 14th Head of Government since 2009

The most criticized President in the history of Nigeria. He was noted for his shoeless story and resource control hat. He signed the Freedom of Information Bill but failed to declare his assets in his capacity as President. He claimed the asset declaration as vice President should be fine.

President Jonathan's government faced lots of attack from an Islamism terrorist group called Boko Haram from the North East of Nigeria. He created Alimonjiri Schools to help the North. Under his

watch most criminals were granted pardon including
the former governor of his home State. He was the
first President from oil producing State in Nigeria.
His political base the South South and South East of
Nigeria could not stand critics of his administration.

Prof. Attahiru Jega
Chairman of INEC 2011 to date

Prof. Attahiru Jega's appointment was hailed
by all Nigerians and the international community. A
former activist of the ASUU and political scientist
from the North, he was probably the first
Northerner to Head any Nigeria electoral
commission since independence in 1960. He was

determined to reduce the political parties from 65 to a manageable number of three or five, which led to many mergers in the country.

He introduced trail blazing system and picture ID for voter registration, which drastically reduced ballot rigging by illegal voters across the nation, but the award of more polling stations to the North his region drew attention from his critics.

Part Three

DNA is like God: It is everywhere.

~ Oracle

INTRODUCTION

When a nation obtained freedom without shedding blood, there will be a tendency for mismanagement of the end result of the so-called freedom. The political history and governments of Nigeria since 1945 is full of amazing negative revelations, which seem to have no end. It is more like a continuous soap opera on the television, and it goes on and on.

You wonder if it was even real or not. Politicians stole recklessly from the government treasury, as if there was no tomorrow, and the court system and constitution were used to pervert justice through endless adjournments and immunity. The legal system was used to let financial criminals walk away from justice. They killed each other over religion and when you looked at everything, when you take the time to read the Quran or the Bible, you wonder if it was in the name of God or the devil himself. Nevertheless, just like the pages of a book, they flipped on and on to the next pages in their daily activities without caring. It was sad.

They turned their eyes away from positive developments around them. When they were reminded of the benefits of good governance like other nations based on fairness, Justice, respect for human dignity, establishment of State and city police for internal security, and a mayoral system of administration for all the cities to get the nation out of dark minds and ideas, they said it could not work in Nigeria. They used conservative religious doctrines to perpetuate hate crimes. They closed their eyes to all the commandments of the holy books despite their proclaimed love for the Church and Mosques. They celebrated laziness and corruption. They picked and chose on what they wanted to do. In most cases, they selected those that made the country move backward as leaders in the twenty-first century.

Nigeria may end up being the only nation that keeps on using the same old tools to fight corruption through centralization of the Federal police system. They still rely on one man, the Inspector General of Police, to fight crimes, a system they inherited from the British. They believed it could help solve crimes in every part of the country, a society of almost 225 tribes dynamically changing with the twenty-first century tools. When that same Inspector General of Police could lock a state governor out of his office and could chase the President of the Senate to his village, or withdraw the security network around a state Governor, you wonder if it was real or just the imagination of a writer. It was real, the story of Nigeria and the lesson of history.

What an irony.

In the last fifty-three years, Nigerians have gone through lots of problems. They fought a twenty-seven months civil war which ended in 1970. The government claimed more than two million people died when they had no statistics to support the figures. They probably made it up; it could even be more. They called it a war between the Christians and Muslims but it was more than that, it was a war based on greed, corruption and absolute power grab. They had written and set aside four constitutions. They changed government with military coups or recycled it among the same political class since 1960.

They forgot the terrorist group called Boko Haram was a development of social economic disparity and disadvantages in education and wanton stealing without equal opportunities. The Oracle said it was probably the last foot soldiers of the Caliphate and Bornu Empires, the heartbeat of the foundations of Islam in West Africa, which the clashes of civilization in the twenty-first century revealed. But as crises were becoming the instrument for change, the youths deprived of the benefits of citizenship and good governance and unending unemployment, lack of electricity, water and a shrinking atmosphere of opportunities, began to question the Amalgamation of 1914 of the North and South of Nigeria, what could be done.

It was almost getting to that level when those with good intentions will give up on the activities of daily living that were recklessly consuming the lives of more than 160 million blacks in South of Sahara. Sooner or later from a bird's eye view, the fire and the flame of these inequalities will be seen from a reasonable distance, and all the birds will flee the nest.

What a people! And what a society!

Zents Kunle Sowunmi (ORACLE)
Brooklyn, New York USA

Politicians and diapers have one thing in common. They should be changed regularly and for the same reason.
~ Author unknown

1

How It All Started

The two Igbo words Oriaku and Okpataku came from one of the books the Oracle's generation read in the seventies: *Toads for Supper* by Professor Chukwu Emeka Ike, who later in life worked as the Registrar for the West African Examination Council in Lagos. Reading in those days was what most of us enjoyed.

It was not uncommon for most of our generation before the age of 16 years to have read all the books by Nigerian writers. Like books by the first African Nobel Prize winner Wole Soyinka, late Chinua Achebe, who was Nigeria's most celebrated author of the books during our time, *Things Fall Apart* (1958) and *Arrow of God* (1964); T.M. Aluko of *One Man One Matchet* fame (1964), the late Ola Rotimi noted for his play book, *The Gods are Not to Blame* (1971) and a host of others in Africa like James Nguigi of *Weep Not Child* (1964) and Camera Laye of Guinea *The Africa Child* (1953).

However, when the recent events of body politics in Nigeria started growing in a way that beclouds the dreams of our generation and the future of Nigeria youths, this writer fondly called Oracle, could not think of a better title for these sequences, which eventually became this book, than to borrow from Professor Vincent Chukwu Emeka Ike's *Toads for Supper* and (1965) *The Naked Gods* (1970). His books were almost at par in African culture with *No Longer at Ease* (1960), which was a follow up to *Things Fall Apart* by Chinua Achebe in those days.

Oriaku is a vulture; it is a consumer of other people's wealth, while Okpataku means the producer of the wealth. In the book *Toads for Supper* Professor Ike likened women as eaters of other people's means of livelihood, though it is not politically correct to classify women in this category in the twenty-first century, depending on which side of history one tends to look at. To classify Nigerian politicians as Oriaku and Okpataku for the sake of seeing the nature of human behavior to public trust, which the Oracle in previous political contribution classified as Angels and Demons of Nigerian politics, using proper African words of Igbo origin like Oriaku and Okpataku, this writer believes, will drive home the points more than the use of angels and demons. What we have here is more than just a story; it was, and probably still is, the way of life in Africa south of Sahara.

However, one is bound to ask how will this analysis apply to Nigeria as an entity alone? If we can take a scissors-like view on the activities of those who had the opportunity to direct the affairs of the largest concentration of the black race on earth, how and why they failed or succeeded from 1945 or 1960 will be explained, as well as all the events that led to the independence of Nigeria from the British government, particularly on how greed and corruption finally became the problem for the young nation in 1960.

Furthermore, Herbert Macaulay (1946) the grandson of Bishop Ajai Crowder (1891), whose photograph is on one of Nigeria's currency denominations will be the starting point of this analysis.

The foundation for the nation's political structure was unitary in nature. Macaulay, a man whose background could be traced to the Creoles or Saaro from Sierra Leone and Lagos in Nigeria, was also the grandson of the first African Bishop, Ajai Crowder, who translated the Bible into three Nigerian local languages. Samuel Ajai Crowder was among the last batch of the slaves freed in the 1830's and who became a missionary. His zeal for freedom probably rubbed off on his grandson Herbert, who saw the freedom of his colonized country as ultimate.

Northern Nigeria was a British protectorate from 1900 until 1914 in the present country of Nigeria. The protectorate included the pre-colonial States of the Sokoto Caliphate, the Bornu Empire, and the Kano Emirate. The first High Commissioner of the protectorate was Frederick Luggard, who created a system of administration built around native authorities.

Southern Nigeria was a British protectorate in the coastal areas of modern-day Nigeria, formed in 1900 from union of the Niger Coast Protectorate with territories below Lokoja on the Niger River. On the recommendation of Luggard Southern and Northern Nigeria were unified in 1914.

Macaulay passionately wanted to see his people out of the control of the British Empire. Along with Dr. Nnamdi Azikiwe, he formed the National Council of Nigeria and the Cameroons (NCNC), a Nigerian political party from 1944 to 1966. (Cameroon was included because it had become an administrative part of Nigeria in 1945, after Germany lost it to Britain and France after the Second World War. Herbert Macaulay was its first President, while Dr. Nnamdi Azikiwe (1936) was its first secretary.

Macaulay died in 1946, and his political party faced internal upheaval from the group led by Chief Obafemi Jeremiah Awolowo. The turmoil led to the emergence of other political parties in Nigeria.

In the West of Nigeria, Action Group emerged on March 21, 1951, after Chief Awolowo returned from the United Kingdom with a law degree to challenge the legitimacy of the NCNC, which was more of Lagos Colony Party, and East of Nigeria, with some tentacles of political Octopus around Nigeria.

In the North of Nigeria was the Northern People's Congress (NPC) led by Sir Ahmadu Bello and a host of other parties led by late Mallam Amino Kano (1983) who led Northern Elements Progressive Union (NEPU), and later in life PRP. Late Senator Joseph Tarka (1980) led United Middle

Belt Congress into alliance with the Action Group of the western Nigeria in 1958.

However, the Action Group was a political party in the West of Nigeria. It was a more purposeful and determined radical group than others, meaning, Chief Obafemi Awolowo became the first serious political radical that changed the face of Nigerian politics. What was closer to his radical leadership was Mallam Aminu Kano's group from the heart of Hausa Fulani group and Joseph Tarka of the United Middle Belt. They never had the political control of governance like Chief Obafemi Awolowo. These three groups would in the future be the foundation and the face of the progressives in Nigeria's political system.

What the United Kingdom saw as a challenge or the fear of a loss of control of a post-independence Nigeria, was indeed the future of a possible government of a new country under the Action Group, which might not be in the interest of Her Majesty, the Queen of England. It must be stopped.

Somehow, the United Kingdom played on the ignorance of the political parties of the time to destroy the unity of the tribes through divide and rule and misinformation strategies. This turned the fragile unity within the 225 tribes of a colonized Nigeria against one other, meaning, those who labored in truth and demanded freedom of the country from the British were those sidelined by the system the British foisted on the nation in 1960.

The nation's foundation at independence was based on deceit without clear-cut goals. Liars, backbiters, and those who danced to the diabolical plans of the British were those given the flag of independence on October 1, 1960, not those who asked for it.

It was a sad beginning for the young nation.

When one gets to a position of authority by deceit instead of planning or labor for its growth, it is not unexpected to see failure as the option instead of success. Such was the fate of Nigeria, those who became Nigeria leaders in October 1960 lacked foresight or purposeful leadership on how to direct the ship of the new nation. Instead, they went for the destruction of the Action Group party, because the foundation of economic growth of Western Region under Awolowo as Premier made a mockery of the Federal government's economic plans.

Instead of building, they were pulling down the ship of a new nation and political independence meant nothing to them. Sadly, the foundation inherited in 1960, was more like dog-eat-dog strategies, a ruthless mindset in which causing harm to others was an acceptable means to achieve a goal.

The Oracle once wrote in 1993 that when a political party wins an election, it must learn to be humble and magnanimous in success, and it must demonstrate the feat with love to embrace the loser. It must avoid the temptation to destroy the opposition because the effect of it may eventually come to destroy the whole system of government itself. The loser must congratulate the winner and the winner must respect the loser in his acceptance speech. This is how the First World nations preserve democracy.

Furthermore, this book will examine all the contributions of each leadership to the growth of Nigerians or Nigeria as a country. After gaining independence, Nigeria's government was a coalition of conservative parties: the Nigerian People's Congress (NPC), a party dominated by Northerners and those of the Islamic faith; and the Igbo and Christian-dominated National Council of Nigeria and the Cameroons (NCNC) led by Nnamdi Azikiwe, who became Nigeria's maiden Governor-General in 1960. Alhaji Tafa Balewa the first Nigeria Prime Minister.

Forming the opposition was the comparatively liberal Action Group (AG), which was largely dominated by the Yoruba and led by Chief Obafemi Awolowo. Southern Cameroon opted to join the Republic of Cameroon while some parts of the Northern Cameroon chose to remain in Nigeria. It made the land mass of the northern part of the country far larger than the southern part.

Domination of the Northern Region by the NPC and NCNC control of the Eastern Region were assured. Action Group control of the Western Region was weakened and then collapsed because of divisions within the party that reflected conflicts within Yoruba society. This loss of stability in one region gradually undermined the political structure of the whole country.

Between 1963 and 1964 less than four years after the independence Action Group party was almost disbanded. The Western Region was partitioned into two with the creation of Mid-Western Region, most likely to weaken the Western Region from aspiring to government at the Center, because creation of regions out of the North or East were never encouraged even though there were needs for it.

The nation under Prime Minister Tafawa Balewa and ceremonial President Dr. Nnamdi Azikiwe could not point to any legacy of development in terms of energy or electricity, water, roads, or railways development, nothing in terms of industrial development or economic development program, instead the duo were obsessed with destroying Action Group than developing Nigeria.

Prime Minister Tafawa Balewa and President Azikiwe lacked foresight, and purposeful leadership, and by the time the first military coup happened in 1966, nothing concrete could be pointed to in terms of growth or infrastructure of the country.

Despite Chief Obafemi Awolowo's shortcomings, the Western Region enjoyed a golden era when he was Premier. When Chief Obafemi Awolowo died in 1987, Harold Wilson a former Prime Minister of Great Britain said, "Awolowo leadership quality could be considered equal to any country in the first world, but he was wasted by Nigeria's Federal system."

In other words, Wilson said, Nigeria had a leader of the same quality like the United States, Britain, and France as far back as the fifties.

What a shame!

Chief Obafemi Awolowo with his contributions to Nigeria, as the Federal Commissioner for Finance and Deputy Chairman Federal Executive Council under Gen. Yakubu Gowon, assisted Nigeria during a twenty-seven months long civil war without borrowing a kobo from any institution, be it international or internal. He was an Okpataku of Nigeria. He was a contributor not a taker, nor was he a cog in the wheel of progress of Nigeria. He believed in the rule of law and true Federalism.

Even though it will be hard to sell Chief Obafemi Awolowo's achievements as Federal Commissioner and Deputy Chairman Federal Executive Council to the Igbo tribe of Nigeria because he was accused of the war strategic policies during the civil war that led to the deaths of several thousands of Igbo because food and medications were cut off from the war zone.

In his book, Naiwu Odion explained that Chief Awolowo made the decision after Biafra leader Col. Ojukwu refused to give assurance to international organizations like the Red Cross that vehicles used to supply medication and food to the war areas would not be used to smuggle in ammunition. As a result of his refusal, the Federal government cut off supplies to the East of Nigeria during the civil war. The Igbo never failed to blame Chief Awolowo on that decision instead of blaming Ojukwu who made it impossible because of his refusal to grant the request.

In the West of Nigeria, as Premier between 1952 and 1959, Chief Obafemi Awolowo laid the foundation for educational development with free education at all levels, and his government awarded scholarships to colleges in and out of the country. His education program was free to all the people in the region, not for his tribe alone.

There was also rural integration and industrial complexes and other infrastructure, the first television in Africa at a time when TV was relatively new. His government built the tallest building (Cocoa House) in Nigeria. He developed real and industrial estates in Lagos and Ibadan. Rural development, rubber plantation at Ikenne, and other projects were brought to Nigeria like Coca Cola, all of which placed the Western Region far ahead of the other two regions.

It was as if his government was in a hurry to catch up with the First World, unlike other regions in the East and the North of Nigeria. By the time the products of his educational and industrial revolution matured the rest of the country became envious. Instead of blaming their leaders for lack of development in their regions, they blamed the Yoruba or Chief Awolowo for their misfortunes because the future of the country would be dominated by the educated powerful middle-class produced by the West of Nigeria.

By 1962 Western Region had two Federal universities—Ibadan (1948) and the University of Lagos (1962) and a regionally controlled University of Ife (1963) Furthermore, the western Nigeria civil service was strongly committed to progress under Chief Simeon Adebo and Attorney Gen. Chief Rotimi Williams.

With Chief Awolowo already in jail for treasonable felony, and his region in turmoil, it was a sign that the first Republic was heading for a disaster. The 1964 election which would have saved the first Republic was rigged, with active support of the Federal government under Balewa and President Dr. Azikiwe, yet all the warning signs were ignored. They thought the problems were only in the Western Region. It was not.

The problems became bigger than they expected, before it eventually swallowed the nation itself with the January 15, 1966, military coup d'état led by Majors Ezeokwu, Ifeajuna, and Ademoyega, which led to the death of Prime Minister Balewa, Ahmadu Bello, the Sardauna of Sokoto, and uncompromising leaders in the West like Chief SL Akintola who had refused to vacate office when he lost the election.

The 1966 coup was faulty because all the Igbo leaders escaped from assassination, while leaders in other regions in the country were killed due to the reckless compromise of Major Emmanuel Ifeajuna who handled the Eastern Region of the coup operation. Chief Richard Akinjide one of the Ministers of the Balewa's government revealed that civilian never handed over government to the military; they took it, because acting President, Nwafor Orizu an Igbo man refused to swear in Zana

Diphcharima as acting Prime Minister. He was waiting for direction from Dr. Azikiwe who was suspiciously away in the West Indies at the time of the coup like most of the leaders in East of Nigeria

One of the reasons given by the 1966 coup plotters for the removal of the corrupt and unprogressive leadership of Dr. Azikiwe and Sir Balewa was to have Chief Awolowo released from jail to become the Prime Minister of Nigeria. However, the coup, which favored the Igbo leadership and the subsequent emergence of Gen. Aguiyi Ironsi as the new military Head of State, contradicted the assertion that the coup plotters had Chief Awolowo in mind at all. Instead, it marked the beginning of the nation drifting into an unknown military government journey for the next thirteen years.

The new Head of State Gen. Ironsi had the opportunity to correct the mistakes of the past but he never did. If he had released Chief Obafemi Awolowo from jail he could have had the support of the Yoruba. The appeal letter by Chief Awolowo to Gen. Ironsi for pardon was rejected because Ironsi was still preoccupied with the imbroglios between Chief Awolowo and Dr. Azikiwe back in the days after the death of Herbert Macaulay.

Did Majors Emmanuel Ifejuana, Kaduna Nzeogu, and Adewale Ademoyega ever inform Gen.

Ironsi about their plan for the release of Chief Awolowo? If they did, there was no written or verbal record to support that assumption, more like beer parlor talk, by those who thrive on sentiments to win affection.

Obafemi Awolowo's Letter from Prison

TO MAJOR GEN. AGUIYI IRONSI PRESSING FOR HIS RELEASE AND THAT OF HIS COLLEAGUES (DATED 28TH MARCH 1966) CONFIDENTIAL

The Supreme Commander and Head of the Federal Military Government, Lagos.

Thro: The Director of Prisons, Prisons Headquarters Office,

Private Mail Bag 12522, Lagos.

Sir:

PREROGATIVE OF MERCY:

SECTION 101 (1) (a) OF THE CONSTITUTION OF THE FEDERATION ACT 1963

1. I am writing this petition for FREE PARDON under Section 101(1) (a) of the Constitution of the Federation Act 1963, on behalf of myself and some of my Colleagues whose names are set out in the Annex hereto.

2. Before I go further, I would like to stress that the reasons, which I advance in support of this petition, in my own behalf, basically hold good for my said Colleagues. For they share the same political beliefs with me, and have intense and unquenchable loyalty for the ideals espoused by the Party, which I have the honor to lead.

3. There are many grounds, which could be submitted for your consideration in support of this petition. But I venture to think that SEVEN of them are enough and it is to these that I confine myself.

(a) In the course of my evidence during my trial, I Stated that my Party favored and was actively working for alliance with the N.C.N.C. as a means, among other things, of solving what I described as 'the problem of Nigeria', and strengthening the unity of the Federation.

In October 1963 (that is about a month after my conviction and while my appeal to the Supreme Court was still pending), a Peace Committee Headed by the Chief Justice of the Federation, Sir Adetokunbo Ademola, made overtures to me through my friend Alhaji W. A. Elias to the effect that if I abandoned my intention to enter into alliance with the N.C.N.C., which, according to the Committee, was an Igbo Organization, and agreed to dissolve the Action Group and, in co-operation with Chief Akintola (now deceased), form an all-embracing Yoruba political party, which I would lead and which would go into alliance with the N.P.C., I would be released from prison before the end of that year.

I turned down these terms because I was of the considered opinion that their acceptance would further widen and exacerbate inter-tribal differences, and gravely undermine the unity of the Federation.

TODAY, THE MILITARY GOVERNMENT, OF WHICH YOU ARE THE HEAD, LEAVES NO ONE IN ANY DOUBT THAT IT STANDS FOR NIGERIAN UNITY. BUT IT MUST BE EMPHASISED, IN THIS CONNECTION, THAT IF I HAD PRIZED MY PERSONAL FREEDOM ABOVE THE UNITY OF NIGERIA, I WOULD HAVE BEEN SET FREE IN 1963. IN THAT EVENT, THIS PETITION WOULD NOT HAVE BEEN NECESSARY, AND THE WORK OF

CONSOLIDATING THE UNITY OF THE COUNTRY TO WHICH YOU AND YOUR COLLEAGUES NOW SET YOUR HANDS MIGHT HAVE BEEN MADE EXTREMELY MORE INTRACTABLE AND IRKSOME.

As recently as 20th December, 1965, identical peace terms (the only variant being that the alliance with the N.C.N.C., which was now a reality should be broken) were made to me here, in Calabar Prison, by a delegation representing another Peace Committee Headed by the self-same Chief Justice of the Federation and purporting to have the blessing of the Prime Minister, with the unequivocal promise that if I accepted the terms my release would follow almost immediately. I rejected the terms for the reasons, which I have outlined above.

(b) One of the monsters, which menaced the public life of this country up to 14th January, this year, is OPPORTUNISM with its attendant evils of jobbery, venality, corruption, and unabashed self-interest.

From all accounts, you are inflexibly resolved to destroy this monster. That was precisely what my Colleagues and I had tried to do before we were rendered hors de combat since 29th May, 1962.

On two different occasions I was offered, first the post of Deputy Prime Minister (before May 1962), and second that of Deputy Governor-Gen. (in August 1962).

If I would agree to fold up the Opposition and join in a National Government, I declined the two offers because they were designed exclusively to gratify my self-interest, with no thought of fostering any political moral principle, which could benefit the people of Nigeria.

The learned Judge, who presided over the Treasonable Felony Trial, commented unfavorably on my non-acceptance of one of these posts and held that my action lent weight to the case of the Prosecution against me.

I must say, however, that in all conscience, I felt and still feel that a truly public-spirited person should accept public office not for what he can get for himself — such as the profit and glamour of office but for the opportunity, which it offers him of serving his people to the best of his ability, by promoting their welfare and happiness.

To me, the two aforementioned posts were sinecures, and were intended to immobilize my talents and stultify the role of watch-dog, which the people of Nigeria looked upon me to play on their behalf, at that juncture in our political evolution.

(c) This leads me to the third ground. From newspaper reports, it would appear that you and your Colleagues— like all well-meaning Nigerians are anxious that on the termination of the present military rule, Nigeria should become a flourishing democracy. Now, democracy is a political doctrine, which is very intimately dear to my heart. It was to the end that it might be accepted as a way of life in all parts of the Federation that I campaigned most vigorously and relentlessly in the Northern Provinces of Nigeria, from 1957 to 1962, to the implacable annoyance of some of my political adversaries.

It was to the end that this doctrine might survive the severe onslaught of opportunist and mercenary politics that I refused to succumb to the temptation of the National Government.

Many views some of them well-considered and respectable have been expressed about the value or disvalue of opposition as a feature of public life in a newly emergent African State. Speaking for my party, I submit that the Opposition which I led did, to all intents and purposes, justify its existence and was acclaimed by the masses of our people as essential and indispensable to rapid- national growth.

This was so, because it was unexceptionably constructive. The abrogation of the Anglo-Nigeria Defense Pact was one of the feathers in its cap. Some of the policies, which the Government of the day later adopted — such as the creation of a Federal Ministry of Agriculture and the introduction of drastic measures to correct our balance of payments deficit — were among those persistently and constructively urged by the Opposition inside and outside Parliament.

The point I wish to emphasize here is that it was not out of spite or hatred for any one that I chose to remain in Opposition instead of joining the much-talked-of National Government. I did so in order to serve our people to the best of my ability in the position in which their votes had placed my Party, and to ensure that the young plant of democracy grows into a sturdy flourishing tree in Nigeria.

(d) Since the declaration of emergency in the Western Region on 29th May, 1962, political tension has existed in Western Nigeria. My conviction on 11th September, 1963, together with the surrounding bizarre circumstances, has led not only to the heightening of that tension in Western Nigeria but also to its profuse and irrepressible per Collation to the other parts of the Federation. The result is that it can be said, without much fear of contradiction, that today the majority of our people are passionately concerned about and fervently solicitous for the release of me and my Colleagues.

The work of reconstruction on which you and your Colleagues have embarked demands that all the citizens of Nigeria in their respective callings should give of their maximum best, a state of psychological tension, however much it may be brought under control or repressed, does not and cannot conduce to maximum efficiency.

In spite of themselves, people laboring under emotions, which this kind of tension automatically generates, are bound to make avoidable mistakes, which in their turn have adverse effects on national progress. It is, therefore, in the national interest that this tension should be relaxed, if possible, without further delay.

(e) A petition of this kind is, by its very nature, bound to be replete with self-adulation. I hope and trust that, in the circumstances, this is excusable. It is in this hope and trust that I assert that my Colleagues and I have the qualifications and capacity to render invaluable services to our people and fatherland. Every day that we spend in prison, therefore, must be regarded as TWENTY-FOUR UNFORGIVING HOURS OF TRULY VALUABLE SERVICES LOST TO OUR YOUNG COUNTRY. Even my most inveterate enemies have given the following testimony about me: 'AWOLOWO HAS STILL A GREAT DEAL TO GIVE TO THIS COUNTRY.'

No country however advanced and civilized can afford to waste any of its talents, be they ever so small. Nigeria is too young to bury some of her talents as she was compelled to do under the old regime. It is within your power to restore my colleagues and me to a position where our fatherland can again rejoice at the contributions, which we are capable of making to its progress, welfare, and happiness.

(f) Nigeria is now SIXTY-SIX MONTHS old as an independent State. The final phase in the struggle for Nigeria's independence was initiated by my Party in the historic Self-Government motion moved by Chief Anthony Enahoro and supported by me on 31st March, 1953.

IT SHOULD BE REGARDED AS MORE THAN IRONICAL, AND AS

PALPABLY TRAGIC, THAT TWO OF THE ARCHITECTS OF THAT INDEPENDENCE AND, INDEED, THE PACE-SETTERS AND ACCELERATORS OF ITS FINAL PHASE SHOULD BE UNFREE IN A FREE NIGERIA. In precise terms, I have spent FORTY-SIX out of the SIXTY-SIX MONTHS of independence in one form of confinement or another. I happened to know that the leaders of the old civilian regime, in spite of themselves, did not feel quite easy in their conscience about the plight into, which they had maneuvered me in the scheme of things; and I dare to express the hope and belief that you personally view my present confinement with concern and disapproval.

(g) It is usual — almost invariably the case — on the accession of a revolutionary regime, for political prisoners and, indeed, other prisoners of some note, to be released as a mark of disapproval of some of the doings of the old regime, or in token of the new dawn of freedom, which comes in the wake of the new regime. It would be invidious to quote unspecific instances.

However, in the case of my colleagues and myself, by courageously and adamantly opposing the evils, which your regime now denounces in the former civilian administration, I think we are perfectly justified if we expect you to regard us as being in tune with your yearnings and aspirations for Nigeria, and therefore entitled to our personal freedoms under your dispensation.

4. In view of the foregoing reasons, which clearly demonstrate?

(I) that I have always and, under trying circumstances, steadfastly and unyieldingly

(A) Stood for the UNITY OF NIGERIA,

(b) Been opposed to POLITICAL OPPORTUNISM with its attendant evils,

(C) fostered the growth of DEMOCRACY in Nigeria;

(ii) That my incarceration:

(a) Has led to the heightening of political tension

Among Nigerians, which tension can only be relaxed by my release?

(b) Has deprived our fatherland of invaluable services such as we have

Rendered before, and can still render now and in future, in greater

Measure; and

(iii) that the evils, which my colleagues and I condemned and valiantly refused to compromise with in the old civilian government are what you now quite rightly denounce, and are taking active steps to remove in order to pave the way for national and beneficial reconstruction.

I most sincerely appeal to you to be good enough to exercise, in favor of myself and my Colleagues, the prerogative of mercy vested in you by Section 10 (I) (I) (a) of the Constitution of the Federation Act 1963, by granting me as well as each of my Colleagues a FREE PARDON. If you do, your action will be most warmly, heartily, and popularly applauded at home and abroad, and you will go down to history as soldier, Statesmen, and humanitarian.

Yours truly,

OBAFEMI AWOLOWO.

THOSE CONVICTED FOR TREASONABLE FELONY.

1. THOSE STILL SERVING THEIR TERMS

1. Chief Obafemi Awolowo 2. Chief Anthony Enahoro 3. Mr. Lateef K. Jakande 4. Mr. Dapo Omisade 5. Mr. S.A.Onitiri 6. Mr. Gabby Sasore 7. Mr. Sunday Ebietoma 8. Mr. U.I.Nwaobiala

2. THOSE WHO HAVE ALREADY SERVED THEIR TERMS.

1. Mr. S.A. Otubanjo 2.Mr.S.J.Umoren 3.Mr.S.Oyesile.

3. THOSE THAT HAVE NOT YET BEEN TRIED.

1. Mr. S.G. Ikoku 2.Mr.Ayo Adebanjo 3.Mr.James Aluko

Gen. Ironsi failed to release Awolowo and his group from Calabar prison; he was murdered in a second military coup by Major Theophilus Yakubu Danjuma. The group from the North eventually installed thirty-two-year-old Lieutenant-Colonel Yakubu Gowon as the new Head of State to appease

the North, which felt cheated with the outcome of
January 1966 coup.

Head of State Major General Aguiyi Ironsi
with his trusted buddies, 1966

The second coup took the East of Nigeria out
of the loop. About 300 of Igbo military officers and
several thousands were killed in the North of Nigeria
by the aggrieved Muslims over the death of their
political leaders by the first coup. Col. Emeka
Odumegu Ojukwu, who was appointed the Military
Governor of the East by the late Gen. Ironsi,
refused to accept the leadership of Col. Gowon as
the Commander-in-Chief of the Armed Forces.
Governor Ojukwu was faced with the death of

several thousand of his Igbo men and women killed daily in the North without any help from the Federal government and after the failure of Aburi Conference to resolve the problem. He opted out of the Federal Republic of Nigeria by declaring Biafra a new country.

Some critics thought he did it for his personal ego, but no one was clear on what they expected of him in situation with several thousand of his people dying without the help from the government at the center.

The declaration was initially challenged with a careless approach by Col. Gowon. He had been promoted to General to give him military power and position over aggrieved officers like Col. Ojukwu and Col. Banjo who believed a senior officer like Brigadier Ogundipe, a Yoruba, ought to have been appointed the new Head of State. But Ogundipe had taken a foreign position. In actual fact, Col. Ojukwu could not have been sincere with his assertion as subsequent events would reveal how he headed the government of Biafra and how he ordered the execution of Col. Banjo years later when he (Banjo) refused to advance his troops on his Yoruba nation after finishing up with Mid-West of Nigeria.

However, under Gen. Gowon, Nigeria had more money than the government before him, and once said, *"The problem of Nigeria is not about money but how to spend it."*

Gen. Gowon's government was even paying the salaries of workers in South American nations such as Grenada because of their African heritage, as if Nigeria owed them some form of reparation for years of slavery.

In 1974, his government paid the Udoji Award to Nigerian workers. It became the foundation of Nigeria's first hyper-inflation as the minimum wages went from twenty-three naira to eighty-seven naira per month, and different types of loans were introduced like bicycle loans for Nigerian civil servants.

The nation graduated from mini-cars to imported cars on Nigeria's single lane roads and the government embarked on road constructions in Lagos but excluded other cities, which created unhappiness within other tribes.

The new status and facelift of the Lagos State, with High rising buildings and roads, became a concern to others tribes and the beauty of Lagos was seen as a Western Region achievement rather than something benefitting all of Nigeria. Had Gen. Gowon's government planned even development in most of the cities in Nigeria, along with his National Youth Service Corps (NYSC) program, which to preserve the unity of the country with his no victor, no vanquish policy, no one would have disputed his Okpataku qualification.

However, his government did not stay focus, and corruption was all over his administration like cosmetic powdered on the face of whore. By the time Gen. Muritala Mohammed kicked Gen. Gowon out of office in August 1975, his achievements of uniting the country were overshadowed by his failure to hand over government to the civilians, which was one of the reasons Chief Awolowo resigned from his government in 1971 a year after the end of the civil war.

Gen. Gowon could not determine what he wanted, whether to stay as life military Head of State or be transformed into a civilian President. At one time he wanted to be crowned as Field Marshal of the Nigeria Army by the Queen of England since Idi Amin Dada of Uganda had already awarded himself a title, which was challenged by members of the British Commonwealth as if only the Queen Elizabeth had the right to bestow such a title.

Gen. Gowon's activities left history confused, as he was simultaneously an Oriaku and Okpataku. Later in life when he wanted to run for the office of President, General Obasanjo humorously asked Gowon to tell the nation what he forgot in office in 1975 after nine years in power that he wanted to go back to get in 1992. It became a question he

Obasanjo too would have to answer several years later.

The next chapter will look further into Gen. Gowon and other events that led to his removal from office, the activities of Gen. Muritala Mohammed, and the introduction of Gen. Olusegun Obasanjo and President Sheu Shagari.

When the jury takes long to come out it is not a good sign for the accused to come out clean.
~Unknown Author

2

The Era of General Gowon

Gen. Gowon's attitude towards transition to civilian government after the civil war in 1970 was faulty before he was pushed out in August 1975. It could be likened to that of Gen. Babangida years later in the nation's history, before he too was forced out in 1995.

Gen. Yakubu Gowon was the youngest leader ever to rule Nigeria; he was thirty-one years old when he became the Head of the military government after the assassination of Gen. Ironsi in a military coup led by Major Theophilus Danjuma.

General Gowon released Chief Awolowo
from Jail to win the support of the Yoruba, a
decision which Gen. Aguiyi Ironsi rejected when
he had the same opportunity

Gen. Gowon had superiors like Colonel
Adeyinka Adebayo, who was immediately appointed
the Governor of Western State, and Brigadier
Ogundipe. They lacked the support of the
perpetrators of the second coup like Major Danjuma
who led the group that executed Major Gen. Aguiyi
Ironsi and his host Lt. Col. Adekunle Fajuyi, the
Governor of Western Region. Col. Ojukwu, the
governor of the Eastern region, did not want a boss
of average intelligence, which was his assessment of

Col. Gowon because the new Commander-In-Chief had no university degree and Ojukwu had a master's degree from Oxford in the United Kingdom.

Gen. Gowon shifted the goal post of transition to civilian rule every year, until the progressives like Chief Awolowo left his government in 1971, and subsequent events exposed him for what he was: a man who loved to be in power, without clear-cut transition plan.

General Gowon looked for favors from Britain, as if Nigeria never had her independence. It was indeed sad to note how he was selling Nigeria cheap to the international community and was later accused of negotiating oil-rich Bakasi peninsula away to Cameroon for support during the civil war against Biafra.

It would not be unreasonable to classify Gen. Gowon as a stooge of the British Government as most of the stolen wealth under his leadership could be traced to British banks. Despite having a good heart, he was a very weak Head of State. However, he never compromised the unity of Nigeria, during the civil war; the unity was even coined out of his last name: Go on with One Nigeria.

Gen. Gowon had only one goal in mind, which he never attained: he wanted to be crowned a Field Marshal of Nigeria Army just like Gen. Idi Amin did in Uganda during the 1970s. Instead of awarding himself the title directly, Gowon wanted to be made a Field Marshal by the former Colonial master, Queen Elizabeth, because it would look dignified more than the crude method of Idi Amin Dada of Uganda.

Gen. Gowon was the architect of the second Festival of Arts and Culture (FESTAC) in Lagos, which was originally scheduled for October 1975 to coincide with the arrival of Queen Elizabeth, but all these plans changed as a result of bloodless 1975 military coup.

FESTAC, first hosted by Dakar Senegal in 1966, was pushed forward and hosted by Nigeria in 1977. However, because of Nigeria's wastefulness on the festival, no country could host the festival again. President Abdoulaye Wade of Senegal did something similar to the festival between 2009 and 2010, but it fell short of Nigeria's standards.

Some people believed FESTAC due to the display of masquerades and other fetish symbols was the assembly of evil spirits. Some religious fanatics even asked Nigeria, as a country, to seek God's spiritual deliverance from the festival's after-effects. Whatever it was that came from the festival, the country has never known spiritual peace since, probably the reason no nation showed interest in hosting the festival again for a long time.

FESTAC 77 Theater in Lagos Nigeria

Furthermore, junior military officers, like Col. Yar'Adua, and Major. Jeremiah Usenni, along with some of the architects of the 1983 coup, took advantage of the tension between Gen. Gowon and Brigadier Muritala Mohammed over issues predating the twenty-seven month Biafra wars, over keeping the Igbo nation in Nigeria or to let Ndigbo to go, which Gen. Muritala Mohammed tactically supported.

Generals Gowon and Muritala Mohammed were both from the North, which became a Muslim region after mystic, philosopher, and revolutionary reformer Othman Dan Fodio (Uthmān Ibn Fūdī in Arabic) waged a jihad (holy war) between 1804 and 1808 and created a new Muslim State, the Fulani Empire. The British defeated the Caliphate in 1903. Gen. Muritala Mohammed, a Moslem and Hausa Fulani, was a superior Northerner than Gen. Gowon, a Middle Belt Christian. It was a silent war between a superior Northerner who could trace his history to the Sokoto caliphate and a minority from the same North previously controlled by the Caliphate.

However, Gen. Gowon, who knew his boundary within the Northern power control structure from history and tradition, was able to bend to the strategic control of the Hausa/Fulani. He appointed Gen. Muritala Mohammed Federal

Commissioner for Communication after the end of the civil war. However, Gen. Gowon was a tougher Head of State toward the south than to his base in the North. He went after radicals like Professor Wole Soyinka, Chief Gani Fawehinmi, Dr. Tunji Braithwaite, and Kami Ishola Osobu; most of them were regular visitors to the detention camps.

After the war, Brigadiers General Obasanjo, Danjuma, and Muritala Mohammed became the three musketeers of the Nigeria Army. Muritala Mohammed, whose wife Ajoke from Abeokuta, the same town as Gen. Obasanjo, was considered the leader of the trio, but Gen. Danjuma was as deadly and ruthless as a Tiger with his probing eyes. He constantly reminded Gowon on who led the coup that brought him to power that killed General Aguiyi Ironsi and Col. Adekunle Fajuyi. He was a happy killer.

In August 1975, while attending the Organization of African Unity (OAU) meeting in Addis Ababa, Ethiopia, Gen. Gowon was toppled in a bloodless military coup. It was announced by the heavily mustached Brigade of Guards, Commander Col. Joseph Nanven Garba, who came from the same Middle Belt like Gen. Gowon, probably to assure their continued cooperation of the whole Northern Region.

Commander Brigade of Guard then Col. Nanven Garba announced the coup against General Gowon in August 1975

The likeable Col. Garba was eventually appointed the Federal Commissioner for External affairs by the new government headed by Brigadier Gen. Muritala Mohammed; he became a diplomat, and politician who served as President of the United Nations General Assembly from 1989 to 1990. When General Gowon heard his government was toppled, he quoted Williams Shakespeare and described the world as a stage. Ironically, it was a stage he never knew when to leave. He became a joke to the international community, and all he could do was to go back to the country of his first love, Great Britain, to pursue a degree in political science at Warrick University to prove to Col Ojukwu his ability to acquire a better university education than the Oxford master's degree of Ikemba of Nnewi Odumegwu Ojukwu. He did and he went as far as doctorate degree in political science, a step ahead of Ojukwu Master's degree in history at Lincoln College, Oxford University.

The emergence of Gen. Muritala Mohamed as Head of State and Gen. Olusegun Obasanjo as his deputy was a saving grace for Nigeria's crumbling political system, and the beginning of a purposeful leadership, in Nigeria and Africa. The coup plotters, led by Col. Yar'Adua, had approached Gen. Muritala Mohammed to Head the government. He initially refused because if had he participated in the coup he believed he would have been seen by Northerners as a person who lacked forgiveness.

The coup plotters also approached Gen. Obasanjo to Head the government and he too refused. He advised them to convince Gen. Muritala Mohammed to Head the government; instead, they approached Gen. Danjuma with the same proposal. He too refused the position but directed them to convince either Gen. Olusegun Obasanjo or Muritala Mohammed for the position. It was like a game of chess.

When Col. Sheu Yar'Adua and Jerry Usenni approached Gen. Muritala Mohammed again, it was more like blackmail than a proposition. He had no choice than to accept it or be killed. He brought into his government his two trusted generals. He appointed Gen. Olusegun Aremu Obasanjo as his Chief of Staff Supreme Headquarters, comparable to a vice President, and Gen Theophilus. Danjuma was named Chief of Staff. Army Col. Yar'Adua, one of the leaders of the coup, was appointed Federal Commissioner for Transport, the highest office granted any of the 1975 coup plotters.

Literarily, Gen. Muritala Mohammed became the face of the progressives within the new political class. He announced a transition program for a civilian government that would take place in 1979. He created a dynamic new foreign policy for Nigeria and made the country a respectable and acceptable presence in African affairs. It was indeed a pride to be a Nigerian again. Perhaps what was closer to the joy he brought to the nation could be compared to the day the British flag was lowered for the green white green flag of Nigeria in 1960.

However, he went beyond his fight against corruption. His government implemented massive retirements and firings of career civil servants and university lecturers. He called them dead woods. Most of them never had any home of their own; they lived in the government quarters. With just two weeks' notice, most of the egg heads of the Nigeria universities and top civil servants became homeless.

It was sad.

Gen. Muritala Mohammed created seven new states from twelve to nineteen by military decree. The new states further destroyed the regional loyalty started by Gen. Gowon with states creation. He expelled out of his office inside Dodan Barracks three American diplomats for urging Nigeria not to support MPLA Antonio Augustinho Neto in Angola.

Muritala Mohammed dug his own grave with some of his irrational actions, which changed the status quo, during his six months leadership. Corruption was unheard of until one of the tabloid newspapers revealed his Deputy Lt. Gen. Obasanjo, a former Federal Commissioner for works in the administration of Gen. Gowon, was involved with some shady cement importation deal. Muritala Mohammed was in a quandary. If he fired or court marshaled his deputy, Obasanjo's replacement would have been Gen. Oluleye, a man considered too clean and decent. The military consensus was that Oluleye was not a team player; a typical Ekiti man from Aramoko, too clean and probably too sincere for anyone shady or something to hide. Oluleye was not a buyable person.

Gen. Muritala Mohammed set up a panel to investigate Obasanjo. It was chaired by Justice Babatunde Belgore; the panel's findings did not meet public expectations because Gen. Olusegun Obasanjo was cleared of any corruption.

The outcome of the finding of the panel on Obasanjo reflected poorly on the judgment of General Muritala Mohammed, but in all, he was a decent man and his love for Nigeria was never questioned. The Press reported how he gave back his properties in Kano to the government as soon as he was appointed Head of State. Unfortunately, Muritala Mohammed was assassinated on February 13, 1976, in a military coup led by Lt Col. Buka Suka Dimka. Muritala Mohammed was Head of State for only six months before he was killed.

There were some conspiracy theories concerning his death. Some attributed it to disagreement with the late President Gerald Ford of the United States of America's administration over the support for MPLA Angola over its Liberation movement from colonization. A more local view was that he was killed on a Friday on his way to the Mosque because he did not have his juju or voodoo with him, which exposed his weakness to the soldiers loyal to the former Head of State, Gen. Yakubu Gowon.

Perhaps it was mother luck but still others believed Generals Obasanjo and Danjuma must have known of the coup because both escaped being killed by Col. Dimka's group. No clear reason could be given as to why Gen. Muritala Mohammed was killed or why Generals Obasanjo and Danjuma escaped being killed. Most people suspected Muritala Mohammed simply stepped on too many toes. But his plans and goals for the country were faithfully carried out by his successor, General Olusegun Obasanjo from 1976 to 1979.

General Muritala was in this car when he was
assassinated on February 13, 1976.
Displayed at Onikan Museum Lagos

On the day Muritala Mohammed was killed, the Oracle, as this writer was fondly called was a young staffer at the University of Ibadan with the National Achieves Bindery department. Like most others within the University campus, we all cried and wondered if nothing good would ever come out of Nigeria. Gen. Muritala Mohammed's death was the first time Nigerians of different tribes would be touched to the point of tears and complete love over the death of a leader since 1945 when Herbert Macaulay died which brought the country together.

Obviously, Gen. Muritala Mohammed did his best for his country. He was perhaps one of the few men with a total love of Nigeria in his heart. His death was a big blow to Africa, which had found her voice in the world affairs through his leadership, and a pride, which made Nigeria a bigger brother to all countries in Africa. All the people from all the 225 tribes in Nigerian wept from all cities across the nation, from Ikoyi Lagos in front of the Federal Secretariat where they killed him to Sokoto, Kano, Maiduguri, Enugu, Port Harcourt, Ibadan, Abeokuta and Benin even inside my department in the Bindery section of National Archives. We could not hold the tears. We held each other for support. Our boss, Benedict Chigbata Okafor, kept on speaking in his Igbo language on why anyone would kill the best of his children; that was what Dimka and his group did to Nigeria, they killed the best in us.

It was tears for the nation; even the new Head of State Lt Gen. Obasanjo was almost in tears as he took over the leadership of the bereaved nation. In his first address to the nation, he promised to reorganize the careless and porous security network of the country and to punish the coup plotters. There was no Security Service (SS) then, nothing except Criminal investigation Department (CID), which was not enough to handle the task ahead. General Obasanjo had to start from scratch to create the new security network for the most populous nation in Africa. It was not an easy task for him and the nation.

All Nigerians, particularly his Yoruba ethnic group from Abeokuta, were wondering if Gen. Obasanjo was going to be assassinated like Gen. Muritala Mohammed in next few weeks or months. If Nigerians had any misgivings about Obasanjo over his role with the cement probe, his emotional speech and the love he displayed for the late Muritala Mohammed won him the sympathy of the nation. His sins were forgiven and the nation was ready to move on with him. He was the only person the Military and people of Nigeria could trust. If a nation needed a bigger shoulder enough to lay its head on at a time when it was almost helpless, Obasanjo was the man of the moment for Nigeria, in 1976.

Left: Gen. Muritala Mohamed *Right:* Professor Bolaji Akinyemi a brilliant political Science scholar and Director of Nigeria Institute of Internal Affairs

History would classify Gen. Muritala Mohammed as Okpataku, a giver, and one of the best to ever rule Nigeria. Even though his leadership was less than seven months it was better than most Heads of State or Presidents that came after him.

The Federal Government set up military tribunal for the coup plotters. It was later revealed there were even enemies within the tribunal itself. Gen. Bissala, the same man who coordinated transporting Muritala Mohammed's corpse to Kano through Lagos Airport was an appointed member of the military tribunal until one of the accused pointed him out as a member of their group and the panel chairman, Gen. Olufemi Abisoye, ordered him arrested.

Sometimes in the life of a nation, the moment can pick a man for history and sometimes if not in most cases a man can pick his moment for history.
~US Senator Dick Durbin of Illinois

In politics stupidity is not a handicap.
~Napoleon Bonaparte

3

General Olusegun Aremu Okikiola Obasanjo

It was the United states Senator Dick Durbin of Illinois in 2007 when he introduced then Senator Obama running for the presidency of the United States of America who said, sometimes in the life of a nation, the moment can pick a man for history and sometimes if not, in most cases a man can pick his moment for history. Obasanjo would be a man history and moment picked for the good and bad of his country and corporately for the interest of his continent Africa. This chapter will look at Gen. Olusegun Obasanjo, referred to as Uncle Shege in the late 70s and OBJ twenty years after.

Gen. Muritala Mohammed was a bundle of energy as a military Head of State. He had laid a very strong foundation that was difficult for his successor Uncle Shege to deviate from. Even if Gen. Obasanjo wanted to create his own agenda, he never showed it or never had the guts to even contemplate it. He knew the group that gave him the power was watching, and their leader Col. Yar'Adua had been appointed the chief of staff supreme Headquarters, essentially a deputy Head of State. OBJ had to tread gently. He kept General Danjuma in his post to keep a tab on the Army and other 1975 coup plotters.

However, the Yoruba took the elevation of Gen. Obasanjo with mixed feelings. It was good for the Egba; his hometown people thought Federal largess would at least extend to Ogun State. But it was not a good sign for the Chief Awolowo loyalists and political associates. As events would later show both were disappointed in a reversed and opposite trend because Gen. Obasanjo proved unpredictable. His loyalty was to Nigeria, not to his sub-ethnic in the former Abeokuta province or the Yoruba. Despite his facial Yoruba marks he was a complete detribalized Nigerian.

Furthermore, Gen. Muritala Mohammed had left a road map for Nigeria such as setting up a panel to relocate the Federal capital city from Lagos to Abuja, how to fund the new seven states, and appointing 50 wise men to draft a new constitution with Chief Rotimi Williams as the chairman. Chief Obafemi Awolowo declined to serve under Rotimi Williams.

Gen. Muritala Mohamed did not understand the politics of the West or the Yoruba where leaders of Chief Awolowo's status could not serve under a junior partner like Chief Rotimi Williams. It would be degrading for the leader of the Yoruba to be reduced to the level of ordinary member under a man he once appointed his Attorney General and Minister of Justice in the old Western Region during the 1950s. Among the Yoruba, seniority is often based on age; and position, to compromise it could be likened to the Bible story of Esau who sold his birthright for food.

Chief Awolowo openly reprimanded General Muritala Mohamed for not consulting him on the appointment before the radio announcement, and it became the first known disagreement between Chief Awolowo and Gen. Muritala Mohammed. The Press wondered who included the name of Chief Awolowo in the committee since OBJ was the Chief of Staff Supreme Headquarters. There was never any clear explanation.

The government did not find a replacement for Chief Awolowo; only forty-nine men wrote the 1979 constitution. Chief Rotimi Williams, known then as *Timi the Law*, Chaired the panel and he often displayed his years as a lawyer with tattered academic or legal gowns that he never bothered to replace. To him the rags were a sign of experience in his profession.

The outcome of the 1979 constitution was tampered with; most of the recommendations in the draft constitution were removed or doctored by Gen. Obasanjo's government, which created the basic fundamental complications for the civilian government in 1979, from a people used to parliamentary system.

As the country's leader, Gen. Obasanjo had a problem from the beginning on how to find significant among the Yoruba nation. He had the Awolowo loyalists politically and Fela Anikulapo Kuti socially to contend with. Fela was a Nigerian musician and composer, a pioneer of Afro-beat music, a human rights activist, and a political maverick. Surprisingly, most of Obasanjo's traditional enemies were from his tribe the Yoruba. They saw him in the same way the Jews saw Jesus: a man who came to destroy the laid-down plans of Chief Awolowo for an egalitarian society based on Awolowo doctrines. Obasanjo was like a ruthless General on the battlefront. In the early 1970s, he destroyed the dreams of his adversaries and none of them survived the blows.

On the social side, along with Fela Kuti mates were the radicals: the Nigerian student union leaders and all the egg-Head groups with academic members like Professor Wole Soyinka, Professor Ayodele Awojobi, and Dr. Tai Solarin and lawyers like Kami Ishola Osobu, Tunji Braithwaite, and Gani Fawehinmi. All the radicals became tenants of the new prison yards Gen. Obasanjo built on Snake Island and Kirikiri in Lagos.

At one time, Gen. Obasanjo was so intolerant of criticism of his military government that it bordered almost to the point of being paranoid. Afro-beat king Fela Anikulapo Kuti was so irritating to his leadership that in February 1977 his family house in Lagos, called Kalakuta Republic, was besieged by Nigerian soldiers for a second time and set on fire. His followers mostly women were raped and brutalized. He lost many possessions but the most tragic part of the arson was that of his seventy-eight-year-old mother who was thrown out of a two-story balcony and died months later as a result of the injuries she sustained. Fela himself ended up with a cracked skull and broken legs. He never recovered financially either.

In addition, Fela served time in detention for weeks for his role of safeguarding his person and property. This incident led to the then very famous songs "Unknown Soldier" and "Sorrow, Tears &

Blood.". The whole of Nigeria was traumatized with the way Obasanjo handled the whole problem in which the government probe panel by Justice Anya declared that unknown Soldiers attacked Fela.

The attack was a retaliation of Fela's boycott of the Second World Black and African Festival of Arts and Culture (FESTAC) in 1977, and his accusation that the military dictatorship was corrupt. It proved Fela was bigger than the whole FESTAC itself. He was also an unusual character, when he had a commercial disagreement with Decca his recording company over nonpayment of his royalties; Fela went into history book on how the primitive Egba nation and Ijesha used to collect overdue payments. It was called Dogoo among the Egba and Osho maaloo among the Ijesha. He moved all his families of his band to the frontage of the company. They lived there in the open until the company paid up.

Surprisingly, Chief Awolowo, who was never a political associate of Fela, was also against FESTAC. He said, "Only a nation which could not move forward would be marching backward and FESTAC was not a progressive event to celebrate." His criticism of FESTAC events along with his previous refusal to participate in drafting the 1979 constitution made Awolowo a target for the military. He was a difficult target so the approach to get him could never be as blatant as how Fela was attacked.

Gen. Obasanjo hated trade unionism in any form with a passion. He destroyed the Student Unions and most of their leaders were rusticated from the colleges and universities, Gen. Obasanjo also restructured the Nigeria Labor Congress, which remained a toothless bulldog to his authority. Eventually, Alhaji Hassan Sumonu, a clean and harmless trade unionist, emerged as the first President of the reformed NLC, which only listened to the General, not the problems of the workers until Sheu Shagari became the civilian President in 1979.

The youths in Nigeria, particularly the University students in the 1970 saw Banji Adegboro as a hero of their unfinished student revolution. Those who were not yet in the universities would interact with the students of the University of Ibadan freely and they just listened to his persuasive use of the Queen's English, all of which threatened the Federal Commissioner for Education, Col. Ali.

Later all the Nigerian student unions led the Ali Must Go riot against the military. But again, the opposition was punished and/or crushed. For example, food subsidies and other social benefits to the students and other opponents were cut off. Obasanjo called the program low profile, which meant cut your coat according to your cloth.

On the political side, he found no favor with the Yoruba that saw his actions as a leader and a potential impediment to Awolowo's Presidential ambitions. Chief Obafemi Awolowo was likened to Oduduwa, the progenitor of the tribe. Obasanjo was compared to the Esu laalu (Satan) who messed up the good work of Obatala the god of divinity. He did not help the matter himself when he referred to himself as *Ebora Owu* not the type of name one could find in the Bible, but literary meant the evil one from Owu Community of Egba in Abeokuta, his hometown in Ogun State.

As soon as the altered 1979 Nigeria Constitution was made public, Chief Rotimi Williams rejected the outcome. There was no referendum by the people to accept or reject the new Constitution as expected in a very enlightened society, what we had was the signature of the Military Head of State and the doctored document became the law of the land. Those in the West felt exonerated that their leader Chief Awolowo opted out of the constitution drafting committee.

It was even reported in the news media that Gen. Obasanjo had a meeting with all the five Presidential candidates before the election: Chief Awolowo of Unity Party of Nigeria (UPN), Dr. Nnamdi Azikiwe of Nigeria Peoples Party (NPP), Alhaji Sheu Shagari of National Party of Nigeria

(NPN), Alhaji Ibrahim Waziri of Great Nigeria Peoples Party (GNPP), and Mallam Aminu Kano of People Redemption Party (PRP). Obasanjo told them not to expect the best candidate to win the 1979 Presidential elections. The Press felt he was ironically referring to Chief Awolowo because he was obviously the best and most prepared out of the five Presidential candidates.

The military favored the NPN, because it was a party led by the most corrupt people in Nigeria of that time. Chief Augustus Meredith Adisa Akinloye, the chairman of the party was a onetime associate of Chief Awolowo in the first Republic who disagreed with him over the role of Ibadan politics. Alhaji Sheu Shagari, the Presidential Candidate of NPN, was the man who replaced Chief Awolowo in Gen. Gowon's cabinet as the Federal Commissioner for Finance in 1971. He did not meet the expectation of the office and the standard left behind by Awolowo. They were not Awolowo's favorites.

In fact, most of the NPN members had something on their political resume connecting them to the failed first Republic of NPC and NCNC and those who politically disagreed with Chief Awolowo like his one-time surrogate Chief Anthony Enahoro and meekly, Chief MKO Abiola one of the beneficiaries of Awolowo's government scholarship programs.

Interestingly, Gen. Gowon said the only thing Alhaji Sheu Shagari, who served as his Federal Commissioner of Finance, could do independently without supervision was to light his cigarette. In other words, he was lazy and trying to put on the big shoes of Awolowo in the Finance Ministry exposed his inadequacies.

Other candidates for the presidency could not be trusted by the military. Chief Awolowo of the Unity Party of Nigeria (UPN) had openly said he was going to probe the military over mismanagement of war funds and FESTAC, allegations directly pointing to Gen. Obasanjo. However, Alhaji Ibrahim Waziri of GNPP was only shouting the slogan *politics without bitterness* because he was edged out of NPP for Nigeria's first ceremonial President Dr. Azikiwe to come in as a candidate to give Awolowo a run for his money. When Alhaji Ibrahim Waziri pulled out of NPP the only innovation apart from his red-capped Head was to add great to the NPP name, he called it GNPP. It was funny and equally preposterous.

Dr. Nnamdi Azikiwe was a career and traditional political adversary of Chief Awolowo since the death of Herbert Macaulay. It was even rumored that the military was responsible for the emergence of Dr. Azikiwe in the political arena to neutralize Chief Awolowo's influence with his popular four cardinal programs to pave the way for the NPN victory. Azikiwe was later called a ranting ant by Dr. Chuba Okadigbo when the accord between NPN and NPP failed.

Mallam Aminu Kano, the Presidential candidate of People's Redemption Party, (PRP) was too straightforward and regional to pose a threat and he could not be used by the military. He was also out of the loop of the conspiracy. The only option was Alhaji Sheu Shagari, a man with a middle school education, who was more of a willing niff and a reluctant candidate for the office of presidency. Shagari had wanted to be just a Senator but he found himself as the Presidential candidate of NPN and later a president of a country too complex for his average education.

Those who made it their business to trace the secret ballot paper in the 1979 Presidential elections said Gen. Obasanjo actually voted for the NPN. His subsequent relationship with NPN after the election was an indication of where his vote went. Gen. Obasanjo was the champion of low profile policy. He replaced the use of Mercedes Benz as official cars with Peugeot 504 SRs in all government departments and that of his office. He cut lots of wasteful spending from the government, and introduced Operation Feed the Nation. It was not a surprise he became a farmer when he left office, with a Land use degree, that enabled him to grab innocent farmers' lands all over the country.

Uncle Shege saved lots of money for the coming civilian government. He also signed many decrees that remain the foundation of Nigeria's national security today. His government established the National Security Organization (NSO) and its by-product, the State Security Service (SSS). These agencies and related laws were intended to stop coups, and to execute those behind the 1976 coup.

Ironically, the same anti-coup law he signed himself was used to sentence him to death twenty years later. OBJ's government, like Chief Awolowo did in Western Region in the fifties, introduced free and compulsory primary education all over the country but the Awoists could not give him credit. Even though the foundation of some of his actions could be found in Awolowo's doctrines, to them OBJ would remain evil.

Gen. Obasanjo kept faith with all the programs of late Gen. Muritala Mohammed, with the implementations of the new seven states, the foundation for the relocation of Federal Capital from Lagos to Abuja, and many more. In doing so, the mustached general destroyed all those who stood in his ways.

In fairness to Gen. Obasanjo, he remained a detribalized Nigerian. To him Nigeria interest came before everything as long as he called the shots. The Yoruba expected more from him than he gave, which made his people the Yoruba to hate him with passion. It got to a point they doubted if he was actually a Yoruba man.

Why a man of his status would love his country more than his ethnic group in a multi-ethnic society of 225 tribes would forever remain a misery to the Yoruba nation within Nigeria. Charity begins at home they say; in the case of Obasanjo it began abroad, far away from Abeokuta or the Yoruba nation.

In one of the books written by Allison Ayida, a former Permanent Secretary at the Ministry of Economic Development recounts how Gen. Olutoye Oluleye met with Gen. Obasanjo in his office. He discussed what could be seen as a Yoruba fraternity of talk between brothers. He advised Gen. Obasanjo to reduce the powers and authorities of the Hausa/Fulani in the country and most importantly, to redeploy Brigadier Yar'Adua to another powerless ministry.

Gen. Obasanjo listened and then called a meeting of all members of his cabinet, including the entire Hausa/Fulani group that Gen. Oluleye spoke against, and asked the grey hair Oluleye to repeat exactly what he told him in confidence.

In the Military, you could not refuse the order of your Commander–in-Chief. Gen. Oluleye almost to point of tears and complete disappointment in the Yoruba fraternity between him and his Oduduwa brother obeyed the command and at the end of his statement in the presence of Hausa Fulani mafia, Gen. Obasanjo demanded for his resignation from the Army. From that day, the loyalty of Gen. Obasanjo to Nigeria or Fulani was never in doubt.

Gen. Danjuma later confessed that from that day it was very difficult for him to doubt Obasanjo's loyalty to Nigeria. Several decades later, he was rewarded with civilian presidency not by his people but by the same Fulani oligarchy after he came out of jail about twenty years after.

The resignation of General Oluleye from the Army eliminated a man whose straight forwardness would have made him a replacement for Obasanjo during the cement probe, which the Gen. Obasanjo sailed through with the help of Gen. Muritala Mohammed.

Sadly, in October 1979 when Gen Obasanjo returned to Abeokuta, his place of birth, on a horse like a primitive wartime general, his people, the Egba, were disappointed because the general did not begin his charity at home. Abeokuta remained a primitive City with no modern roads or infrastructure except for the new Ogun river bridge that led to his house. The people wondered what the advantage of his presidency to them; if there was any, no one could see it.

However, the Federal government under President Sheu Shagari supplied his agricultural farm at Sango Otta with a direct electric line from Agbara for his own personal usage. His people wondered if they ever had a Head of State in the city. It was sad and pathetic. Later in life, Gen. Obasanjo said he loved his early life as a villager at Ibogun, a life of ignorance where everyone lived with no lights, no modernization of anything; simple life at the mercy of nature. In the opinion of this writer the society General Obasanjo bequeathed his people and Nigeria when he bowed out of office in October 1979 was a nation like a village of his dreams.

Finally, will General Obasanjo be considered an Oriaku or Okpataku? He left his critics and friends confused and it will be appropriate to suspend any meaningful tag on him since he came back as President of Nigeria twenty years later. President Sheu Shagari's lazy actions, however, made him more of an Okpataku than an Oriaku.

In the country of Mexico in the North of America an air-conditioner is called a politician because it makes lots of noise but doesn't work very well.
~Lan Deightom

If you plan to have something important to you done, quickly do it yourself, if you want it delayed set up a committee to look into it for you. Dr. Onaolapo Soleye 1987 Faculty of the Social Sciences University of Ibadan

As a tribute to Chief Awolowo who died in 1987 at the age of seventy-eight, the military President Gen. Babangida said, Nigeria politics was all about Awolowo and those who were against his policies. The same statement was confirmed by Chukwu Emeka "Emeka" Odumegu Ojukwu, leader of the defeated Biafra movement, who said, Chief Awolowo was the best President Nigeria never had. But in truths and facts, the story of the political giant of the siege of Nigeria or Yoruba politics died with the emergence of Gen.

Obasanjo. Even Gen. Gowon knew that the hero of post-1979 political dispensation was Gen. Obasanjo.

Somehow, the 1979 Federal elections were marred with controversy over the two-thirds majority condition in the electoral law before a winner could be determined. None of the five political parties that participated in the Presidential election met the condition.

The Federal military government under Gen. Obasanjo, for the sake of administrative peace, gave the victory to President Sheu Shagari; the man Gen. Gowon had said was incapable to handle a complex country like Nigeria.

In fairness to Shagari, he had more votes than Chief Awolowo, but the law must be followed and he did not meet the electoral requirement. Gen. Obasanjo's motivation to rush to conclusion without waiting for the final outcome of the court was unknown and baffled the political class that had rested everything on the yet to be determined Supreme Court ruling on the two-thirds requirement of the electoral law on who actually won the election.

Was it a pressure by Major Gen. Yar'Adua, the leader of the coup that brought him to power, or his own hidden contempt for Awolowo and his legacy? Historians recalled Obasanjo said he watched Awolowo's political career as a kid when he came to

Abeokuta to address a rally in the 1950s seeking the votes for presidency of Nigeria. In 1979, the same Awolowo was still seeking the same mandate; obviously to him, Awolowo must be using the wrong strategy for the goal of getting the mandate.

How Shagari, a man with little knowledge or understanding of the Nigerian founding fathers' goals could lead the most populous black nation was the problem yet to be defined by all. Perhaps Gen. Gowon's assessment gave Shagari too much credit on his ability to light his cigarette independently; according to late Dele Giwa, the pioneer Editor–in-Chief of Newswatch, and former Editor-in-Chief of Concord when Shagari became the President, his political adviser Dr. Chuba Okadigbo was given the responsibility of lighting the President's cigarette.

However, the warm embrace Gen. Obasanjo expected from his people, the Yoruba, was not there when he left office in October 1979, and he was seen more like a saboteur of the dreams of Chief Awolowo than a soldier who put Nigeria unity above all. If his own people hated him, he did not attempt to either win their support or beg for forgiveness. To the Yoruba, Gen. Obasanjo was a heartless SOB who destroyed the dreams of Chief Awolowo, their hero, and his road map for his vision of Nigeria.

As mentioned previously, Nigeria's unity was compromised prior to independence in 1960 by

Britain's divide-and-conquer strategies to split the country into three administrative regions: East, West, and North.

Furthermore, we saw how the British encouraged the North to focus more on the military recruitment with many of the siblings of the Emirs and opinion leaders as young military officers. However, in the South, the military as a career was for those with no family to give them head start in life, so they did not command the same respect like their Northern counterparts who joined the Nigerian Army.

When Gen. Obasanjo handed over power to the civilian government in 1979 all the service chiefs left with him except Gen. Alani Akinrinade who was immediately relieved of his position in April 1980 by the new President. However, President Shagari was a disaster from day one in office. He did not know what to do with the leadership of the nation. Obasanjo left the nation with a parting gift of a new national anthem, a new national pledge, and security network for the unity of Nigeria that will be difficult to remove.

President Shagari's NPN signed an accord with NPP to form the national government like NPC and NCNC had done in 1960. His government was based on the parliamentary system instead of an executive leadership or Presidential system in the constitution, and Nigeria floundered because Shagari did not know how to move the nation forward.

The first four years of Shagari's administration was the greatest setback for the hope and aspiration of the nation. Perhaps his limited education affected his abilities. At the time, qualified candidates were around but the military scared them away, and his inferiority complex could be felt from all his toothless policies. His brother-in-law Alhaji Umaru Dikko, a mathematician and the Transportation Minister, became the de facto President of the kitchen cabinet.

An article by Dele Giwa and Ray Ekpu in Newswatch magazine on his presidency, "Bicycle Government," explained how President Shagari combined stupidity with ignorance in affairs of Nigeria. By time he completed his first term in office as President in October 1983, Nigeria had lost all the foreign reserves that the military government of Gen. Obasanjo amassed through the Low Profile Policy of cut-your-coat-according-to-your-cloth. Nigeria became a debtor nation to London and Paris clubs, with an uncontrollable interest rate that foreign nations took advantage of, Nigeria leadership in Africa affairs had been eroded and the nation needed a savior.

In a civilized society like the United States, with an almost identical constitution, the presidency is the embodiment of the hopes and goals of the country. That is the reason for the expanded primaries system (EPS) debates within parties that are organized by various bodies at least 18 months prior to the election, including Press releases. The citizens are required to ask questions from any candidate and no candidate to any political office can refuse to attend debates or refuse to answer to questions. It is just normal to be civil in any political set up. It was not the same process that made Alhaji Sheu Shagari President of Federal Republic of Nigeria in 1979 and 1983.

The use of expanded Primary System (EPS) is a recommended solution in which no party member, no matter how powerful he or she is can ask any aspiring political contestant to step down without facing the law. All the books and articles the candidates read or wrote in the past would be used to understand his or her goals for the country. In most cases, unprepared and stupid leaders will drop out at the primaries before the general or Presidential election.

The way United States keeps its Presidential system vibrant and away from those without plans or commitment by vetting a candidate's political views as well as their social lifestyle, marital responsibilities, attitude to work ethics, and women are looked into by the Press to enlighten the public on the mentality of a likely leader.

However, in Nigeria, the process that got Shagari elected as President had none of the above qualities. Some party leaders like Chief AMA Akinloye said they talked to God or Allah in Mecca and God or Allah had selected Shagari as President of Nigeria and voting for any other candidates would be seen as not obeying the command of Allah.

What kind of God would allow his people to continue to suffer for the sake of nothing was enough ground to doubt everything religion in whatever form stood it for. NPN made a mess of fiscal policies or any form of accountability. The National Party Nigeria members were celebrating acquisition of private jets all over the country and billionaire status on the pages of newspapers. Some even had champagne brands named for them, and commercial banks were forced to open at night so they could withdraw money whenever they ran out of cash while out every night partying. It was the era of reckless spending without respect for accountability under an irresponsible leadership.

Sheu Shagari had no qualities of a President in charge of a nation; all he wanted was to pray five times a day, which he did faithfully. Even at executive meetings, he would excuse himself to pray. The cabals in his government knew when to slide things in, as most dubious contracts and deals were done whenever the President was praying.

It was more than what Chief Awolowo could stomach. He wrote an open letter to the nation and the presidency of the danger ahead and how the future was being mortgaged by the ruling government's careless spending. NPN called him a frustrated politician. NPN chairman Chief Akinloye asked Awolowo to see the robust cheeks of its members and all the sagacious Chief Awolowo needed to do was to abandon UPN for NPN and he too would have a robust cheek, if he so desired Chief Akinloye mockingly advised.

In between all these, a retired Gen. Obasanjo could do nothing. He knew he made the mistake of handing over the government to a man who was not up to the task. But it was too late for him; moreover, naïve President Shagari was advised by Dr. Okadigbo to seek his independence from retired Gen Obasanjo, which was what he did. He cut off communication with the man from Temperance farm Ota, refusing to take Obasanjo's phone calls, and the whole country waited for the October 1983 Election to kick NPN out of office.

The NPN had used the policy of rice importation throughout the country in the past to secure public support but the election fever was already gripping the ruling party. The people wanted more than just rice; they wanted a change of government.

The 1983/84 National Youth Service Corps (NYSC) program was done in fear; everyone knew it would be the worst service time in Nigeria in the election year. However, Nigerians in their wisdom or otherwise through massive rigging re-elected Shagari as President.

As expected, Chief Awolowo went to court again to challenge the result of the election. He lost, like he did in 1979. Unfortunately, rigging was not only at the Federal level, it was done in most of the States controlled by the progressives and UPN.

In the early morning of the election in October 1983, Chief Bola Ige the UPN Governor of Oyo State had stumbled into the prepared result of the election that was yet to take place in his state, he announced the plan of the NPN to remove him as governor with the fake result.

Uncle Bola Ige had a problem: he talked too much. Some called him the Cicero of the land. He was a neatly dressed man, always in safari jackets with a pair of glasses. His appearances would remind a casual observer of a secondary school teacher, but he was a lawyer and could speak Latin, English, Yoruba, and Hausa fluently. Uncle Bola Ige was educated in Ibadan and his wife was a judge. The shape of his mouth and front dentures with gaps made his opponents uncomfortable. He was an Ijesha man born and raised in the land of the Oluyole, Ibadan.

Nigerians thought he was just an alarmist, but the evening after the election result was released, the document was identical to what Chief Bola Ige released before the election. Chief Augustus Meredith Adisa Akinloye, the National Chairman of NPN, told the public to ignore Chief Bola Ige. He said only a bastard from Ibadan would vote for the re-election of Bola Ige in Oyo State, where no governor had ever won a re-election. The government controlled television station NTA in the State was busy displaying the gap-toothed mouth of the Governor instead of the seriousness of his allegations. Some said he was talking like someone with hot meal of local yam in his mouth. Bola Ige truly had a funny set of frontal teeth, but the problem was more than the dentures of the Governor; it was the very crude and untidy way the NPN cheated in the election.

It was the same problem with Ondo State but if democracy was a game of numbers, the NPN method of stealing elections could not hold in Ondo State. Chief Omoboriowo, the NPN governorship candidate who was declared the winner, could not govern from Akure, the State capital. He operated from Lagos and he was protected by the NPN-controlled Federal government; Ondo State was politically too hot for him.

It was the same riggings in the East of Nigeria as Governor Jim Nwobodo of Anambra State lost to Chief CC Onoh of NPN. Alhaji Abubarkar Rimi of Kano lost to Alhaji Barkin Zuwo of PRP. NPN was bent on controlling everything from the Senate to governorships in most of Nigeria's nineteen States and the presidency.

The reason why NPN stole gubernatorial elections in some of the States in the old West was to create a base for Chief Akinloye to win the nomination of the party after President Shagari completed his second term, scheduled to end in 1987. MKO Abiola had been frustrated out of the party by Chief Adisa Meredith Akinloye who had no visible competition in the West of Nigeria according to the Zoning arrangement of the Party. However, he went about it in a very crude and untidy way. He already had his slogan for the future election, called Adisco 87.

Three months into the second term of President Shagari's presidency, in the midst of unhappiness all over the country and unfulfilled expectations of the youths, in the early hours of New Year's Eve 1983, Gen. Buhari became Nigeria's military leader in a bloodless coup that was announced by Brigadier General Sanni Abacha.

Nigeria under President Shagari was like a patient who had cancer and a degenerative disease like Alzheimer's or Parkinson's at the same time. It marked the beginning of everything that was evil about politics in Nigeria, and the ugly smell of corruption that never left the nation.

It was the foundation on how the for future politicians and became a monster for many years to come. Such a man must never be respected or be seen in political arena of any civilized society. Yet in Nigeria, Shagari shamelessly attended the Council of States meetings many years after he was removed from office like every other past leaders.

Gen. Buhari took over in January 1984 and set up many probe panels on the activities of the past civilian government. When President Shagari was questioned on what he was doing when the enemies of the nation were destroying democracy with blatant stealing and abuse of office, he gave the most astonishing statement: he said he was praying.

The whole country was stunned at some of the revelations about Shagari's mental attitude and performance. Was it his level of education or he was just a dumb leader? How could the chief executive of a nation of 150 million black people who had taken the oath to uphold the constitution be praying while crimes were committed in his office?

Was he Oriaku or Okpataku?

One of the penalties for refusing to participate in politics is that you end up being governed by your inferiors.

~Plato

5

Only those who read the article "The Bicycle Government" by Dele Giwa the pioneer Editor–in-Chief of Newswatch in the 1980s could understand the gravity of the damage done to the Nigeria economy by President Shagari and how the gains of the past military government of Gen. Obasanjo were lost. And those who could have given the country purposeful leadership were made to watch the parade of Nigeria's affairs from the sideline.

It was sad; the change of government with a military coup on the New Year's Eve became inevitable since all efforts to have a legitimate change through the ballot box was frustrated by the government in power. Nigerians greeted one another across the nation with the slogan: Happy New Year! Happy new Government, even if it was undemocratic, the country was happy to see the end of maladroit leadership of President Shagari's government and other governors across the nation, most of them with arrested education were all detained.

Gen. Buhari was probably the tallest and slimmest Head of State ever to rule Nigeria. A Muslim, he was born on December 17, 1942, in Daura, Katsina State. He had the look of a hungry lion in the savannah, with the strength of a bull and unquestionable love for the nation. He identified corruption as the number one problem of the nation and was determined to fight it out. In his first speech to a reassured nation, Gen. Buhari tried to justify the takeover of government by accusing the civilian as hopelessly corrupt. He silenced his critics with many draconian laws.

Gen. Buhari's number two man Gen. Tunde Idiagbon was also a thick-set officer with a receding hairline he concealed under his military beret cap. He had two tiny eyes that were greenish like a snake, ready to bite.

Gen. Idiagbon had a master's degree in strategic military studies, which made those with limited education around him uncomfortable in any debate that required analytical thinking. His smiles could be closer to that of hyena chasing a prey. In all, Gen. Idiagbon was a brilliant Army officer who knew his stuff. He surrounded himself with smart officers like Col. Adedotun Gbadebo as his principal staff officer who later became the Alake of Egbaland.

Gen. Tunde Idiagbon's role in the government was the war against indiscipline, until he became a nuisance to everyone. He forgot corruption had been embedded in Nigeria's system. Years before Gen. Gowon left office in 1975, it had developed into the DNA of the nation. How to remove it from the system would be the challenge Generals Buhari and Tunde Idiagbon inherited from ousted President Sheu Shagari.

The level of corruption the military met in 1984 was very disturbing and disgusting. A civilian Governor like Jim Nwobodo of Anambra state who visited one of the residential halls at the University of Ibadan, his Alma Marta, the lucky student who was using the same bed the Governor had used as a student was awarded unbudgeted money by Gov. Jim Nwobodo.

In Kano State, the sum of five million naira cash was found in the governor's bedroom in the government house. Governor Barkin Zuwo displayed the worst ignorance of banking rules and accountability with the Statement: "Government money, in government house. Shikena."

Many of the governors were found guilty and locked away with minimum jail terms of twenty-five years. The most pathetic of them was Governor Jim Nwobodo who was sentenced to 125 years and in tears, like a fool, he asked the Judge if in reality, the judge believed, he would be able to come back from jail alive or complete the jail term.

The Judge also humorously told him, "God Bless your heart in your new journey in jail."

Jim was a man who believed in bleaching his skin to look like a fair-skinned Oyinbo Nigerian. By the time he came out of jail without access to his Ambi bleaching cream he was as black as charcoal and the Press made a lot of funny jokes with his new natural complexion.

Ogun State governor Olabisi Victor Onabanjo was jailed for diverting the State resources to Unity Party of Nigeria his political party. Even in jail, he could not see anything wrong in what he did. Dr. Adelekan, the chairman of the Ogun State Housing

Corporation, was the most unintelligent kleptomaniac out of all the politicians. A few days after the coup he literally removed the corporation's electric generator and it earned him a twenty-five-year jail term. When he was released from jail years later, he relocated to the United States to practice medicine.

Most of Nigerian politicians believed in voodoo or the use of it to improve their lives or fight their political enemies. They joined fetish secret societies to perform rituals that would be too much to describe in any publication.

In the course of these ungodly associations, they used lots of voodoo medicated cream to buff on their bodies, charms, and spiritual dresses in and out of their environment. It was lack of access to it that made the strong man of Ibadan politics Chief Adelakun, fondly called Eruobodo, to request the Federal military government if he could be released from jail to go home to use his local voodoo cream because his skin was turning greenish. He was reminded that jail was different from staying in the comfort of a five-star hotel.

Chief Adelakun was one of the political thugs of Chief Awolowo in the 1950s. He was made Commissioner of Local Government affairs in 1979 by Chief Bola Ige, the new Governor of Oyo State, to the discomfort of Awolowo who questioned the rationale of Bola Ige for elevating a thug to a position that required someone with more than average intelligence. Bola Ige was too weak to see the mistake he was getting himself into until he found out that Adelakun had used his office as Commissioner to get ten acres of land each from all the traditional rulers in the State.

Gov. Bola Ige redeployed him to Ministry of Health, which he refused, and his replacement at the Ministry of Local Government died in a suspicious way and the comment from the Chief made him a suspect.

"Only a stronger man can replace a strong man, not a weak man," he told the Press.

Adelakun had left the Unity Party of Nigeria to join the NPN with a public display on how he shredded the membership card of UPN into pieces. He mocked Chief Awolowo in front of the historic Mapo Hall in Ibadan. Surprisingly, two weeks after, Chief Awolowo came to the same location to assure his loyalists, and to rebuke Eruobodo.

"The public destruction of UPN card membership can only lead to one thing for Eruobodo, tearing his life into pieces and going into perdition," Awolowo said.

It was exactly what happened to Chief Adelakun and he never recovered from it. He died in jail of skin cancer. After several months in jail and human rights abuse of the Gen. Buhari's government on the politicians and the ordinary civilians, the goodwill of his government deteriorated and public opinion changed in the same way; like the Jews in the desert turned against Moses and his God when they were starving.

Nigerians wanted Gen. Buhari and his number two man uncompromising Gen. Tunde Idiagbon out of office. It became a concern to the military establishment itself. It was not long before a crack was noticed and it was the opportunity Gen. Ibrahim Babangida was waiting for to strike the same administration he was part of as Chief of Army Staff with Col. Mepaida as his ADC.

In fairness to Generals Buhari and Tunde Idiagbon, Nigeria was a mess when they took over. They had to start from the scratch to inculcate discipline on the society already polluted by the disarrayed and dishonored National Party of Nigeria leadership. However, Nigeria lacked the ability to sustain any revolution unlike countries in the North of Africa or Middle East; after few days of unrest, they easily give up.

The government introduced many programs with good intentions, but it used the military tactics to implement them. It made the civilian population uncomfortable. For any student of history, with the knowledge of French revolution, one should be able to understand how a bit of freedom given to the peasants consumed Louis XVI of France himself. It marked the beginning of a revolution that changed the history of France.

Within four years of civilian rule, Nigerians were used to an unregulated society under President Shagari but Gen. Buhari's styles were too harsh for them, and even too militant for the society. His government failed to apply the same principles of even discipline to everyone. It was based on a pick and cherry-picked mentality. President Shagari, a Moslem, a Fulani from the North like Buhari, was placed on House arrest and his civilian deputy or vice President from the South, and a Christian, Dr. Alex Ekweme from the Igbo tribe, was jailed. It exposed the insincerity of his government on tribal lines and the Nigeria Press loved it. Everyone was looking for how to hit back at the holier than thou government of Buhari and Idiagbon.

When the government changed the naira currency notes, it turned its eyes away from fifty-three suitcases brought into the country illegally through Muritala Mohamed Lagos International Airport by a Northern Emir of Guwandu through the deposed Emir Jokolo who was then a Major and ADC to Gen. Buhari. The Press made a great deal of that nepotism. But Nigerians failed to understand from the history of the Caliphate, the Emirate of

Guwandu was next to Sokoto in rank because it was the political base of the brother of Othman Dan Fodio. In the defunct Caliphate, which was abolished by the British in 1903, power rotated between Sokoto and Guwandu with Kano Emirate being the problem child for the Caliphate.

In between the various probes going on all over the country, and arrests and jail terms in multiples of twenty-five years for anyone found guilty, the government made attempt to kidnap Alhaji Umaru Dikko, the brother in-law of the deposed President, with the hope that all the assumed blamelessness of the former President would be exposed. The kidnap attempt failed in Britain. The government denied the failed attempt and those involved were jailed.

Secondly, at a time under-aged children were barred from holy pilgrimage to Mecca, Gen. Idiagbon took his own twelve-year-old boy to Mecca, and the enemies of the government took advantage of it to stage a coup through Gen. Babangida who was rumored to be under investigation for a drug related case. It was a coup, which was sponsored by MKO Abiola whose brother in-law was suspected to have been arrested for another drug related case; both of them had fiduciary reasons to stage a coup on a government that was increasingly becoming a problem to the society.

Furthermore, all the military governors in all the nineteen States were abusing the rights of the people all over the country. People were openly caned and even made to frog leap on the streets of Lagos for crossing the streets inappropriately. In Ogun State Gov. Oladipo Diya was harassing civilians without any respect for rule of law in a State that had produced Nigeria's first four Chief Justice for the country and the cradle of western civilization in West Africa. It was shameful.

The new military Governor of Lagos State, Air Commodore Gbolahan Mudashiru cancelled the new Metro railways contract. Alhaji Lateef Jakande government planned and signed the contract with a French company for the sum of 800 million dollars; that alone, turned the Lagos Press against the government. When Gen. Buhari's administration jailed two Guardian journalists for publishing the classified document and executed the two Lagos drug lords, the nation was fed up.

Reciting the National Anthem and National Pledge became the condition for promotions and dismissal from government jobs in all the States of the country. It was horrible because most Nigerians were used to the old National Anthem than the new one, which Gen. Obasanjo forced on the nation before he left the office in 1979.

Gen. Buhari despite his good intention and slogan that Nigeria had no other place to call their own, his government lacked economic know how, as it turned to the era of transatlantic trade of 17th Century through the primitive trade by Barter. His government rejected the IMF loan and the conditionality to devalue the country currency. However, the government received praises from all Nigerians for lowering inflation and curbing imports of needless goods. He reduced crude oil theft while simultaneously using pledge trade policy to barter; he seized illegal bunkered crude oil for needful goods and machineries.

It was the period Nigerians called *Andrew wants to check out*. Nigerians were fleeing the country overseas for the greener pastures because the era of free money and over-invoicing was over. Gen. Buhari failed to understand the Nigeria Press based on the values of the West or the Yoruba, and in between these unknown principles, there were five lines you dare not cross, or abuse, if you want your government to be popular through the Nigeria Press.

- Chief Awolowo for his programs that changed the lives of those in the Western Region,

- Fela Anikulapo Kuti for his radical music and a family history of change for African women through his mother Chief Mrs. Funmilayo Kuti,
- Professor Wole Soyinka for his academic excellence and his radical history of taking over the radio station in the sixties to force the government to announce the result of election, they called him Kongi and the first African to win the prestigious Nobel Award in Literature
- Dr. Tai Solarin for his selfless humanitarian services despite his atheist behavior, and founder of Mayflower college Ikenne in the present Ogun State, and
- Gani Fawehinmi one of the most respected radical lawyers in Africa.

These groups of five were treated as the custodians of natural expectations of good government; natural justice, freedom, and respect for an egalitarian society were regarded as the integrity of the people.

Gen. Buhari and his Deputy Idiagbon were just too excited to jail Fela Anikulapo Kuti for ten years, for having on him, his undeclared foreign currency all, which made the western Press upset. That action was described by Amnesty international as a fabricated political witch-hunting. It was more as if Gen. Buhari came to complete what Gen.

Obasanjo could not do with Fela in the seventies.
General Buhari crossed the line.

Fela had suffered a lot of victimization from
the military in the past. His business and properties
were burnt down at Oju-elegba in Lagos in 1978.
The military had thrown his seventy-eight-year-old
mother, the first woman to fight for women's right
in Nigeria, out of a two story building, which
eventually resulted in her early death. Mrs.
Funmilayo Ransom Kuti was more than Fela's
mother alone. To all the women in Nigeria, she was
the custodian of their rights on how women should
be in Nigeria. She fought for universal adult rights
and equal job pay for women in Nigeria. Her action
in the past led to the abdication of the Alake of
Egbaland Oba Ademola in the 1940s.

In all, Fela had won both the legal and public
sympathy. The case of adduction of twenty-seven
young women made Obasanjo government to look
stupid. To beat the law; Fela married all the women
in one day according to the traditional right and law
of the land to escape military kangaroo justice, all of
which made a fool of the Federal military
government. His music never failed to remind
Nigerians to stand up against the control of the
military in any form. Fela was indeed a pain in the
butt of the military.

To all Nigerians, Fela with his pidgin lyrics of his songs, which spread to every part of the world, was more like a Freedom fighter than the military projected him to be. He was in the class of Bob Marley, Stevie Wonder and Jimmy Cliff; those were his friends.

Furthermore, Gen. Obasanjo a retired Army former military Head of State came out to defend the actions of Gen. Buhari's government as an offshoot of his 1979 military government because most of them served his government as military administrators. By the time the government jailed the two journalists for publishing what the government later called classified document, and Gen. Idiagbon was asked if the document was truthful, will it still be justified for the government to jail the journalists? The response was disturbing and diabolical, Gen. Tunde Idiagbon said, "If the truth will embarrass the government don't publish."

However, Buhari's government provided a complete departure from the past; it made the poor Nigerians and the middle class to believe in the country again with his popular slogan.

"We have no other country to call our own," he said repeatedly. Zig Ziglar a motivational speaker in the United States of America said if you keep repeating a statement, you might end up believing in it. That was the psychological effect of the Buhari words on Nigerians. Gradually they started believing in the country, they could line up at the Bus station and post office, they learned to respect the feelings of others, the need to rush and kick each other over simple issues was reduced, the policy and war against indiscipline was working.

As Nigerians were positively changing their attitudes, the gap-toothed Gen. Ibrahim Badamosi Babangida (IBB) from Minna in Niger State kicked him aside after eighteen months in office in 1985 through a palace coup that was actively supported by the Press and political class.

The eighteen months of Gen. Buhari and Tunde Idiagbon was hectic for all Nigerians used to laidback attitudes. Most people heaved a sigh of relief when the government was kicked out by IBB and all the gains were thrashed away with SAP (Structural Adjustment Program) which IBB introduced, which was spearheaded by Chief Olu False, the Secretary to the Federal military government. The local currency lost its value for the first time and didn't recover for several decades.

When Gen. Tunde Idiagbon travelled out of the country on a pilgrimage to Mecca and Medina with his twelve-year-old son, and a helpless Gen. Buhari was relaxing, Gen. Babangida the Army Chief of Staff sent a signal for a meeting with all the service chiefs in his office. He placed all of them on house arrest and it was the simplest way to organize a coup d'état with Gen. Idiagbon out of the country. It was easy for Brigadier Sanni Abacha, a man with knocking knees to announce again another coup like he did in December 1983, which brought Gen. Buhari to government. But this time Gen. Babangida was named the new military President, which was a complete departure from Head of State system of the past.

Retired Gen. Babangida is not literarily a tall guy, probably around 5.8 ft. tall, thick set, with a killer instinct, infectious smiles, and gap toothed and in most cases, it could be difficult to separate his smiles from his annoyance. Call him a man with the smiles of hyena on his face; you will be very close to it. He could be killing you with a deadly knife pushed slowly into your heart while still displaying the same smiles on his face.

IBB had the same hyena smiles on his face on March 5, 1986 when he ordered the execution of his 'best friend,' Major Gen. Mamman Vatsa who was by his side when he married his wife several decades before, Vatsa was probably the best poet and writer ever to come out of Nigeria Army. He was the Head of Brigade of Guard, and a patron of Nigeria Arts. Despite pleas from friends and academic society worldwide, IBB's surrogate General Bali announced the execution of Vatsa on March 5, 1986. Bali without regret told a surprised nation with a quote from the Bible that the wages of sin is death.

Fondly called IBB by his friends and the Press because of his initials, he looked harmless, and could be easily taken as a friend, but that was all you could get from him. IBB was a ruthless General and probably involved in all the successful military coups in the history of Nigeria. Major Okar, who planned the 1990 coup against IBB, called him homosexual. It was not refuted and in a real sense of it IBB could be the ugly side of General Obasanjo.

It will not be appropriate now to focus on Gen. Babangida government because his government represented all that was evil again in Nigeria. It was worse than former President Shagari's government; in his tenure, corruption was almost legalized as spurious government funds were deposited into people's private accounts to influence public opinion. Some were courageous enough to expose the government, like Wole Soyinka and Olikoye Ransome Kuti. Both of them returned the funds deposited into their private accounts to the government treasury. Incidentally, they were all indigenes of Ogun State and whatever the gains of IBB in his eight years as military President, he destroyed it with the annulment of the June 12 election in 1993.

However, the IBB government changed the license plate tag through Federal Road Safety Corp. chaired by Professor Wole Soyinka. His government also could be credited completion of third mainland bridge in Lagos and establishment of People's Bank, which was chaired by Dr. Tai Solarin. IBB knew how to corrupt any public officials better than any of his predecessors. Dr. Tai Solarin was an avowed atheist and socialist. He never wore anything more than his short nickers. By the time IBB finished with him, Tai Solarin was wearing typical flowing Agbada dress as the Chairman of the People's Bank and smiling to his last premolars.

Furthermore, IBB and his many projects that were badly executed or not relevant to future development of the country all died or faded away as soon as he left office.

Imperiously, Dele Giwa the editor-in-chief of Newswatch who had lots of incriminating documents against Gen. Babangida, from his days as the editor of Sunday News Concord, his head was blown off with a parcel letter bomb, purportedly sent from Dodan Barack in Obalende Lagos, which was then the seat of government.

Despite the denial of the government in the complicity, the manner in which the government went about to destroy evidence and prevented the court from hearing the case brought by Dele Giwa's lawyer, late Gani Fawehinmi, placed a red flag on the proverbial hands of Esau with the voice of Jacob. IBB could not pass a simple lie test on what and who was responsible for the death of Dele Giwa.

Afro-beat king Fela Anikulapo Kuti, who was jailed by the past administrations, was released to appease his fans. IBB was like the house mouse, Mickey, as he was biting the country he was also mouth fanning it at the same time. He appointed Fela's brother Professor Olikoye Ransom Kuti, a respected World Health Organization consultant, as the Federal Minister of Health.

When the Nigerian Press, jokingly asked Fela if his brother had joined the rank of those stealing the nation's resources as a minister in a government he thought was corrupt, Fela said, "I know my brother can never steal from the government, but I noticed since he became Minister his butt has been shooting out."

By the time Gen. Babangida stepped aside in 1993, his eight years in office was more of setback, or probably a nightmare for the Nation than any progress he made. His government could be classified as Oriaku.

Maybe, if the two party systems his government created were left intact, the unity and progress of the country would be very easy to harmonize, but it was destroyed or pulled down by

Gen. Babangida who annulled the 1993 Presidential elections won by his friend or enemy MKO Abiola while late Gen. Sanni Abacha nailed the coffin of Democracy with his draconian almost five years military dictatorship.

Politics is the game of telling lies and getting away with a straight face.
~Unknown

6

After all the efforts of Gen. Babangida to prolong his stay in office had failed and he was forced to choose between his life or to stay as a military President in a country that saw his true colors, IBB did what most cowards would do: he stepped aside.

He left a baggage of problems and disunity among the Yoruba. He even went deeper to destroy the unity in the very hometown of the Egba in Abeokuta, which was based on the control of five councils of Obas and separate groups like Ake, Gbagura, Ibara, Oke Ona, and Owu. Appointing Chief Ernest Shonekan as Head of the interim government was disrespectful to the serving generals and was calculated to drive a wedge between MKO Abiola from his kinsmen and women.

To understand more about the politics of Ogun, your may wish to read my book *Ogun State Policy of Manipulation* (2013), with details on the way things were controlled and managed then in Ogun State.

Oba Oyebade Lipede belonged to the Ake section of the Egba as well as the new Head of interim government, High Chief Ernest Shonekan. MKO Abiola was from the minority group of Gbagura. The whole of Nigeria expected the people of Abeokuta to support and defend the June 12 mandate of MKO Abiola. They could not understand why and how the Alake of Egbaland could be looking favorably with a finalized nepotism at interim Head of State Ernest Shonekan as his very own rather than MKO Abiola as an Egba man.

MKO Abiola had his problems with Alake of Egbaland in the past. He had made too many promises, which he never fulfilled to His Royal Highness the most respected Oba Oyebade Lipede and his people.

MKO Abiola was a force of nature, everything about him was bold and flamboyant, and everything he touched was successful. A moderately tall man with horse faced like, with a very funny hesitant pitch voice. When MKO smiled, he showed his last premolars. When he danced, he raised his two index fingers up in systematic rhymes that made his political enemies jealous because of the Awolowo two-finger victory signs. A man with big protruding eyes and wide nose, he had plenty of money in all currencies of most western nations not just in his pocket, but also in all the corners of the world banks and all these attracted women to him like the honey to the bees.

MKO owned the Concord Newspapers conglomerate, which also published in local languages; he owned properties and investment all over the country and beyond. The more he accomplished the more he wanted, and his political ambition bothered the North and the military. MKO Abiola's presence could be found in every business, from investment in Habeeb Bank with retired Gen. Yar'Adua, the Summit Oil and Gas Company with retired Col. Dan Suleiman, ITT, Radio Communication, bakery, and printing. His investments like his women were all over the world.

MKO Abiola was a shameless flirt like most men. When he talked to women, he did it with humor and respect. He knew the weaknesses of women, and it was difficult to get a reject from any woman because he was a master of the game. He once stopped an attractive black woman at Ita-Oshin at the outskirt of Abeokuta to direct him on how to get to Lafenwa Abeokuta.

"Hello Angel, can you direct MKO to Lafenwa?" Abiola asked.

"Yes. I can even tell you how to get to your house at Sabo Road in Abeokuta," she said.

MKO smiled, he gave her a large sum of money before he took her away for the night.

MKO Abiola came from a very challenging background and openly admitted his humble upbringing. Behind his generosity was the greed to grab more. He was also an employer who paid his staff better than anyone in the country; it was easy for him to attract the best hands in his business.

Despite his generosity MKO Abiola was more of a Lagos man than Abeokuta his place of birth, and his people were technically disappointed in him. He was able to use his handout of gifts to those around him to prevent the real expectations of the people from a man of his caliber.

Late Chief Awolowo once said Chief MKO Abiola was a man larger than life who failed to use his influence to help his people or the nation, and that might be true, all the requests of MKO Abiola to his people to start new ventures in Abeokuta were generously given to him, but MKO Abiola never implemented any of them.

MKO was given industrial lands at Obada Oko at the periphery of Abeokuta on Lagos road, for MKO soft drinks, ITT power generator plants, Abiola farms, and many more, MKO got the lands, and he fenced them with a signpost of the companies but never developed any of them. At one time the Alake of Egbaland asked him openly if he had a problem with his home town, because the city would like to benefit from his business connections. With a smile and total respect for the crown, he told the king, he had none, but love for the City of his birth and origin.

However, when he visited the Abeokuta Club, Engineer Yomi Adenekan, the Publicity Secretary of Abeokuta Club at the time and the arrow Head of all clubs for all Egba, asked him, the same question. MKO Abiola gave him a thumb down answer and even ridiculed Engineer Yomi Adenekan who was the Director of Works for Ogun State, as a man who only lived on government contracts and could not understand the indices and requirement of business location. That statement from MKO Abiola would be his nemesis in future with late Engineer Yomi Adenekan.

Based on MKO Abiola, assumption Abeokuta did not have all the requirement of a business location. Six months after that encounter, he acquired several acres of industrial land on Apapa Road for his printing and publishing company in Lagos and his home town Abeokuta, and the respectable Alake of Egbaland Oba Oyebade Lipede were all left gasping. That was the problem MKO Abiola had with Egba before his election was annulled by military President Gen. Badamosi Babangida in 1993.

Chief Abiola had no backward integration policy like the Ijebu in the State of his birth and origin like that of Otunba Subomi of First City Merchant Bank or Chief Bayo Kuku of his caliber in the Ijebuland. When he visited the same Abeokuta Club later to ask for the support of the Egba for the actualization of the June 12 election de-annulment, he faced late Engineer Yomi Adenekan again, who had the last laugh on him.

The Egba are noted for one thing, they don't forget anything good or bad. Life to them is like the Law of Moses, you do it, you pay for it, and that very day after MKO Abiola had told the members of the club how he was expecting them to support and work for the de-annulment of the June 12 election. Engineer Adenekan told Abiola openly, "The Abeokuta, and indeed the Egba you said, was not good for investment was now ripe for use as a tool to fight a course that would benefit Chief Abiola alone. Because we do not think Abeokuta or the Egba nation would even benefit from a likely MKO Abiola presidency, as a result, we are not ready to set out our children to be killed by the soldiers for a man who never put our interest at heart in the past."

With that, MKO Abiola's desire to have his Egba people behind him for the actualization of the June 12 mandate failed from his hometown and no single Egba man was killed for his dream in

Abeokuta or in Egba community. Clearly, it could be said he was given the middle finger by his own people.

However, MKO Abiola, despite his money and influences, was indeed a man from the minority Gbagura sub-ethnic group of Abeokuta, with Oba Laloko as the king, apart from Alake of Egbaland, Oshinle of Oke Ona, and Olowu of Owu all other two groups (Ibara and Gbagura) are not really a force in the Egba Council of Obas.

The appointment of Chief Ernest Shonekan, an Ake man, and a High Chief of Alake as Head of Interim was seen more of a blessing than the flamboyant son, MKO Abiola's caliber, which was almost the general consensus of those who never really liked MKO Abiola.

Let us back up a bit on the above. At a time Gen. Babangida was shopping for the Head of Interim, Retired Gen. Obasanjo former Head of State was the unfulfilled Oliver Twist of Nigeria politics. He was interested and he was disappointed when Gen Babangida finally settled for Chief Ernest Shonekan, a former UAC Chief Executive, and a High Chief from Ake section of Abeokuta or the Egba instead of him the Balogun of Owu of the same Egba Kingdom.

Furthermore, Gen. Obasanjo who belongs to the Owu section of the Egba and the rivalry of the

Owu and Ake was legendary. Also very deep in the City of Abeokuta over which of the two groups that first came but events supported Oke Ona as the first settlers through Sodeke but the Ake had the support of all other polished true Egba than the Owu or the Oke Ona people. That could be seen more like the Ibadan people and in most cases, the link between the Owu and Orile Owu in Oyo State gave credence to that separation of interest within Egba Community.

There was no record, which indicated Chief Ernest Shonekan ever had the support of Gen Obasanjo. From day one in office, however, Chief Shonekan did what late Alake of Egbaland had requested from previous administrations without success for the Egba or Abeokuta; he awarded the duali-zation of Lagos-Abeokuta road contract to Julius Berger. The company moved to site immediately, and the Interim government of Chief Shonekan looked promising to the Egba or the Alake of Egbaland than Chief MKO Abiola's unreliable dream of the June 12 in limbo of Hausa Fulani and military oligarchy.

At one time the King of Egbaland in Abeokuta said, "If what the Egba were looking for in June 12 they could find it in Interim government, it will still be the same."

Meaning it was time for the Egba to move on. With that statement, Alake was ready to dump MKO Abiola and his fruitless dream of the June 12 mandate. A view that was seen by those with objective view on the local politics of Egba nation, as if the king was ready to defend the interest of Ake over that of Gbagura in the political imbroglio.

Ordinarily, the average Egba people were disunited on who to support between Abiola and Shonekan. With the new Lagos /Abeokuta road, which had claimed many lives in the past, under-construction, interim government was more of a reality than that MKO Abiola, a friend of the North, to them in the past, he did not have the sincere interest of the Yoruba, Egba or religious tolerance, which the Egba were noted for secretly. However, the Egba without anyone voicing it out might have dumped MKO Abiola and his June 12 mandate.

Furthermore, as events continued to unfold, Chief MKO Abiola's June 12 mandate and political imbroglio were reduced to his personal problems, that of NADECO, his family and business associates alone, but not that of his own people. In the same pathetic way, Chinua Achebe described the tragedy of Okonkwo in the book "Things Fall Apart" and how he perceived his people of Umofia, when he realized he had made the greatest mistakes of his life for killing the court messenger without the support of his kinsmen before he went to commit suicide. It was the same feeling here for MKO Abiola.

Bashorun MKO Abiola knew he had to do it alone, without his roots, it was sad as Are Ona kankanfo of Yoruba was stripped of his pride among his people. It was then he knew no one could clap with one hand, which was the popular slogan at most of his philanthropy donation events. He reasoned he had been doing just that with other people excluding his home base.

Chief MKO Abiola reflected on what he had done for his people in the past years in the areas of education, millions of naira donations to many schools, and scholarships, two time winners of Challenge Cup through Abiola Babes football club, which placed his hometown on sport history. He wanted to know where he went wrong. He could not see it in the same way his people saw it, maybe, if he was given the support he asked for, he would have redeemed himself or behaved like a better citizen of the city of his birth, but history and subsequent events never gave him the chance he asked for.

Maybe MKO needed to ask for forgiveness from the Awolowo loyalists or the dreams of Awolowo he destroyed with his newspapers despite the fact that the government of Western Region in the fifties led by Chief Awolowo gave him scholarship to study Accounting in Glasgow in the

United Kingdom, which opened up his world. His role against Awolowo's political career made him an ungrateful beneficiary of a program that helped many from poor homes in the Western Region.

The above analysis could not fulfill the opening paragraph and the next chapter on IBB will attempt to explain the expectations and implications of the problem left behind by Gen. Babangida with Gen. Sanni Abacha and the death of Chief MKO Abiola.

Poetry is about grieved, politics is about grievance.

~Robert Frost

The Oracle says when you have money, and too much of it, political power may not be the best Abraham Maslow's hierarchy of needs to attain, that was why MKO Abiola had all his smiling friends as enemies at a time he needed their support, and why he did not realize the green snakelike smiles of his so called friends or enemies was beyond imagination. He was set up to run for the office of presidency by those who had a hidden agenda, by the frustrated political class that wanted Gen Babangida out of office at all cost after he had destroyed the Presidential ambition of Gen. Yar'Adua, Kingibe, and Falae all within the Social Democratic Party (SDP) and Shinkafi and other Presidential candidates from NRC

Chief MKO Abiola was never a foundation member of SDP, those who brought him to run for the office of President, knew how close he was with the sit tight military President Babangida. They knew their history was way back to when the IBB was only a Captain in the Nigeria Army, they knew how both of them sponsored the coup that removed Gen. Buhari from office in 1985, they knew how MKO Abiola used his newspapers Concord shamelessly to give legitimacy to the government of military President IBB, they knew, when Gen. Babangida men with the Air force beat up the Chief in Lagos after one of his sons Deji had problem with the Air force men, at Ikeja in Lagos, they knew everything and many ugly deals between the duo from crude oil, banking and Liberia war deals. It was a setup, which MKO Abiola himself never discovered, like an unsuspected prey he walked into the trap.

The Oracle says if you really want to catch a monkey throw him a piece of banana. Sadly, as it may sound to the readers or supporters of unending political drama of Nigeria, Are Onakakafo of Yoruba land Chief MKO Abiola was the banana thrown at IBB before he could be removed from office.

However, IBB was not the only monkey that wanted the banana, others were the oil cartel of serving and retired military Generals and faceless cronies of AGIP (Any Government in Power) like the Obas and Emirs, contractors, oil dealers, who knew, and heard the comment of MKO Abiola on how oil price and the level of millions of unaccounted barrels of oil left Nigeria shore, which the MKO Abiola promised to look into as an

Accountant and as a President, if he had won, those were the hidden facts behind the annulment of election of June 12, 1993.

As soon as MKO Abiola won the nomination of his party SDP in Jos and failed to select Alhaji Abubarkar Atiku, a surrogate of Gen. Yar'Adua as his running mate, the mafia Head of the party SDP, his adversaries started to work against his electoral success or the future of his presidency, and they realized his presidency might be difficult to control.

IBB was also interested in planting a trusted allied as the vice President to a government controlled by SDP if Abiola had won the election. He wanted Pascal Bafiyawu, his surrogate, the serving President of the Nigeria Labor Congress NLC to represent his interest in a possible Abiola presidency.

However, all the serving civilian governors wanted Alhaji Babagana Kingibe who sponsored or mentored most of them for offices. It was a power struggle, somehow, MKO Abiola wanted his business associate retired Col. Dan Suleiman as his running mate, but in his wisdom or otherwise, he went for the wishes of the Governors with the selection of Alhaji Kingibe as his running mate. It was the first noticeable crack in his Presidential bid.

It was the first time in Nigeria where the issue of religion took the back seat because the State and people of Ogun, and indeed the Yoruba, never mixed religion with politics, old western region was and still the base of religious tolerance in Nigeria.

To the Yoruba, a government should be measured by achievement not by the religion of the leader. The West never had any history of problem or war on religion, every religion including traditional religion or fetishism was allowed to thrive side by side. It is not uncommon to find Churches, Mosques and Ile Ogboni on the same street.

The North was happy to have a Muslim/Muslim ticket for the office of President and vice President of Nigeria. To the rest of the South, most importantly among the Igbo, and Yoruba tribes, it was the generosity and good heart of MKO Abiola that mattered. The predominantly Christian south never questioned the control of the two powerful offices in the land by the Muslims. To them, MKO Abiola who went to a Christian school, Baptist Boys High School, with proper understanding of Christian values would do the right thing, they thought!

Why the Christians in the North also did trust MKO Abiola could not be ascertained after Olu Falae was banned. The next reliable person was MKO Abiola, a good friend of President Babangida, and his religion was no longer a factor. Regrettably, despite the fact that everything was looking good on paper for a brighter future for the politics of Nigeria, it left the military President Gen. Babangida on behalf of the military deflated and Retired Gen. Yar Adua out of the loop. Both of them kept away their differences and plotted against the election, a plan to derail the progress made by the progressives was conceived.

An outsider and a traditional adversary of the Yoruba political class had to be used while the duo operated from the political chess backroom. Association of Better Nigerians ABN emerged with Chief Arthur Nzeribe who was mandated to challenge the result of the Jos Convention that confirmed the nomination of MKO Abiola as the flag bearer of the party, from a favorable Judge.

It was very easy for the military to manipulate events in their favor like in the past. All they needed then, was to call in the Chairman of Federal electoral Commission (FEDECO) or so, deposit some money in his account as it was the practice in the past and he would be singing the type of song they wanted, that was the system then.

Somehow, it turned out differently, the Chairman of the electoral commission, Professor Humphrey Nwosu, turned out to be a man of honor. He ignored all requests and body languages of the military, including the court order, which was fraudulently obtained overnight. He relied solely on the law, which categorically stated that the election or the outcome of it could not be halted by the court after the convention.

The electoral law had been drafted in such a way that gave no jurisdiction to any court to stop the electoral process, and it was the weapon the electoral Chairman Professor Nwosu relied upon. Legally, he was right to have gone ahead with the election, but with the military, he was not a team player, and the power of a dictator was stronger than any rule of law.

On June 12, 1993, almost 14.8 million Nigerians went to the polls to vote. It was peaceful. No single misunderstanding was recorded all over the country. It was the most successful and peaceful election ever held in the country since independence in 1960 according to all the international and local observers. The weather itself was approved by the gods: there was no single rain to disrupt the flow of traffic and people. Even the sun itself was friendly. It was a change of government, everyone was happy to participate.

However, Nigerians never checked what the Holy Book said about being watchful, even when everything is going well. The Holy Book says watch and pray, even when it is not going well the Holy Book still ask for prayers, with prayers prosperity of any believer including the nation could be protected.

In the primitive history of the Yoruba, when God (Olodunmare) asked Obatala to undertake in the creation of the universe, he consulted the Oracle who asked him to make supplement or sacrifices to Esu laalu Onile Orita for his journey to be peaceful. Obatala failed to heed the message of the Oracle, when he finished the work, he got drunk with palm wine, and Esu destroyed most of his creations, that was how some became hunch back, Albino, blind, short and tall, even fat, because Obatala failed to listen to the Oracle.

Until today among the traditional worshipers of Obatala a separate allocation was also made for Esu as a form of respect for his activities and it has been a taboo for worshippers of Obatala to drink palm wine again. Chief MKO Abiola failed to pray against the hands of the devil in the election that would determine his fate with history.

Nigerians were proud to vote for the candidates of their choice. The method of the voting system was very simple by any imagination. All a voter needed to do was to line up behind the candidate of his or her choice emblems in the public. The electoral officer counted and announced the result. Everyone got a copy of the result in the affected ward, which was collated at all local governments, the same day. The collated results from all local governments were also checked at the

States level. By the time the result was sent to national office of electoral commission even a caveman knew the winner already. It was the best foolproof result against fraud in any third world nation; the system was called Option A4.

However, as the Federal electoral body was announcing the results State by State, it was obvious from all the open results, which everyone in the country knew the result already that MKO Abiola had won the election. By the time the first fourteen States were announced in favor of MKO Abiola, the military and all enemies of Democracy had to look IBB directly in the face, to either cancel the election or be killed himself because they were not ready to accept MKO Abiola, a womanizer with lots of money and influence as their Commander-in-Chief. Some even called him a CIA agent of the United States.

With only five lines statements on a plain sheet of paper, without shame and respect for the public, the result of the best election in Nigeria was annulled. It marked the beginning of fruitless journey in Nigeria, the chain of events that killed and sent many into exile including the life of the winner of the June 12 election in 1993.

The whole nation was disillusioned based on the flimsy excuse of the court statement obtained overnight in a diabolical way, which could not pass simple lie test. It was a shame to the integrity of the Nigeria judiciary and ruling Armed forces under IBB as both institutions plotted against the result of the best and freest election ever had in Nigeria.

However, MKO Abiola despite his shortcomings had a very good heart. He loved the poor and very likeable to all tribes. But he was not a true politician. He was a practical business man and a good man running for the highest office in the land of the Blacks, which was the reason IBB had him by the balls, by appointing his home town man Chief Ernest Shonekan, as the interim Head of State to divide his base and Yoruba community. IBB succeeded because money was the root of all evil, as MKO Abiola was running about like chicken without head.

Unfortunately, IBB actions had him as a very dirty player or Oriaku. If he had transferred power to Chief MKO Abiola all his past sins would have been forgiven, including unresolved murder cases like the death of Newswatch pioneer Editor-in - Chief, or the plane crash of military officers around Ejigbo in Lagos, which was rumored to have been plotted by his government. But like evil genius he called himself, it was difficult to see his mind and how he could live with himself with all the mess he left behind. Sometimes average Nigerians would wish his regime never happened in the history of

Nigeria, but it did, and Nigeria has never been the same again!

Was Chief Ernest Shonekan appointment as Head of Interim government a betrayal to the dreams of Chief MKO Abiola? Was he a part of Chief MKO Abiola dream plan? Or was he just a decent man left with history to be judged? Why will a High Chief of Ernest Shonekan caliber from Abeokuta treat MKO Abiola with such a Brutus knife at a time he needed his kinsmen and women? Will History justify his action as brutal and unfriendly? However, will those with sympathy for him rate him as a man who was there with his shoulder big enough for his country and when the IBB needed a getaway plan?

At the unseen apex hands of politics in Nigeria, the loyalty and control of power belonged to the group that became the friends of the British that edged out those that specifically asked the British for the independence of the country in 1960. As soon as you crossed the line of Rubicon to request for a change of plan from the laid down policy since 1960, the tendency is to be eliminated, that was the secret code of Nigeria political set. *See no evil, talk no evil!*

MKO Abiola's presidency was likely to cross the line to the other side and he was sidelined by all his so-called friends in power and he died in hands of those who wanted Nigeria tied to the apron of control of the same power that has put the nation in chain since 1960 or with the forceful spirit of the Amalgamation of Nigeria in 1914 by Lord Frederick Luggard.

Furthermore, some unanswered questions in the minds of readers would be why did Abiola not declare himself as President when he had the result of all the states to justify his action? Why did he have to wait for almost a year until it was too late before he did it at Epetedo in Lagos? If he had declared himself the winner and followed it up with the result in a court of law, IBB and the military would have been defeated in their ugly game. It was probably the mistake on the part of MKO Abiola. He listened and took advise from the wrong people most of them never really liked him.

Finally, on this part seven, If MKO Abiola was the banana thrown at IBB to get him out of office by those who wanted him out at all cost after so many failed and prolonged transition elections and primaries; Chief Ernest Shonekan could be described as the returned dirty banana from IBB to the nation with a bitter pill of Gen. Sanni Abacha.

Senator Chief Author Nzeribe

He led the group ABN that was used by the military to annual the June12, 1993, election. Nzeribe was a professional arm dealer and a maverick politician. Critics of General Ibrahim Babangida believed Author Nzeribe was used by the military to derail the 1993 presidential election; his connections with Uche Chuckwumerije the Federal Minister of Information of the time in the brouhaha could not be ascertained both of them, ended up as Senators of the Federal Republic of Nigeria.

Gen. Oladipo Diya
Chief Staff Supreme Headquarters

General Oladipo Diya was lucky or blessed to escape death from his boss General Sanni Abacha in a botched military coup. Diya, a former Military Governor in Ogun state during General Mohamadu Buhari regime. He emerged as number two man in the regime of General Sanni Abacha after the provisional government of Ernest Shonekan was kicked aside.

General Diya's demand to have the Capital of a proposed Ijebu State in his home town Odogbolu was one of the reasons given for the denial of new State by the Awujale of Ijebuland.

Major Hamza al-Mustapha
Chief Security Officer too late
Head of State Sani Abacha

Hamza al-Mustapha was the Chief Security Officer of Gen. Sanni Abacha, military Head of State of Nigeria from November 1993 to June 1998, After Abacha's death he was arrested and tried for murder and attempted murder. On January 30, 2012, a Lagos High Court sitting at Igbosere convicted Al-Mustapha for the murder of Kudirat Abiola, the wife of the acclaimed winner of the June 12, 1993, Presidential election, Chief Moshood Abiola. He was sentenced to death by hanging.

Gen. Jeremiah Usenni

A professional Coup plotter since 1967, despite being the most senior military officer after the death of Gen Sanni Abacha, he was not appointed the military Head of State because his stand was against the transition plan and the general interest of other Generals as later revealed by Major Hamza Al Mustapha to the truth Commission.

General Usenni was with the late Head of State Gen Sanni Abacha who died few hours after he left the maximum dictator in early hours, whatever his role in the death of Abacha was never revealed because he was a suspect, and probably why he did not succeed the later military dictator.

Gov. Olusegun Osoba
Ogun State Governor from January 1992 until
November 1993 and May 1999-May 2003

Aremo Segun Osoba was elected on the Social Democratic Party platform, and was removed from office by the administration of General Sani Abacha. After the return to democracy in 1999, he was elected again as Governor on the ticket of Alliance for Democracy; he held office between May 1999 and May 2003. He also served as a titled chieftain of the Egba clan as well. Unconfirmed source said he persuaded MKO Abiola to run for president in the annulled 1993 election.

Senator Bola Tinubu

One of the leaders of NADECO, an associate of MKO Abiola, Tinubu was a two-term Governor of Lagos State, leader of APC, and most likely to be the President of the Senate in 2015 or Vice President of Nigeria. He will in future be credited and known as the politician who rebuilt the opposition into a formable party from the funny 65 political parties in Nigeria to a two party system. And probably the heir to the vacant political shoes of late Chief

Obafemi Awolowo among the Yoruba, the Oracle
says probably.

If it walks like a duck, it moves like a duck, it looks like duck, it must be a duck.
~ **Senator John McCain**

A Friend on the Facebook, Mr. Najim, wanted to know if MKO Abiola had selected Atiku as vice President what would have been the result of the election. It was very simple to predict what could have happened because President Obasanjo who later in life benefited from MKO Abiola failed legacy did and MKO Abiola would have gotten the same treatment Gen. Obasanjo got from the same inheritor of political machine of late Gen. Yar' Adua.

Just as this writer fondly called the Oracle was thinking on what to write about the eighty-four days in office of Chief Ernest Shonekan as the Head of the interim Government after Gen. Babangida stepped aside, as fate would have it, the Oracle was on the same ARIK flight to Abuja with the High

Chief of Egbaland in the last week of November 2011, the trip would be my first visit to the seat of power in Nigeria, since 1990 when I visited the FCT, at a time it was a virgin land. Nobody in the South of Nigeria with the complete love of Lagos wanted to go, with lots of constructions going on then.

Abuja was a virgin city then, for the risk takers and the Igbo knew the future of the city before other tribes in Nigeria. Like the Oracle used to say, "If you really want to know if there will be prosperity in a city, check the population trend, if it has Igbo people, stay there, because there will be money and opportunities for the future and unimaginable growth.

However, if you don't see Igbo, please move on, only the Ndigbo can see the color of money in a city before any tribe in Nigeria. It is the truth and will always be because these group of hard working Africans from East of River Niger and Benue, are risk takers, and fearless in midst of difficulties." They were the first to understand the potentials of Abuja as the new Federal capital.

My then boss and chairman of the company I worked for in Lagos as Marketing Manager, Chief Ononuju, Ogbuefi Chiyelugo of Omunakwo from Ogbaru local government in Anambra State was shipping tons of cement and building materials to Abuja and we were skeptical and ignorantly laughing at his dream of a city. We thought in our innocent minds that Abuja as Federal Capital of Nigeria would be a waste and would never take off; but the Chief was one of the first set of people to see the potentials of Abuja, the hidden diamond in the heart of Nigeria.

When you learn to take risk in anything in life, you believe in yourself, you trust in your fate and luck and with it, the blessings will come. Abuja would in future be a blessing to all Nigerians and the risk takers would decide the future of the city that looked like Las Cruces in the State of New Mexico in the United States with all its topography and infrastructure.

What the Oracle saw of Abuja would have to be written in another spectrum for us not to be Abuja crazy or carried away with the topic at hand i.e. The Political history of Nigeria or Oriaku and Okpataku of Nigeria politics since 1945.

In a subtle and formal Yoruba way, the Oracle greeted the High Chief of his hometown Abeokuta with respect and he became comfortable. From the fifteen-minute discussions, I had with him; he was a man still in search of his relevance with history.

Chief Shonekan, a simple polished businessman in the hands of fate and history, and we concluded with the consolatory words that it was not how long in office but how effective he was.

Chief Ernest Shonekan was the first Head of State to be sworn in Abuja, the new Federal Capital of Nigeria. It was during his short time in office as Nigeria Head of Interim government, Ondo State became an oil producing State in Nigeria, and to the people of Abeokuta it was the time the Lagos Abeokuta Express road that had witnessed lots of accidents with many deaths in the past was dualized or the contract was first awarded to Julius Berger before it was cancelled by Lateef Jakande the Minister for Works under Gen. Sanni Abacha.

Furthermore, Ernest Shonekan became the man Gen. Babangida trusted with the presidency in 1993 when he had to step aside. He was the former Head of UAC in Nigeria or West Africa. Though MKO Abiola's generosity could be felt everywhere like the current of electricity, Shonekan's legacy was very specific. He had established a branch of UAC his company at Ibara Abeokuta.

However, MKO built the Library for Ogun State Polytechnic, which has since been renamed after MKO Abiola, and the defunct Abiola Babes football team, which placed Abeokuta on the sport history of Nigeria with two Challenge Cup championships, and a secondary school on Ibadan Abeokuta Road, apart from other donations to Mosques and scholarships to several thousands of individuals all over the country.

That was it; however his people wanted something much more tangible like manufacturing companies, like late Chief Lawson did in the 1960s with his Top Brewery or like Chief Odutola did with 33 Brewery at Ijebu Igbo. The closest thing Chief MKO had to a viable ongoing company in his home town would be his wife's company, Zidikayat Nigeria Limited.

Furthermore, at the time of MKO imbroglio with the military, only the mosques, schools and political associates benefited from his generosity, which was even better. But the Egba was like the Oliver Twist, a society that wanted to see companies and factories like Chief Lawson did with Top Brewery, with that, MKO Abiola was grossly misunderstood because the hearts of Egba politics revolved around Gen. Obasanjo his school mate, who made the Federal government to grant the creation of Ogun State and Abeokuta as the seat of government in 1976.

However, between MKO Abiola and the High Chief Shonekan of the Ake powerful section of Egba nation, readers would recall that Gen. Obasanjo had also lobbied to be Head of Interim government before Gen. Babangida selected Chief Shonekan and it became a problem between the two. It would be appropriate here to explain that Gen. Babangida and Gen. Obasanjo had a history of cooperation in the military and civilian lives, based on the military seniority and mischievous pranks.

At one time Gen. Babangida revealed, Gen Obasanjo saved his military career at a time he did something that was not appropriate and stupid. When his response to the query given to him by the Army Authority was reviewed, it was Gen. Obasanjo who assisted him to doctor a favorable feedback that freed him from a problem that could have ended his career with the Nigeria Army. Whatever it was, he never disclosed it, but knowing how bad IBB was as a reckless military officer, it must have been very terrible.

Some rumored it has to do with homosexual, which late Major Okar later accused him off publicly on the national radio broadcast when he tried to over-throw his government in the late eighties, he never denied the allegations, but there was no clear cut evidence to support the allegation, probably a rumor, IBB was married to one of the most attractive ladies in Nigeria Maryam who died in December, 27th 2009 over a complicated Ovarian Cancer at the age of 61.

The gap-toothed General was indeed a grateful man in the manner of respect he accorded his former boss. But Gen. Obasanjo was a difficult man to please. Later in life Femi Fani Kayode one of the Ministers in the civilian government of Gen.

Obasanjo and a friend of both, said anyone who tried to please Obasanjo would be wasting his time.

Gen. Sanni Abacha became the monster Chief Ernest Shonekan inherited from Gen. Babangida; the relationship was like a friend asking you to watch over a lion for him in his house.

Lagos, the seat of the Ministry of Defense that Sanni Abacha held onto with an iron grip, became the house where the lion was kept and Ernest Shonekan stayed far away in Abuja. Gen. Abacha would not come to Abuja for any Federal Executive meetings and the Interim Head of State was helpless and when Gen. Sanni Abacha finally threw him out after eighty-four days in office, Chief Shonekan was even relieved himself, probably happy because he was not killed.

Head of Interim Government Chief Ernest Shonekan had no power or significant influence with the military, at the same time and he was seen as the antagonist of his people, the Yoruba. They felt he should have been courageous enough to reject Head of Interim offer of Gen. Babangida for two reasons, the power of decency, and blood of the people killed since the failed Presidential attempts of Chief Awolowo in 1959, 1979, and 1983 and the political predicament and spillover of Chief MKO Abiola in 1993 was likely to influence.

To a man of his caliber, history had nothing
to do with it. He believed in the power of the
moment, in most cases very difficult for people with
ideology with greed for power and even ambition to
understand that behind the history of every action in
life, lies the future of decency and when a man dies,
that would be the platform on which he would be
judged, regrettably, that was where Chief Shonekan
failed the Yoruba particularly the Egba, including his
place in history.

Furthermore, Chief Shonekan was reviled by
the political class in the country who saw him as a
man who came from nowhere to harvest where he
did not sow. as the rest of the country would say, he
was a beneficiary of other people's labor. If he was
seen like a quisling, they were selfishly wrong,
quisling would have been someone with a pact to a
previous agreement, and he was never a party to
assist Awolowo or MKO Abiola in any form in their
political dreams. He was purely an independent
business guru.

Truthfully, from the Oracle's objective
analyses of the High Chief, he has not been able to
reconcile himself to that part of his misunderstood
life, based on the idea that not all food could be
edible and Head of Interim was a food in bad taste
to all Nigerians who believed in the power of the
ballot box. The offer, which Gen. Babangida placed

on his table, ought to have been rejected, if only he could understand the mood of the nation, he did not.

Chief Shonekan was a man with a big head, with his broad face, he could look like Evander Holyfield the former professional World Heavy Weight Boxer Champion in his youthful years, when he smiled his teeth were hidden, a sign of higher IQ when he conversed with his peers. He was a master of boardroom politics but Nigeria was bigger than any board debate of UAC.

Chief Ernest Shonekan who the Oracle had a 15 minute chat with at Abuja international Airport in 2011 was a quiet man, very intelligent, and easy to communicate with but in his heart, he could be seen, as a man still in search of something. That something may still be troubling him or his legacy for a long time and to this writer known as the Oracle, he was a fine gentleman used by history for either good or bad of his country.

9

A politician is a fellow who lay down your life for his country

~Texas Guinan

For the lovers of history and politics, Nigeria is a country of intrigues news, what you see is not what is happening, like how MKO Abiola rightfully, described it: "Politics in Nigeria is like calling a dog a monkey, and when you look at the dog for long time after being told the same thing all over again and again the dog would be looking like a monkey."

That was how the politics of Nigeria was played in the nineties and it may be like that for a long time. Surprisingly MKO Abiola who defined politics of his time could not apply any remedy to it before he was arrested.

How the Nigeria politicians back bite one another and still moved on to work together could never be read in any political history books. In real sense of it, Nigeria political arena and human feelings have no relationship, they stepped on each other toes, and moved on, as if it never happened, so readers of this sequence expecting to see feelings and emotions or respect for agreement would be living in a fool's paradise.

By the time late Gen. Yar'Adua heard from the grapevine that he was likely to be disqualified from the Presidential race by the military President Gen. Babangida after he had defeated Chief Olu Falae in the Social Democratic Party primaries even in the South West of Nigeria at a time the North was likely to produce the two Presidential candidates for the two political parties in Nigeria, he asked for a meeting with the military President, also known as the evil genius, IBB agreed to a meeting in the presence of Gen. Yar'Adua's father, a former Minister in the First Republic, he was the Godfather to Gen. Babangida, infact the Old man wrote the letter of recommendation for Gen. Babangida to join the military.

In the presence of the elder Yar'Adua, Gen. Babangida placed his fat hand on the Quran and he told the late Gen. Yar Adua, that he had no such intention, naively, he believed IBB, who assured him he would even be much more comfortable with Yar'Adua as a worthy successor than any other person like Alhaji Umar Shinkafi a former Director General of State Security Service (SSS). Yar'Adua was a devoted Muslim; he thought any man who could swear by the Quran must be sincere.

He was wrong!!

From the mode the primaries of the two approved parties went, it was likely the North of Nigeria was going to produce the two flag bearers of the two approved political parties, a development, which those in the South West of Nigeria could not stomach and Gen. Babangida knew it and he played on the feelings and emotions of the development from North and South dichotomy.

Retired Gen. Sheu Yar'Adua a possible SDP Presidential candidate believed President Babangida, they hugged each other, and he made calls to his associates that everything was okay, forty-eight hours after the meeting with the Godfather after IBB returned to Lagos, Gen. Yar'Adua was having his favorite Tuwo for dinner when he heard on Nigerian Television (NTA) the ugliest news that affected his blood pressure.

Gen. Babangida banned Gen. Yar'Adua and others from the race and the need to look for a new set of candidates came up, no one thought of the feelings and sadness of Yar'Adua, but a selfish political class moved on as if nothing happened and, if elderly Yar'Adua was the godfather to Gen. Babangida. His son Gen. Yar'Adua was the same to Abubarkar Atiku.

Damboro unba, Shege which meant bastard in his local language Hajia, his wife, sensed this could trigger his blood pressure and quickly summoned Alhaji Abubakar Atiku for a strategic planning meeting.

The whole political arena was disorganized all over the country, including alliances and re-alliances, the decision of the military affected all the cream of the candidates from the two political parties and how to find the new leaders that will meet the new regulation of the ever changing, dynamic transition process of IBB became the issue.

Alhaji Abubarkar Atiku was also monitoring events from his hotel room; the last meeting had been hectic. The leader had told him all things would be okay. Everyone in the country knew his stronger ties to Gen. Shehu Yar Adua. From his days with the Customs, he had adopted Gen. Yar'Adua as his political father after a study of the role, Yar'Adua played in ensuring how Gen. Obasanjo became the military Head of State in 1976. He wondered why he did not take the position himself when Gen. Muritala Mohamed was killed on February 13, 1976. Gen. Yar Adua, had told him there was time for everything, even if Obasanjo had refused or killed in the abortive coup, Yar'Adua would still have conceded the position to Gen. Danjuma, what a man with a great heart he told himself. He listened to Yar'Adua faithfully like a student would do to a teacher he admired and respected him a lot, he drank from the fountain of his wisdom and he knew in his heart only death could deny him his loyalty to the retired General.

Atiku got a call that morning from his wife Titilayo; she would be coming to see him. She never gave him details, because she knew he never loved details. She was still as beautiful as she was when they met, and his love for her had expanded his love for the Yoruba, her tribe in the West of Nigeria. He loved Yoruba owanbe parties, how they sprayed money on dancers and musicians, their traditional Aso Ebi and the cap called Abeti Aja.

Titilayo made him to understand the five political taboos of the Yoruba: talk no evil of Chief Awolowo because after Oduduwa the most important man to them is Chief Awolowo, she had also told him to smile when Fela the Afro-beat King did all his yabis, respect Professor Wole Soyinka for everything he stood for, acknowledge the unusual generosity of Dr. Tai Solarin on education and health care and finally, read and agree with all the comments of Lagos based Lawyer Gani Fawehinmi.

If you could understand those five principles you will be in the good books of the Yoruba, it was what he did to understand the Yoruba politics one of the three most powerful tribes in Nigeria.

However, the telephone call from Hajia to meet with Gen. Yar'Adua his mentor was not unexpected after he heard the sanction of the political leaders on the biased Nigerian Television Authority NTA, he knew he was the Plan B of the General and his political machinery had sidelined the Gen. Yar'Adua sick brother, Musa Yar'Adua, a lecturer in one of the institutions higher learning in the Central North who could have been his next surrogate, but he was too soft and had some socialist tendencies, unlike his ruthlessness and tactical brother, beside, his health bothers everyone including the General. Atiku called his driver as he prepared to meet with his mentor.

In the South West of Nigeria somewhere in Lagos, in a meeting with Senator Tinubu, Governor Osoba, a former Managing Director of the Daily Times of Nigeria came into limelight, from those who read this writer's book on the *Ogun State Policy of Manipulation since 1976* Aremo Segun Osoba was a man who built everything about his career on friendship.

"Until when a man knows how to service his friendship truthfully, he should not expect any growth in life," he said,

That was the philosophy of Aremo Osoba and most of his fans believed him. To him friendship was about trust, just like late Colonel Olu Akiode of the military intelligence wrote, friendship must be for mutual benefit, and like the Oracle would say, friendship is not adequate, if the relationship is financed by one party, it must be mutually exclusive, like simultaneous equation not one answer, two or more, that is life and that was how it was for him.

Aremo Segun Osoba was not literally a tall man, he could be around 5'9" with a round mouth, penetrating and curious eyes. He wore glasses and was always neatly dressed, a man who finishes up his backdoor meetings before the actual meetings to disorganize his adversaries hoping to catch up with him in the actual meetings. By the time Osoba would attend the meetings it would just be formalities. He had studied the intra politics within the military, from his days as a reporter with the Daily Times.

Fondly called Segun in his early career, he was the first reporter on the ground when Nigeria's First Prime Minister Alhaji Tafawa Balewa was assassinated. His story was read all over the country, which made him a favorite of his boss Alhaji Ajose.

He rose up through the ladder to become the Managing Director of the Daily Times, one of the largest newspapers in Nigeria, due to the training and backroom politics he got from the doyen of the Nigerian press Alhaji Ajose.

Osoba's contact in the ruling military authority had told him, the ban would be coming, which was very pleasing to the political class in the West. They could not believe it, when Yar'Adua defeated Olu Falae in the Yoruba land in the SDP primaries and he too, like Atiku looked for "Plan B" on the next candidate to run for the office of President under SDP, that will be from the South of Nigeria, hopefully, from his tribe and selfishly from his home town in Abeokuta, that was how, Governor Segun Osoba came up with the plan to draft Chief MKO Abiola into the SDP, which could be described as the Party of the Progressives, Segun had one thing in common with MKO Abiola, he love to acquire traditional titles, as the Governor he almost made a nuisance of it, as he became a chief in every city and village.

MKO Abiola from history was never a progressive politician; he was a compassionate conservative politician with a soft spot or feelings for the economically challenged because of his background. He was an executive member of National Party of Nigeria NPN in the second

Republic, but was frustrated out of the party in 1982 by late Chief Augustus Meredith Adisa Akinloye the National Chairman of NPN, both of them were interested in who would be the flag bearer of the party as soon as President Shagari completed his abortive second term in 1987.

MKO Abiola's larger than life was noticeable in Ogun State as the NPN Chairman in the State and by the time AMA Akinloye disorganized his political base in Ogun State MKO Abiola with his suspension by the local politicians in State from NPN, MKO Abiola had to leave the party that was in 1982.

Who mandated Chief Segun Osoba to request MKO Abiola to run for office? It could not be ascertained, some rumored that Governor Segun Osoba from Ogun State must have influenced MKO to run for the office of President after he had a meeting with Senator Bola Tinubu and Chief Anthony Enahoro who were initially skeptical on the loyalty of MKO to the ideas of the progressives he, and others had labored for since 1960.

MKO Abiola was initially a reluctant candidate, he could remember the warnings of his late wife Simbiat who cautioned him on the danger of running for the Highest office in the Land, she had told him to quit politics in 1982 from NPN, which he did and his business and influence had gotten up beyond Nigeria, Africa and in other continents.

Secretly, he knew Simbiat was never wrong, in any of her advice, Allah knows, he loved her so much and he wondered why she had to die so young and so innocent of everything around her, he felt lonely and deprived of genuine advise from everyone around him because they all wanted something, money, influence and connections, which he had but Simbiat, his High school sweetheart, was everything to him.

MKO knew the day his first wife died, he would have to face an untrustworthy life alone in which his ability to take a meaningful direction would be a challenge, in his heart of heart, he longed for her to speak to him.

Kudirat, his second wife was a paragon of beauty, he could remember how he felt the day he first saw her, her eyes, height, and her smiles were too much for him, he could not sleep for days and he knew, if he was unable to make her his wife, he would never be at peace with himself, he worked so hard to win her heart, his religion and the tradition of his tribe was an excuse to marry more than one woman, sometimes he wondered where the idea of one man one wife came from, a friend told him the Bible said two shall come together and become one, but is David not a man God loved so much that he said he could have destroyed Israel if not because of his love for David, did he marry one wife?

What about Abraham, who was described as the friend of God? If God did not like his polygamous life he would have told his friend. He wondered how the Christians interpreted their Holy books. He thanked Allah for being a Muslim, a religion that embraced some areas of his forefather's tradition...

After the meetings and discussions with the disorganized SDP leaders, who had given him forty-eight hours to consider himself a likely candidate of the Party from the West to challenge Senator Arthur Nzeribe, Atiku, and others, MKO asked for more time to consult with friends particularly IBB the military President. He was granted the privilege.

IBB had disqualified all the early starters like Yar Adua and Olu Falae, when MKO contacted his friend Gen. Babangida of many years for clearance and approval, IBB told him to go ahead, both were collaborators to the fall of the regime of Gen. Buhari and his dream for a disciplined and better Nigeria in August 1985.

However, between 1984 and 1985 Gen. Babangida was rumored to be under investigation by Generals Buhari and Idi-Agbon on a suspected Gloria Okon drug issues, MKO Abiola's brother-in-law was also rumored to be held by the government for what was rumored to be drugs related.

During the regime of Gen. Buhari as Head of State, drug dealers or peddlers were executed. The fear of a possible execution was one of the reasons behind August 1985 palace coup. Apart from unfavorable public opinion against the human right abuse of the regime both Gen. Babangida and MKO Abiola in unity worked together to get Gen. Buhari and his team out of office in August 1985.

Like the Oracle wrote above, it was more like simultaneous equations, equations containing multiple variables; you get two answers, at the end of Generals. Buhari and Idi-Agbon's removal from office, in August 1985 MKO got his brother-in-law freed and Gen Babangida got his case thrown out and he became the first military President.

Literarily, the influence of MKO Abiola increased within the government circle he used his Concord group of Newspaper publications and influence within the media to paint the new military government in good light to the public. It was like three for the price of one deal, with Gen Babangida holding the aces.

MKO Abiola was a devoted and loyal friend to Gen. Babangida. He used his Concord Newspapers to promote in good light all the plans of the government, hiding ugly news that would have destroyed the government. MKO Abiola support led to the resignation from the Concord the most respected journalists in Nigeria, Dele Giwa and others. They later started their own first investigative news report in Nigeria, Newswatch magazine.

Dele Giwa was an American-trained Nigerian journalist from Edo State. Along with Ray Ekpu and Dr. Doyin Abiola, they gave MKO Abiola the best newspapers in the country. Giwa and his rebels misunderstood the extent MKO was ready to go to protect his friend IBB, they gave MKO Abiola two weeks' notice to review their work relationship that would give them the right to publish any news without any hindrances from the publisher or else they were ready to quit.

MKO Abiola listened to them in his office and smiled, for three minutes MKO Abiola was still smiling to his last pre-molars and he asked his personal Assistant to get five bottles of Coca Cola for Dele Giwa and the rest. He opened the drinks. He asked for prayers, which Giwa offered, he too joined in praying for the company to grow from strength to strength, and they all took the first and second gulp of the chilling drinking before he asked them to stop, he told them in the most heartless finality of words an employer could use to get rid of unwanted staff, the drink was not about their proposal for a review of the condition of service it was a sendoff party.

He fired them on the spot.

Dele Giwa along with others were dazed, because they never expected it from MKO Abiola, their only consolation was that MKO Abiola allowed them to go away with their official cars, which were Mercedes Benz, they were the best paid, journalists in Nigeria, two months earlier Dele Giwa had taken a couple of University Students to Ile Ife where he grew up in a mud house, the students had challenged him after a lecture that he was a proud man, and he behaved as if he walked on water with his pen as a successful writer and editor..

After he took them to his poor upbringing, which ended up with lack of three square meals most nights, he looked the students directly in the face and said, "I have worked so hard, to be the best I could be in my career, I hate poverty, I parted with it from the day I left the country for the United States and I told myself I would get the best of everything in life I could not from my parent not because they did not try, but because I believe my location in life will always be a factor in my allocation in life, this baby is not coming back to Ile Ife again to live."

That was just two months ago, Dele Giwa had no Plan B what he had was his skills, perhaps as the most investigative journalist the country ever produced, for the first time in his life he became jobless and his marriage was crumbling, he was hunted by his early life at Ile Ife. He talked to opinion leaders and money bags that also had problems with MKO and the military leaders, and he was advised to turn his skills to an enterprise along with Ray Ekpu, Dan Agbese and Yakubu Mohammed they formed a new magazine Newswatch that changed the news media landscape in Nigeria, that was 1984.

Literarily, most of the buried news from the National Concord newspapers became the bedrock of the job the Newswatch magazine planned to finish and one of them was assumed to be the case on Gloria Okon. It was even rumored that it was the reason Dele Giwa was parceled bombed in his house at Opebi, Ikeja in Lagos in 1986 since the case was never brought up in court, the fact behind his death at the age of thirty-nine could not be justified either however, every effort of Dele Giwa's attorney, late Gani Fawehinmi to have security agents like Col. Akilu and Major Togun prosecuted were resisted by IBB's government.

MKO Abiola and Gen. Babangida had history of friendship way back to the time Gen Babangida was only a Captain of the Nigerian Army, and that history was not a happy one with Gen. Sanni

Abacha, and Gen. Obasanjo who played bigger role in this imbroglio.

In the Army, you play friendship with your equals and as soon as MKO Abiola went down the ladder to make Captain Babangida his friend, he lost the respect of Gen. Obasanjo, his High School mate and they were never truly close buddies anymore, the mistrust and sadness of it could be seen at most functions that included the two, they treated each other with disrespect and MKO Abiola with his unusual loud or big mouth could not bring himself to understand Gen Obasanjo, because he was a businessman not a soldier.

However, Gen Babangida knew the ugly relationship between his former boss and his friend, and he did his best to exploit the situation, Gen. Obasanjo, on the other hand, failed to understand the situation of his school mate. It was indeed the beginning of the events that created unhappy relationship between them and when the clamor need to de-annul the election came up, Gen. Obasanjo could not give his support at all, at a conference which put a stamp on the annulment of the election, in far away in East Africa Gen. Obasanjo said MKO Abiola was not the expected messiah for Nigeria.

If Gen. Obasanjo had reminded the North and the military of his own 1979 transition which favored the North maybe things could have changed. It was a lesson he learnt twenty years later, when late President Yar Adua was clinging to office from hospital bed in Saudi Arabia.

MKO Abiola asked Gen Babangida if he wanted to stay in office because he was asked to run for the presidency under the SDP, he did not want to make a fool of himself in any election that would be cancelled by the military, just like IBB did to late Yar'Adua, Abiola his business partner with Habeeb Bank Plc.

As if that was his style of convincing friends or enemies of his sincerity as Gen Babangida again, placed the same fat hand of his on the Quran and promised MKO Abiola his support for the election, despite the fact that the military would not support his presidency. IBB knew the plan of the military not to have a presidency with MKO Abiola as the Commander–in– Chief, but the evil genius was prepared to lead his friend astray or on a wild goose journey.

The reasons why the military was against MKO Abiola could be attributed to four main points, too much money, women, local vocabulary of the Chief, which was often laced with hesitant speech level, and his deep connection to the Black Congressional Caucus of the United States, and none of them could be corrected by the Chief. It was even rumored his relationship with ITT in which he was the vice President for Africa and Middle East technically made him a secret agent of the American government.

MKO Abiola loved women to the extent that a queen to one of the kings in Yoruba land was seduced by him in the story carried by The Sketch News titled: *"Abiola Snatched Olori HOPE."*

MKO Abiola also loved money and he made plenty through contracts with ITT and oil industries; millions of dollars, pound-sterling, Japanese yens, and India rupees all over the world at a time when Nigerian naira was stronger than American dollar. One of his problems was his hesitant speech level, which was natural with him, but Gen Babangida asked the military to ignore those shortcomings, as MKO Abiola would not be elected by Nigerians in an election between North and South or able to win the SDP primaries in Jos. It was the calculation of the military that a Southerner will face a Northerner in the election, most likely the candidate from the North would be the winner, it was the failure to have the above scenario, the previous primaries involving Yar'Adua and Shinkafi was cancelled. It was one of his greatest miscalculations.

The rest on how MKO was elected was history, he won the SDP Primaries, and ignorantly thought he had the backing of his friend, Gen

Babangida, he forgot that Gen. Sanni Abacha was the strength of Gen Babangida and that both had a secret pact that after Gen Babangida would be Abacha as President of Nigeria, it was a pact long signed before Gen. Buhari could be removed from office in 1985.

The details of the agreement was earlier mentioned in the last chapter, that in Nigeria politics when you sleep you do not close your two eyes, MKO Abiola closed his and that would be explained in the next part and answers to most of the questions asked in the first paragraph of this chapter.

*Ignorance makes most men go into a political party
and shame keeps them from getting out*
~Edward Halifax

I f the late Senator Francis Arthur Nzeribe
was used to destroy the mandate of MKO
Abiola, with the Association for Better
Nigeria(ABN) program, with several
court injunctions for the cancellation of the Jos
Convention that approved MKO Abiola as the
winner of the nomination of the SDP it had the
tentacles of the political class of Nigeria
mischievously behind it with the military secretly
financing the problems.

The arrangement to derail the election also
had the backing of all those called AGIP (any

government in power) they included the Emirs, and Obas, and Obis they were not happy with MKO on how he grabbed one of the wives of their members, a King in Yoruba land who was called Olori Hope by Nigeria Sketch when the story first broke out.

It had been a yearly give away things for MKO to ditch out gifts to all the kings, Emirs and Obis in Nigeria, until a King in Yoruba land returned MKO's gift, he alleged, MKO Abiola had put his wife in the family way meaning he impregnated the wife of the king, and stationed her in London far away from his kingdom.

It was a sensational news, MKO Abiola denied it, when he explained his relationship with the king furthermore, MKO unashamedly asked the reporter what he expected from a king who wanted to borrow money from him and at the same time sending his most beautiful wife to collect it, and he even asked the king to return several thousands of naira he had borrowed in past since the king was in the mood of returning money. It was a shameless way to defend adultery.

It was funny, as the Press went to town with it, they added spices to the news, and some even said if the king was always in the habit of sending his most beautiful wife to the Chief to ask for favors, he deserved what he got from MKO Abiola. Nobody blamed the Chief, it was the King who was ridiculed by the Press, morality was not the issue it was the greed of the King in question.

The Olubadan of Ibadan late Oba Asanke did not want such a wife grabbing stuff to happen to him, when MKO Abiola wanted to pay him a visit at his palace, he kept all his wives out of the view of the Chief when MKO came to his palace at Ibadan in Oyo State, when MKO finally got to the palace of Olubadan Oba Asanke and jokingly asked for the welfare of his wives as a matter of courtesy, Olubadan, jokingly told MKO Abiola, he thought the visit was for him not his wives. He told MKO Abiola in the most humorous way to just focus on the visit that involved men alone and both of them laughed over it and MKO Abiola got the joke and the seriousness behind it with a big smile showing his last premolars.

It was not the first time MKO Abiola would be faced with such an embarrassing situation. When Chief Lekan Salami the proprietor of the IICC Shooting Stars Football Club died, it was rumored that MKO Abiola paid more attention to the youngest wife of the late proprietor than the burial events which the gathering was all about, when he attempted to give the bereaved woman his business card, he had to be reminded the event was about late Chief Lekan Salami.

Anyway, because of MKO Abiola's love for women and uncontrollable thirst for them, he made enemies with the kings and military officers as most of their wives had something to do with the Chief. When he died and his family wanted all the women who purportedly had children with him to come forward, more than 65 children underwent DNA testing and many failed but the exact number of children that passed the DNA tests was not released to the public.

Like this writer mentioned earlier, when you plan to catch a monkey, you throw him a piece of banana, MKO Abiola was indeed the Banana used to get Gen Babangida out of office, the pressure was too much for IBB, he had to choose between his life and presidency, because his base, the military wanted him out after he annulled election and the unrest that followed, in 1993.

Gen. Babangida had assured the military, that MKO Abiola was going to lose the Presidential election, but the result as released from the first fourteen States of the country had given victory to MKO Abiola

For the first time, IBB became a nobody within the military. That was the consensus of the military his base. The recent Statement from IBB that Gen. Abacha was left in the interim Government to stabilize the government was bullshit. He had no such power over the man who announced the coup that brought Gen. Buhari in December 1983 and his own government to power in August 1985. IBB knew the military power was with the General with Kanuri facial marks. Gen. Abacha was left behind to fulfill his own dreams.

Gen. Sanni Abacha was his own man, probably a sadist. He knew no fear, it was even said, if the General was eating and there was a bomb blast, Sanni Abacha would finish his meal first without shifting ground. Those who blamed him for destroying the gentleman agreement he had with MKO Abiola obviously did not understand the politics and ugly banana left behind by IBB, which Chief Shonekan the Interim Head State could not curtail.

What was the role played by Gen. Oladipo Diya in this imbroglio? Did he tell MKO Abiola the truth on the information he was passing to Gen. Sanni Abacha? Was he also ambitious or was he contended to be number two man in Abacha's government than handing the abortive mandate to MKO Abiola? Did he carry the political differences of his Ijebu and Egba in Ogun State to a national level?

Those were the hidden facts behind MKO failure to understand Gen. Sanni Abacha who had no pact with him, but was only fulfilling his own part of the deal to be Head of State after IBB outplayed himself with his unending transition programs, and as far as Gen. Sanni Abacha was concerned the Interim Government left behind by IBB never existed, as he never attended any of the Federal Executive meetings called by the Head of the Government Chief Ernest Shonekan in Abuja during his eighty-four days in office. He never left his office in Lagos until he took over as Head of State in Abuja the Federal Capital of Nigeria.

Those who requested Gen. Abacha to send the interim government packing also failed to understand the military. They lost everything, as Gen. Sanni Abacha destroyed the little political structures in operation at the State and local levels and they were all replaced with military personnel as Governors, and Administrators, he went further than they envisaged. He suspended the constitution.

MKO Abiola became the victim of his own political miscalculations, like the Oracle said, MKO was never a true politician, he trusted people too much and like the knife of Brutus, he was stabbed in the same manner Julius Caesar was by his friends and associates, as they scrambled for the crumbs on the General Abacha military table, and MKO and his mandate became history to them. It was the sad part of Nigeria history, as Nigeria politicians stood for no principles only those with it stayed far away from government like Bola Ige and others.

MKO Abiola with the support of few people like Senator, Bola Tinubu, Papa Enahoro and Osoba, and professional radicals like Wole Soyinka, and others had no option than to use his Plan B, which had no serious foundation. He declared himself President at Epetedo in Lagos, with a stalemated mandate, and almost overtaken by events of history. Unfortunately, the so-called June 12 mandate, which was based on the constitution which he was relying on as President had been suspended by Sanni Abacha, his vice President in the election also had become a Minister with Abacha, he was left in the limbo with no wing to fly.

Political observers considered the wisdom or otherwise of his action or inaction only if he knew the political and social economic implication of his Plan B in a system firmly controlled a by a ruthless general from Maiduguri, as history would later record it, the declaration would be his last major public appearance as a free man in Nigeria. What happened to him?

Here is the text of MKO Abiola's Epetedo Declaration, "Enough is enough," given on Saturday, June 11, 1994, announcing the formation of a Government of National Unity (GNU) at Epetedo, Lagos and in which he declared himself President and was subsequently arrested and later tried.

PEOPLE of Nigeria, exactly one year ago, you turned out in your millions to vote for me, Chief M.K.O. Abiola, as the President of the Federal Republic of Nigeria. But politicians in uniform, who call themselves soldiers but are more devious than any civilian would want to be, deprived you of your God-given right to be ruled by the President you had yourselves elected. These soldier-politicians introduced into our body politic, a concept hitherto unknown to our political lexicography, something strangely called the "annulment" of an election perceived by all to have been the fairest, cleanest and most peaceful ever held in our nation.

Since that abominable act of naked political armed robbery occurred, I have been constantly urged by people of goodwill, both in Nigeria and abroad, to put the matter back into the people's hands and get them to actualize the mandate they gave me at the polls. But mindful of the need to ensure that peace continues to reign in our fragile federation, I have so far tried to pursue sweet reason and negotiation.

My hope has always been to arouse whatever remnants of patriotism are left in the hearts of these thieves of your mandate, and to persuade them that they should not allow their personal desire to rule to usher our beloved country into an era of political instability and economic ruin. All I have sought to do, in seeking dialogue with them, has been to try and get them to realize that only real democracy can move our nation forward towards progress, and earn her the respect she deserves from the international community.

However, although this peaceful approach has exposed me to severe censure by some who have mistaken it for weakness on my part, those with whom I have sought to dialogue have remained like stone, neither stirred to show loyalty to the collective decision of the people of their own country, nor to observe Allah's injunction that they should exhibit justice and fair-play in all their dealings with their fellowmen. Appeals to their honor as officers and gentlemen of the gallant Nigerian Armed Forces, have fallen on deaf ears. Instead, they have resorted to the tactics of divide and rule, bribery and political perfidy, misinformation and (vile) propaganda.

They arrest everyone who disagrees with them. Even the seventy-one-year-old hero of our nation, Chief Anthony Enahoro, was not spared. How much longer can we tolerate all this? People of Nigeria, you are all witnesses that I have tried to climb the Highest mountain, cross the deepest river and walk the longest mile, in order to get these men to obey the will of our people. There is no humiliation I have not endured, no snare that has not been put in my path, no "set-up" that has not been designed for me in my endeavor to use the path of peace to enforce the mandate that you bestowed on me one year ago. It has been a long night. But the dawn is here. Today, people of Nigeria, I join you all in saying, "Enough is enough!"

We have endured twenty-four years of military rule in our thirty-four years of independence. Military rule has led to our nation fighting a civil war with itself. Military rule has destabilized our nation today as not before in its history. Military rule has impoverished our people and introduced a dreadful trade in drugs, which has made our country's name an anathema in many parts of the world. Even soccer fans going to watch the Green Eagles display in America are being made to suffer there needlessly because Nigeria's name is linked with credit card and fraud and "419." Politically, military rule has torn to shreds the prestige due to our country because of its size and population.

The permanent seat at the United Nations Security Council that should be rightfully ours is all but lost. For who will vote for Nigeria to get the seat if Nigerian military rulers do not respect the votes of their own people? Enough of military rule he said.

We are sickened to see people who have shown little or no personal achievement, either in building up private businesses, or making success of any tangible thing, being placed in charge of the management of our nation's economy, by rulers who are not accountable to anyone. Enough of square pegs in round holes, we are tired of the military repetitive tendency to experiment with our economy: Today, they say "no controls." Tomorrow, they say "Full controls."

The day after, they say "Fine tuning." The next day, they say, "devaluation." A few days later, they say, "Revalue the same naira upwards again Abi?" All we can see are the consequences of this permanent game of military "about turns," High inflation, a huge budget deficit and an enormous foreign debt repayment burden, dying industries, High unemployment and a demoralized populace. Our youths, in particular, can see no hope on the horizon, and many can only dream of escaping from our shores to join the brain drain. Is this the Nigeria we want?

We are plagued also by periodic balance of payments crises, which have led to a perennial shortage of essential drugs, which has turned our hospitals and clinics into mortuaries. A scarcity of books and equipment has rendered our schools into desolate deserts of ignorance.

Our factories are crying for machinery, spare parts and raw materials. But each day that passes, instead of these economic diseases being cured, they are rather strengthened as an irrational allocation of foreign exchange based on favoritism and corruption becomes the order of the day. Enough is enough of economic mismanagement! People of Nigeria, during the election campaign last year, I presented you with a program entitled "HOPE '93?

This program was aimed precisely at solving these economic (problems) that have demoralized us all. I toured every part of Nigeria to present this program to you the electorate. I was questioned on it at public rallies and Press conferences and I had the privilege of incorporating into it much of the feedback that I obtained from the people. Because you knew I would not only listen to you but deliver superb results from the program, you voted for me in your millions and gave me an overwhelming majority over my opponent.

To be precise, you gave me 58.4 per cent of the popular vote and a majority in 20 out of 30 States plus the Federal Capital Territory, Abuja. Not only that, you also enabled me to fulfill the constitutional requirement that the winner should obtain one-third of the votes in two-thirds of the States. I am sure that when you cast an eye on the moribund State of Nigeria today, you ask yourselves:

"What have we done to deserve this, when we have a President-elect who can lead a government that can change things for the better?

Our patience has come to an end. As of now, from this moment, a new Government of National Unity is in power throughout the length and breadth of the Federal Republic of Nigeria, led by me, Bashorun M.K.O. Abiola, as President and commander-in-chief. The National Assembly is hereby reconvened. All dismissed governors are reinstated.

The State Assemblies are reconstituted, as are all local government councils. I urge them to adopt a bi-partisan approach to all the issues that come before them. At the national level, a bi-partisan approach will be our guiding principle. I call upon the usurper, Gen. Sanni Abacha, to announce his resignation forthwith, together with the rest of his illegal ruling council. We are prepared to enter into negotiations with them to work out the mechanics for a smooth transfer of power. I pledge that if they hand over quietly, they will be retired with all their entitlements, and their positions will be accorded all the respect due to them. For our objective is neither recrimination nor witch-hunting, but an enforcement of the will of the Nigerian people, as expressed in free elections conducted by the duly constituted authority of the time.

I hereby invoke the mandate bestowed upon me by my victory in the said election, to call on all members of the Armed Forces and the Police, the Civil and Public Services throughout the Federal Republic of Nigeria, to obey only the Government of National Unity that is headed by me, your only elected President.

My Government of National Unity is the only legitimate, constituted authority in the Federal Republic of Nigeria, as of now." People of Nigeria, these are challenging times in the history of our continent, Africa, and we in Nigeria must not allow ourselves to be left behind.

Our struggle is the same as that waged by the people of South Africa, which has been successfully concluded, with the inauguration of Mr. Nelson Mandela as the first African President of that country. Nelson Mandela fought to replace MINORITY rule with MAJORITY rule.

We in Nigeria are also fighting to replace MINORITY rule, for we are ruled by only a tiny section of our armed forces. Like the South Africans, we want MAJORITY rule today, which is rule only by those chosen by all the people of Nigeria as a whole in free and fair elections. The only difference between South Africa and Nigeria is that those who imposed minority rule on the majority rule whether it is by black or white, remains minority rule, and must be booted out.

I call on you, heroic people of Nigeria, to emulate the actions of your brothers and sisters in South Africa and stand up as one person to throw away the yoke of minority rule for ever. The antics of every minority that oppresses the majority are always the same. They will try to intimidate you with threats of police action. But do not let us fear arrest. In South Africa, so many people were arrested, during the campaign against the Pass Laws, for instance, that the jails could not hold all of them.

Today, apartheid is gone forever. So, let it be with Nigeria. Let us say goodbye forever to minority rule by the military. They talk of treason. But haven't they heard of the Rivonia treason trial in South Africa? Did those treason trials halt the march of history?

People of Nigeria, our time is now, you are the repository of power in the land. No one can give you power. It is yours. Take it! From this day, show to the world that anyone who takes the people of Nigeria for fools is deceiving him and will have the people to answer to.

God bless you all. Long live the Federal Republic of Nigeria. Long live the Government of National Unity

After this Statement without any functional security and unsustainable network of political support Abiola went home to his Ikeja house to sleep. Like the Biblical story of Jesus Christ, MKO Abiola was taken captive by the soldiers and police loyal to the Gen. Sanni Abacha on a journey he never returned.

It was sad to see the most generous Nigerian philanthropist treated in the most inhuman and undecorated behavior by the political class as the common men and women became those who had sympathy for him and all those who benefited from his generosity left him like a bad habit, as he was taken away by Gen. Abacha.

Weeks became months and Gen. Sanni Abacha made it difficult to even discuss MKO Abiola's release from jail.

Gen. Diya did not understand what he was getting himself into, just like the Biblical Judas Iscariot mistakenly believed Jesus Christ would overcome the Roman Soldiers, so also it was, with Gen. Diya, he had miscalculated and under-rated Gen. Sanni Abacha, he could not get out, it was like driving a car without brake and knowing only an accident could stop the journey. When the accident that was coming finally came he almost lost his life in it.

If MKO Abiola had declared himself President when all the facts of the elections were still fresh in 1993, IBB would have been pressurized to hand over to him, but June 11, 1994, exactly a year after the election made it too late in eyes of Nigerians who lacked ability to sustain any revolution.

Gen. Oladipo Diya was a former military Governor of Ogun State between January 1984 to August 1985, who had been loyal to Gen. Buhari until he was removed in August 1985, Diya quickly switched loyalty to Gen. Babangida who became the first military President in Nigeria, and Diya was promoted to the full rank of General with stronger military postings.

The promotion under IBB placed General Diya as the most senior Army General from the West of Nigeria since Obasanjo left in 1979 until IBB stepped aside, Diya had to look unto Sanni Abacha for survival in the military but the loyalty to Gen. Sanni Abacha had been based on cat and mouse relationship, he knew he would be consumed by the Lion called Abacha, when or how? Only time would tell.

General Diya knew Gen. Sanni Abacha had placed him under his radar for any smart move, when it occurred to him he had been used by the North against his own people, it was even difficult for him to socialize with other Yoruba Generals like Olarenwaju and Adisa without seeking clearance from the Head of State. He was boxed.

Politics determines who has the power not the truth.

~**Paul Krugman**

The Oracle says instead of looking for solution to solve a political problem some mischievous elements in a society like Nigeria in their wisdom or otherwise are always busy looking for more problems to attack the solution James Hadley Chase wrote in one of his thriller books, "You are lonely when you are dead."

MKO Abiola days in jail were lonely and it led to realignment of interests within the political cliques, his friends and enemies had moved on. They scrambled for political appointments like kids scrambled for candies with the Kanuri facial marked dictator called Gen. Sanni Abacha, to them, it was like MKO Abiola never existed in their memories or more like a bad dream, they moved on.

Alhaji Lateef Jakande a onetime Governor of Lagos State one of the leftovers of Chief Awolowo's political surrogates became the Minister of Works and the first job he did after Ernest Shonekan was removed was the cancellation of the Abeokuta/Lagos express road, which was awarded by Interim government of Ernest Shonekan to win the support of the Egba his kinsmen and women. The Egba became unhappy due to the failed political miscalculation on the power shift back to the North.

Conspicuously, MKO Abiola's vice Presidential candidate in the June 12, 1993, election Alhaji Babagana Kingibe was already comfortable as Foreign Affairs Minister, after briefly in charge of Internal affairs Ministry, a department, which somehow controlled the prison yards in the country, which made a MKO Abiola a prisoner in a jail supervised by his former number two man in the controversial last election, what an irony of fate for the former ITT vice President.

Many of them, like Olu Onagoruwa, a radical lawyer, Ebenezer Babatope a onetime Director of Organization of UPN a confidant of Chief Awolowo, particularly in the West of Nigeria abandoned MKO Abiola for the candies and aroma of office under Gen. Sanni Abacha. One of the Ibru brothers and publisher of the most respected Guardian newspaper had joined Abacha as a Minister.

When a house was not built on solid rock ordinary mudslide can push it away, MKO Abiola business was crumbling, including his empire, all the Northern Emirs were stripping him off the traditional tiles he had acquired all over the country. He had lost his first wife Simbiat years before he ran for office of President a decision political observers said he could not have ran for the presidency if Simbiat was alive. She was a beautiful lady from a very rich family in Abeokuta of the well-respected family of the Soaga.

When Simbiat died, all political powers in the country attended, including Gen. Babangida. Both of them cried openly but observers said they all cried for different reasons: MKO Abiola cried because he had lost the only woman who had loved him more than anyone in his life. Simbiat was MKO Abiola's pillar of strength. She had met him when he was a poor little guy on the streets of Abeokuta. Their love had survived through difficulties. The couple was blessed with five children, and in all Abiola businesses Simbiat was the vice President. If money could be a factor for replacement of life Abiola would have given up everything for the life of

Simbiat, it was obvious despite his flirtations that he loved Simbiat more than anyone in the world.

However, the tears from Gen. Babangida were borne out of business. Simbiat was one of the contractors for all the war deals. Under Babangida Nigeria spent millions of unaccountable dollars and Simbiat was rumored and expected accordingly to be the custodian of the kickbacks of the Army generals. Until her death, there was no document on how the deal would be shared. Nigerians love rumors. They thrive on it and they could blend it to a bigger story. It was probably not true.

It was an assumed deal; MKO Abiola refused to be involved since Simbiat was solely responsible for her actions and inactions. Carlisle U.O. Umunnah a New York-based freelance writer said it was indeed five million dollars, which MKO failed to release to IBB. It was the foundation of the problem between MKO and IBB, but that was years before the election.

The management of MKO Abiola's political platform was left with his second wife Alhaja Kudirat. She was determined to be seen like Winnie Mandela of South Africa. The role played by his other wives was to assist Kudirat in reclaiming the June 12 mandate, while they took care of the family, but without the bread winner of the family, it was tougher on the children and wives, it was even difficult for them to separate friends from enemies.

MKO Abiola who was complaining of back pain from the uncomfortable jail house, instead of listening to his health problem, the political class joked about it. They felt it was because he had no access to the intimacy of opposite sex. Life had no meaning to Nigeria political class.

When you are in problem or dying, don't expect anything emotional, like a book they will just flip to the next page, to them Abiola was almost a history and probably a nightmare to be forgotten.

A bird in hand was better than two even three in the bush, to the new crop of Ministers and his former associates, Gen. Sanni Abacha's government was the first bird in hand, MKO was the second in the bush, the third bird was probably the June 12 mandate; they moved on and played lip services to the actualization of the mandate. *O ma she o.!!!*

Alhaja Kudirat Abiola became the arrow Head of NADECO for the actualization of the June 12 Mandate, with the Support of aged Chief Anthony Enahoro, Prof. Wole Soyinka, Pa Alfred Ruwani, Pa Adesanya after the death of Pa Ajasin, and the youths were led by Senator Tinubu, those were the group that gave Kudirat strength and hope.

She became too big for the likeness of Gen. Sanni Abacha, she had to go. At a time MKO Abiola was suffering in jail, most of his trusted friends and traditional rulers were asking him to drop the mandate, and tuck in his tail like a defeated dog and return to Abeokuta like a failure, but MKO Abiola, Bada Bada Barawo, the Are Ona kakanfo of the Yoruba, was never a failure. He had installed the governments in four African countries like Uganda, Sierra loan, Tanzania and Sudan, he had sponsored military coups in and out of Nigeria, he had helped the North to destroy the myths around Chief Awolowo by exposing the sagacious leadership of Yoruba's race as a pretender of socialism with his 370 Maroko Lagos plots. Some even said he had used his Islamic fundamentalist ideas to destroy at sea, a shipload of Bibles. It was the age of rumor.

What more, for a man with special privileges within the United States' Congressional Black Caucus, when Abiola visited Uganda the country Federal Executive meeting was put on hold for him, and for to be treated like nobody by the military in his own country, by those he had helped particularly, the coup plotters of 1985 to remove the purposeful government of Gen. Buhari, and how will the world write his legacy if he had to surrender his mandate? His pride beclouds the reality on the ground. He turned it down.

All the international settlements proposals from various countries like America, Great Britain and many others were rebuffed by Gen. Sunni Abacha. Abiola's incarcerations became the leverage for the dictator to keep a hold on the government. Members of the Federal Executives were even too scared to discussed Abiola's health situation at any of the meetings. Those who tried to mention it, on seeing the ugly grimace on the face of the dictator knew how to reverse their position.

The political scenario was looking like the old folk story in which a primitive society had problems of sicknesses, early deaths, and failures but later discovered the mother of the king was a witch and probably responsible for the problems. They held a meeting to confront the king on the nefarious actions of his mother in which many spiritual deaths had been recorded.

The leader of the group had said, he would present the case to the king and when it gets to the stage to call the king's mother a witch it must be said collectively in a very loud voice to avoid one person being labeled as an accuse or the ring leader, that was the agreed plan.

On the day the king sat down to listen to the people, the leader cleared his throat and presented the story of deaths and ritual killings often associated with witchcraft in the society and he said the society had concluded that the mother of the king had at that stage he expected the people to echo the word witchcraft but to his surprise the people kept quiet, he told the story all over again and again but the people never alter the word witchcraft as expected, he knew he was boxed to the wall and he had to fill in gap himself, to save his neck, he said the king mother was the best mother the society could ever hope for.

The Yoruba political class because of what Awolowo stood for never really loved MKO Abiola who had teamed up with the North against the June 12 mandate, like Ebenezer Babatope, Lateef Jakande and many more, were feeling the heat from dark eye glass screened Sanni Abacha himself, MKO Abiola's matter was faintly mentioned on the pages of the news media except for NADECO and Kudirat Radio the brain work of Wole Soyinka.

Gen. Diya who had thought his influences would be stronger in the government like that of Gen. Obasanjo in the Muritala Mohamed government in the seventies but somehow he had been marginalized to just an ordinary table general, and his families in Ikeja lived in fear, and it was difficult for him to resign from the Government of Abacha without being killed.

Gen. Diya had become a laughing stock among the Army itself, as he was referred to, as a General without support or goodwill from the Army, he could not even get Ijebu State for his people. All he could get out of the risk of being the number two man to the Kanuri dictator was only a local government to save his face from the palace of Awujale and Alaye of Odogbolu and his kinsman Dr. Olu Onagoruwa from the same town with him who also worked as Minister for Justice, had rebelled against the progressives and particularly Lagos radical lawyer late Gani Fawehinmi who openly wept for the loss of loyalty and cause they stood for years.

Unlike Gen. Diya, Late Professor Aluko's opinion, an economist was respected in the government of Gen. Sanni Abacha, when the issue of State creation was tabled at the Supreme military Council meeting, Gen. Sanni Abacha approved Ekiti State for Professor Aluko and Ijebu State, which would have redeemed the image of Gen. Diya in Ogun State was thrown out, at that stage he knew when to keep quiet or take his fate in hands of his gods. Diya could not even consult the fetish Ijebu Alagemo deities for support; he needed a messiah to help him out.

The failure to get Ijebu State from Abacha's government became the foundation of the imbroglio between Gen. Diya and his boss Gen. Sanni Abacha and unknown to Gen. Diya, since he had no strong military support, he was closely monitored by the special intelligence created under Major Al Mustapha and it was not long before he was roped into an abortive military coup along with Major Gen. Olarenwaju, Major Gen. Adisa and other top Yoruba military leaders in the Nigeria Army.

Furthermore, like the heat was placed on Gen. Diya, so it was on other Yoruba military personnel, Gen. Sanni Abacha was determined to curb the Yoruba transferred arrogance from the days of Chief Awolowo with their so called western education, economic power and political sagacity to an affordable and manageable level that will never threaten Northern hegemony for many years to come. Will he succeed?

Many of the Yoruba military officers were demoted, some were bypassed for promotions or roped into spurious coups, Military Officers like Colonel Olu Akiode, Ibukun Sunday Oyewole, and Mepaida became victims and guilty by origin of birth and by association, Col. Olu Akiode and Col Sunday Ibukun Oyewole grew up with the Oracle at Ekotedo Ibadan, I could recall how Oyewole first went to NDA Kaduna, in 1973, how he encouraged all of us to join the Army. We loved the feathers on his beret, it was not long before Olu and Toba Elegbe went to NDA Kaduna, and the Oracle stayed behind to finish his Advanced Level at the Department of Extra Moral studies, University of Ibadan, which was between 1974/76.

It was not long, before Gen. Obasanjo who was declared an institution by a Nigerian court in the time President Shagari, was also roped into an abortive spurious military coup, which was before that of Diya or so. Gen. Obasanjo was jailed on coup attempt, which the international community believed was fabricated to silence the giant of Yoruba military influence in Nigeria. How did Gen. Obasanjo become an institution in the early 1980s?

A police inspector officer who coordinated a police check point had insisted on searching Gen. Obasanjo's vehicle. He made Gen Obasanjo to wait in his car, despite an appeal from the driver and ADC that a former Head of State was in the car. His car was openly searched like all the cars, and no special privilege was accorded the former Head of State, it was very disrespectful to the man who willingly handed over the government to a civilian in October 1979.

When Gen. Obasanjo returned to his office at Otta in annoyance, he felt stripped of his pride and respect as a former Head of State of Nigeria, he sent the soldiers to buttonhole the police officer to his farm at Ota and he had him stripped off of his police uniform, and the officer of the Nigeria police force was caned with twenty-four strokes of Koboko horse whip on his butt.

The police officer was lucky to escape further punishment because Obasanjo had a history of shooting people on the legs. Those who stole from his farm in the past particularly foreigners were shot in the legs before he fired them from his farm, that was the story then, it could be wrong!

However, the officer in tears got back to his duty post. He filed a report to his boss, the case was referred to the Divisional Police officer (DPO) who refused to be involved, but sent the file to his immediate boss, the Commissioner of Police who also refused to help the affected police officer either, he sent it to the AIG in Zone two in Abeokuta for advice.

Zone Two Office of the Police in Abeokuta was filled with officers ready for post but no vacancies, the Federal government had stopped promotions and the AIG was left with no choice than to keep on promising his men things would be fine, regular duty post on the roads within the Zone was the only way to appease these men who looked unto him for the career growth.

The civilian society called the money made on the duty post bribe, but the police called it welfare package, to up their benefits and wages and everything was shared down the ladder. If an officer failed to follow the rules, he might never get outside duty post again, and if a report was received from the public against a police officer for demanding the so-called welfare from the public everything was handled to protect the system. It was a boat nobody was ready to rock.

AIG Kosoko (*not his real name*) had been worried. He was looking forward to the next promotion of his dream post of DIG in the next one year, if he was able to get very close to President Shagari, he could get the post, he remembered the politics he went through before his current post as AIG in Zone two, more like the policy of elimination from his set that graduated from the Police Academy in 1969. It was more like a cat and mouse situation, some secrets and ugly jobs that could have landed him jail had to be done for these politicians.

It placed him in favorable position of trust by the political leaders; he was not ready to allow any little problem to stop him from attaining his dream job. His police career had taken him too many States of the Federation in the last twenty years and had left him with children all over the country. Why his wife Stella from Anambra State had not given him problem had been a concern to him. She asked for money for everything, the more he gave the more she asked; because of his infidelities he could not stop her.

The file on his table, on the case of the Inspector who was canned by Gen. Obasanjo in his farm gave him lots of concerns. It could even derail his ambition to be DIG, he had to be very careful with it, and caution must be his watch word. It would be fine to post that troublemaker out of his zone before he got himself into something deeper than just administrative work, he wondered what they taught them at Police Academy, why would any police officer in his right senses search Obasanjo's car in the public, and how could canning a police officer be justified? He could not reconcile the two equations.

AIG Kosoko robbed his own bottom himself and smiled, twenty-four strokes of Koboko horsewhip in the butt it must be a big pain indeed. He couldn't remember the last time he was canned, his High School teacher Mr. Opabunmi was an expert in placing twelve strokes of cane on the same spot until the students covered his children with (werepe) skin scratching powered that was when he stopped being mean to them. Kosoko led the group then.

Kosoko called his friend in Zone Four who had requested for three police officers to beef off his zone. Instead of looking at the file, he sent a police signal for transfer of the Inspector Dan to Jos. When the Inspector got to Jos three months after he was transferred to Maiduguri, Sokoto and Kaduna, the transfers of the police officer to various zones of the country, it was a calculated attempt of the police authority to run away from protecting the officer, Dan hired one of the progressives lawyers, however, after many adjournments, the court declared Gen. Obasanjo an institution.

The Inspector finally got discharged from the police force.

Under Gen. Sanni Abacha, the institution tags on Gen. Obasanjo had no meaning. OBJ who had said MKO Abiola was not the messiah was also in jail, if he was in jail, to the Yoruba, he deserved it, he never associated with the core interest of his tribe, he never supported the June 12 mandate of MKO Abiola, and he was also seen lobbying to be the Head of Interim government itself before Gen. Babangida left office.

If Gen. Obasanjo never had the tradition Egba Owu facial marks on both side of his face, they would have asked for his DNA but everything about him looked like Yoruba, his talk, his jokes and his love for women was almost identical to that of MKO Abiola himself, only his military background separated him from his tribe, he was a complete detribalized Nigerian who just happened to be Yoruba man, he could have close-fitting in any tribe of Nigeria.

Charity they say must always begin from home, before ending abroad, in the case of Gen. Obasanjo, his own charity started abroad, far away from his kinsmen and he was never really seen at home or any of the local functions, in his home state except his local Baptist Church, or his Agbeloba office on Quarry road.

What the Yoruba failed to understand on Gen. Obasanjo will be discussed in future chapters, his stories will take more than just a page to conclude, but we could just say, the emergence of Gen. Obasanjo as political icon in Nigeria, led to the death of Chief Awolowo political growth. It reduced Chief Awolowo influence to a regional champion among the Yoruba instead of the whole country the sagacious politician aspired to be.

Awolowo supporters may not like this, but it is the truth, as we will conclude in future by placing the two giants of Nigerian politics side by side on the pedestal of political contributions to corporate grown of Nigeria.

Furthermore, in the subsequent chapters, we will look at the life of Gen. Obasanjo in Jail, the five finger hands of leprosy, which Bola Ige called the five political parties introduced by Sanni Abacha, which adopted him as their Presidential candidate, the removal of Sultan of Sokoto a slap on the Old Sokoto Caliphate, the death of Sanni Abacha, the emergence or Gen. Abdul Salam as the Head of State and the road towards the returns to civilian government and how Gen. Obasanjo came of jail to be President again, we will in future see how Gen. Obasanjo dream became the dreams of Nigeria.

Part Four

In politics an organized minority is a political majority.
~Jesse Jackson

Major Hamzat Al Mustapha, the Head of Gen. Sanni Abacha's security squad, decided to open the can of worms on his role in several political deaths in the country authorized by his boss Gen. Sanni Abacha, including many personalities like Papa Alfred Ruwani and Alhaja Kudirat Abiola. There was also a murder attempt on Alex Ibru and a host of others including MKO Abiola, the winner of the June 12 election, Nigerians depending on which side of the country or tribes became much more confused on who was right, between the accused or the prosecutor.

Somehow, a portion of Yoruba leaders mentioned in the ugly backroom deal with the dictator described Major Hamzat Al Mustapha as suffering from hallucination, some called it dementia, and some believed he was trying to find his way out of the political imbroglio, and the Oracle was wondering if they were medical Doctors capable of diagnosing any health issues.

In the language of the Major Hamzat Al Mustapha, MKO Abiola was deliberately eliminated to balance the equation of the death of Gen. Sanni Abacha, who died in the same manner, meaning both were killed or murdered by the same group of people in a country without any value for human lives. And he could be right.

I wrote in the article, "Nigeria: A Country in Fear," that when a Nigerian was murdered the government and people looked the other way and no one was interested in finding out the truth. To the nation, Major Al Mustapha was guilty and should be killed, but no one questioned the legal system that dragged on for ten or thirteen years. Yet in a perfect legal system, we would have anticipated the shift of justice beyond reasonable doubt. His case did not pass the reasonable doubt test.

Let Major Hamzat Al Mustapha get his fair share of justice without condemnation until the court can decide his fate. Let him tender any document he had, fake or original, truth or lies, the court will unveil whatever it was behind the mask on why and how Abacha was killed. June 12 was not only a test of faith in Nigeria, it almost destroyed the love for the country, because of the ambition of Gen Obasanjo and that of Gen. Babangida both had the foundation of the problem of the country, Major Hamzat Al Mustapha was sentenced to death by hanging by the Lagos High Court but a superior Federal court overturned the sentence including Sobowale his partner in the assumed crime. The perpetrators of all political murders in Nigeria again walked away or were never found since the death of Dele Giwa.

At the truth reconciliation Commission Major Al Mustapha almost gave an insight on how MKO Abiola was killed but he was shut down by the Chairman of the panel, he said, a General who asked MKO Abiola to be released unconditionally with his mandate and be made to form a government of National Unity was killed before he got home and three days later MKO Abiola himself died.

Gen. Obasanjo and MKO Abiola operated a cat and mouse friendship from their days at Baptist High School, in Abeokuta, while both loved women and money, both were jealous of each other progress, while the General Obasanjo was very careful with his words, MKO Abiola was careless with his, instead of respect for each other, they nursed hatred for each other's progress. It was the hatred that led to the death of several thousands of Nigeria and deaths of businesses, unemployment, and a breakdown of the system.

The announcement of MKO for presidency was not supported by his school mate Gen. Obasanjo who openly declared MKO was not the Messiah expected for the nation, when the election was nullified.

"When I stayed in my Library for hours, every day and nights, reading and researching for solutions to Nigeria problems, my adversaries are busy drinking, smoking and following women of easy virtue, if they plan to be equal to the level of my intellect, they may have to give up those things they cherished so much."
~**Awolowo**

Gen. Obasanjo was not literarily a tall man, a man with fat tissues around his waist, in his days with the Nigeria Army, he cultivated a funny shooting mustache, with a see-through wide nose, tiny eyes like the Chinese, he walked with pride and confidence of a ruthless General, behind his tiny greenish eyes lays the ruthlessness of a General at war with himself and the society. He had no patience for lazy people, or those looking unto him for favors, particularly from his tribe.

Gen. Obasanjo had no forgiving spirit either. It could be the same spirit he executed the last few months of Nigeria Civil war in which the Biafra surrendered to him in 1970, however, his returns from the civil war changed him from a loving husband of Remi he married 1960 London, in the United Kingdom and he probably came back from the civil war in 1970 with untreated PTSD and unstable personality.

Gen. Obasanjo made his noticeable and acceptable entrance into the Nigeria political arena from the time he took the command of the Third Marine Commando of the Nigeria Army from Brigadier Benjamin Adekunle known then as the Black Scorpion during the twenty-seven months of Nigeria's civil war, which ended in 1970.

Col. Emeka Ojukwu had left the command of the Biafra Army to Philip Effiong on Jan. 8th 1970 for Ivory Coast when he saw the handwriting of defeat and a possible capture by the Nigeria Army on the wall and it did not take the then Col. Obasanjo a long time to finish off where Brigadier Benjamin Adekunle left.

Philip Effiong the new Head of Biafra government on January 12 announced surrender, because the situation was assumed hopeless and prolonging the war would lead to further bloodshed and starvation, he said he had no regret for his action to surrender to the Federal government of Nigeria. Effiong died in November 6th 2003. He was aged 79, Ojukwu on the other hand returned to Nigeria after he was granted a pardon by President Shagari, he tried to win elections in a united Nigeria with many of the political parties he associated with but failed.

He died in 2011 at the age of seventy-eight.

For the sake of the new generation reading this series, it will be okay to just summarize the civil war as a failure of the system created by the British and wrongly managed by the political classes from the gang up in 1960, which led to the deaths of almost two million Nigerians with majority of them from the Igbo speaking tribes of Nigeria, because the battle ground took place in the East of Nigeria. For anyone with feelings and blood in his or her vain, a look at graphical book, The Nigeria Civil War in Pictures by Peter Obe, which was published by the Daily Times in the 1970s, would reveal the complete massacre both unleashed on each other.

It was one of the saddest stories of the entity called Nigeria at a time the nation was begging for fairness and Justice, what the Igbo got in return was inhuman treatment from Nigeria, innocent civilians particularly women and children became the victims, some were starved to death, it was the first time we

read about kwashiorkor and cholera in Nigeria. It
was sad.

When Colonel Obasanjo was in charge of
Third Marine Commando, Chief Awolowo was also
managing the affairs Ministry of Finance for the
country, and both shared in the glory and success of
the war more than the Commander-In-Chief Gen.
Yakubu Gowon.

Chief Awolowo was credited as the most
efficient Finance Minister Nigeria ever had, the war
was prosecuted without a local or foreign debt, while
Colonel Adekunle who was promoted Brigadier,
however, he was removed from the battleground for
some unconfirmed rumors for lack of proper
inventory of dead soldiers and rumors believed it
that he used voodoo that often made him to
spiritually disappear while his boys were left at the
mercy of Biafra Army or he planned to eliminate
some of his immediate officers in his command like
Akinrinade and Alabi Isama.

Brigadier Benjamin Adekunle fondly called
Black Scorpion the commander of the Third Marine
Commando redeployment was not unconnected
with the visitation of Chief Awolowo to the battle
front, which changed the plan of the Federal
government on food and medical supplies to the
Eastern Part of Nigeria. Before the supplies were cut
off since Ojukwu refused to guarantee the vehicles

used to supply medicals and food would not be used to ship in ammunitions. Brigadier Adekunle was posted out of the war zone. He was replaced with Col. Obasanjo a veteran of Congo wars for the United Nations.

However, Col. Obasanjo was credited as the man who took the Biafra flag of surrender of the secessionists from General Philip Effiong on January 10, 1970. Furthermore, the shared glory between Awolowo and Obasanjo was one the problems and foundations of political classes in Nigeria, like Obasanjo, Awolowo also had no forgiving spirit the political class observed.

Gen. Gowon was left with no option, than to compensate the heroes or warriors of the civil war like Obasanjo, Danjuma, and Muritala Mohamed after he promoted them Brigadiers with political appointment. Out of the three, only Danjuma was treated unfairly by Gowon, even though he had led the coup that slaughtered Gen. Aguiyi Ironsi at Ibadan in 1967, which paved the way for General Gowon a Lt Col them as the Chief of Staff Army to become the Head of State.

Brigadier Muritala Mohamed was never truly a friend of Gen. Gowon. Both were tolerated enemies or what could be called friendenemy. The imbroglio could be traced to how Muritala Mohammed the Head of 2nd Infantry Brigade favored the Biafra secession; he did not believe the Igbo should be forced to be part of Nigeria, if they were not willing.

Furthermore, Brigadier Muritala Mohammed was rumored to have looted the Central Bank of Nigeria in Benin city when his troops captured the city, from the Biafra, both of those stories could not be confirmed, as both were used to discredit one another. Somehow, he too, like Brigadier Benjamin Adekunle was redeployed from the battlefield by Gen. Gowon to the Signal Corps, which was the time he became a friend of MKO Abiola, who was introduced to Muritala Mohamed by his wife Ajoke Mohamed, a respectable lady from Abeokuta.

However, after the Emirs in the North of Nigeria settled the problems between Gowon and Muritala Mohamed after the end of the war, he was made the Federal Commissioner of Communication because of his background with the Army Signals Corps and Gen. Obasanjo became Federal Commissioner for Works to replace a Lagos lawyer Femi Okunu just like Mohamed his background was in the Engineering department of the Nigeria Army. Both seemed perfect for the assigned jobs.

Before those appointments were made, Chief Awolowo had left the government of Gen. Yakubu Gowon in 1971, because the Head of State failed to honor his words to transition of the affairs of the country to civilian's government, which was more of a gentlemen agreement. Awolowo had been grateful to Gen. Yakubu Gowon who had released him from jailed in 1967 after late Gen. Aguiyi Ironsi had refused a similar plea in 1966.

Chief Awolowo had joined the government as the most senior civilian in military regime, as Vice Chairman of Federal Executive Council, and Federal Commissioner for Finance in 1967 after he was freed from Calabar Prison from a concurrent jail sentence of treasonable Felony. His polices had assisted the troubled government of Gowon, when the Chief came into Gowon administration with his colleagues and associates with the same political values, like Anthony Enahoro who was Federal Commissioner of Information, Aminu Kano, Joseph Tarka and some of the surrogates of the Sardauna of Sokoto like Alhaji Sheu Shagari more like a union of West and North political leaders which was not the situation in 1960.

Chief Awolowo was replaced by the future President of Nigeria Alhaji Sheu Shagari, one of the laziest ministers ever to handle a ministry in Nigeria. Gen. Yakubu Gowon himself said the only thing Alhaji Shagari could do independently without asking for help was to light up his Benson and Hedges Cigarettes.

Subsequent event proved Gown's assessment of Sheu Shagari right, when he became the President in 1979-1983 he could not even light his cigarettes, late Dele Giwa the Editor–in-Chief of Newswatch wrote, that it was a duty taken over by Dr. Chuba Okadigbo his political adviser to find favors from the President since Alhaji Umaru Dikko made it difficult to get access to him.

The question in the mind of the readers here would be 'Why did Awolowo serve in Gen. Gowon' government? Why did he not stay away like other political leaders of his calibers like Dr. Nnamdi Azikiwe?

When the first coup led by Major Nzeogu failed, and Gen. Aguiyi Ironsi by omission or commission emerged as the new Head of State of Nigeria, the Yoruba elders had approached him to release Chief Awolowo from jail, for him, to get the complete cooperation of the Yoruba nation since the death of Herbert Macaulay in 1946 He said, he wanted Awolowo himself to ask for pardon in writing, when Awolowo did, Gen. Aguiyi Ironsi still refused. (See page 71)

It was the most senseless and stupid decision from a government that was still begging for recognition after the death of political leaders in the North and decedent leaders likes Akintola in the West. Some attributed his decision to the carry over imbroglio between Dr. Azikiwe and Chief Awolowo, which had become Igbo versus Yoruba nations, even though Gen. Ironsi was closer to Colonel Adekunle Fajuyi the Governor of Western Region from Oke Isha in Ado Ekiti. He had no love, respect or sympathy for Chief Awolowo and when you don't love Awolowo and his values or his doctrines in the West of Nigeria, it means you don't love the Yoruba nation. It was and will always be on how Yoruba selected their friends.

Unknown to other Nigerians, Chief Jeremiah Obafemi Awolowo was not just a political leader of the tribe; to them he was the re-incarnation of Oduduwa, the progenitor, of the tribe with spiritual influences all over Latin America, South America and some States in America. Chief Awolowo in the primitive era would have been deified like a god. When late Bola Ige was asked if he believed Awolowo could ever be wrong on any issue, Uncle Bola Ige said,

"I have respect for the following three that can never be wrong to me: God, Jesus Christ, and Awolowo."

The only people that saw anything wrong in Awolowo and his doctrines were regarded as the demons; spiritual and political enemies of the Yoruba nation. They are called Esu laalu Onile Orita by the Yoruba. Those who crossed Awolowo were not forgiven. To Chief Awolowo himself; forgiveness was almost like a sign of weakness. He was a proud man who believed in education and empowerment of the middle class as the only way for an egalitarian society. He was also the apostle of Federalism and creation of more States in Nigeria.

When asked if he believed he had more knowledge than his adversaries, he said, "When I stayed in my Library for hours, every day and night, reading and researching for solutions to Nigeria problems, my adversaries are busy drinking, smoking and following women of easy virtue, if they plan to be equal to the level of my intellect, they may have to give up those things they cherished so much."

Since Gen. Gowon failed to honor his words when he shifted the goal post of hand over to 1975 or 1976, Awolowo resigned from the Government and Gen. Obasanjo became the replacement for him in contest of Yoruba leadership within the government of Gowon and like a bad habit Chief Awolowo was gradually pushed to the background but his resignation deprived the government of honest advice, which Awolowo brought to the table between 1967 to 1971. However, if Gowon believed he could regain his Yoruba support with Obasanjo, a war hero, in his government. He was wrong! No one can compare apples with Oranges. They don't have the same taste.

When Gen. Gowon was removed in August 1975 coup and Gen. Muritala Mohamed became the

Head of State, the appointment of Gen. Obasanjo as his number two man could be seen like Gowon/Awolowo relationship, even though the 1975 coup plotters were Sheu Yar'Adua, Jeremiah Usenni and others, the fact remained the third arm of the group Brigadier Danjuma would have to be brought in to take care of the Army, while the hegemony of Gen. Obasanjo and Muritala would be planted for a long time to come.

Some attributed the hidden hatred for Chief Awolowo political career by Gen. Obasanjo from the day he joined Gowon Administration. Some even dated it back to the issues on money for soldiers at the battled front that was often passed through the shrewd pen of Chief Awolowo as Federal Commissioner for Finance and when in 1979 Awolowo had to seek the presidency in a new dispensation managed by Gen. Obasanjo as military Head of State, he was quick to say "the best may not win" and when Awolowo did not win and he was still appealing the case in court and using the legal procedure to interpret the two third majority clause in the constitution, Gen. Obasanjo ignored his plea and the laziest man became the President.

It was at that point Gen. Obasanjo crossed the line with his tribe the Yoruba and Chief Awolowo in despair and unfulfilled returned to his chambers at Apapa Lagos to lick his wounds and in

1983 he tried and failed again. It was a payback for Gen. Obasanjo and the beginning of a struggle for him that may never win the type of affection his people had for Chief Awolowo. It could even be a wound for Awolowo loyalists that may never be healed even with history. No matter how Gen. Obasanjo tried, if they were expecting him to ask for their favor or forgiveness, they must have misunderstood him. He never tried to ask for any reconciliation either, because he knew he was never going to get it.

Furthermore, despite his unmatchable achievements, in and out of the country Gen. Obasanjo could never be seen as reincarnation of Oduduwa like his people saw Awolowo; however Obasanjo in future will still have to struggle with the legacy of Herbert Macaulay or Lisabi on his home town Abeokuta or corporately in Africa itself as the replacement for Nelson Mandela, time will tell.

The next part will answer some of the questions raised in the first paragraph of this chapter, which will include the deaths of Sanni Abacha and MKO Abiola, Gen. Obasanjo's years in jail, why he wrote the book *The Power of Prayers* from the prison yard, his farms, his second coming as President, and the series will be concluded with the death of President Yar Adua and emergence of President Goodluck Jonathan the man Nigerians love to call a shoeless President or a man with the resource control hat.

Politics is a game for people with short memories.

~Mika Brzezinski. MSNBC

By the time President Babangida played himself out of office in 1993 and it was time to shop for a successor, he had banned all the eligible candidates like Gen. Yar Adua, Shinkafi, Olu Falae, also he had annulled the election that elected his best civilian friend MKO Abiola as President of Nigeria, the Interim National Government ING was a safe face for the evil genius from Minna, in Niger State to run out of Abuja without leaving his tails behind like a fearful dog.

Like the Oracle mentioned earlier, Gen. Babangida ran out of friends and those left for him to consult were his frienemies they wanted him out, his old boss in the Army Gen.Obasanjo was interested in being the Head of Interim, because he felt cheated with only three and half years as Head of State from the government he left in 1979 to the cigarette smoking Alhaji Shagari who crashed his legacy with a failed civilian government, he should be able to manipulate the system to come back to office as Interim Head of State and probably elongate the years to more than four years, so he thought!

From a photograph in the archives, Gen. Obasanjo and Babangida were more than just buddies or Senior and Junior Army officer relationship; they played game of draft, cards and badminton.

Photograph courtesy USAfricaonline.com

Both were the evil genius of each other, they represented the best and the worst of each other personalities, when you look at it sensitively, either of them could be the other side of the coin to each other in a casino game, in the art of manipulation, whatever the fears of the one could be seen in the other, in other words in politics Gen. Babangida was a son that looked like his father and that father was Gen. Obasanjo.

Secretly, Gen. Obasanjo saw the challenges of the eight years Gen. Babangida spent in office to his own three and half years, he could not imagine the officer he groomed and elevated to the Supreme military Council in 1976 after the death of Gen. Muritala Mohammed and subsequent capture of Col. Buka Suka Dimka from the Radio Nigeria Station in Lagos could be so smart, deadly and was able to make it to eight years in office as military President, which was unimaginable. Gen. Gowon's nine years in office was like a mirage and how the unconcluded draft game would be played with him winning, but time would tell.

Gen. Obasanjo did not believe in losing any contest. In fact, he hardly lost any fight in his life, he was also a lucky fighter and when he wins, he destroys his adversaries to the point they never came up again, for example, Chief Awolowo with his so called free education record in the Western Region, was behind him now, he did the same free education program at primary school level for the whole country in 1976. He had emerged as the only recognized General from the Yoruba tribe, indeed, in Nigeria. All others behind him looked like his juniors, he was and will always be first among the first not even among equals. To Gen. Obasanjo, the only equality to the first is he alone, which was how he displayed his personality in his book, *My Command.* In it, he destroyed all friends and enemies as he almost made himself a saint in the book.

Nigerians never stopped wondering at what drives Obasanjo and what keeps him going. Is it the love of the country? Or the love of personal and selfish egocentrism search for an-ending goal? Perhaps the need to stay ahead while others lined up behind, or is it like the words of Gaius Cassius Longinus in Julius Caesar a play by Shakespeare *to bestow the whole world like a Colossus and the petty men walks under it?* What more as we continue to research into what has kept him going?

Gen. Obasanjo wanted to be the Head of Interim government but he was by-passed for Chief Ernest Shonekan by IBB and the Armed Forces Ruling Council, AFRC and he did not forgive

Babangida for it, like Awolowo, there was nothing like forgiveness. You do it; you pay for it was his doctrine as simple as the Law of Moses.

The abortive military coup d'état that finally landed him in jail was a planned event by Gen. Sanni Abacha to curb the wings of Gen. Obasanjo. He was abroad when the brouhaha of the coup was announced, and from the grapevine intelligence information got to him, he was told never to return to the country because the government felt he could be one of the coup plotters, but as proud as he was, when he was told he was to be arrested, he never believed it, not because he was innocent, but he underestimated the maximum dictator was bent on putting him on check for good and when he was found guilty and sentenced to death. Abacha had no secret or loyalty to Obasanjo unlike IBB who openly showed his respect and affection for OBJ.

The arrest of Obasanjo and removal of Sultan of Sokoto Dansuki established Sanni Abacha as the most fearful Head of State in Nigeria even though he was more like a brainless Head of State to most of his critics, and his ruthlessness placed him far ahead of others before him. However, the process of the arrest Obasanjo took cat and mouse stages, more like Abacha was testing the water and level of support Gen. Obasanjo had with the military before he could fully implement his plans, Abacha adopted the Fabian strategies, Obasanjo was first confined to his Ota farm, and after the visit of former America President Jimmy Carter, all the powers or influence Abacha thought OBJ had with the Army was no longer there, Abacha ordered him transferred to Jos Prison.

Gen. Obasanjo days in Jos prison was hectic, he asked one of the correction officers from his home town Abeokuta, in Ogun State, if the public were already fighting on his behalf like they did over June 12 his friendenemy Moshood Abiola.

"Yes sir!" the correction officer said.

"Sanni Abacha is not going to last," Gen. Obasanjo said with pride

"I believe you, sir." He told General Obasanjo

"I hope the casualties are not too many over my jail term." Obasanjo inquired.

"Sir, the public fighting is not that totally Nigerians sir" He said.

"Who are they?" Obasanjo

"You don't want know sir" He said without looking at Obasanjo in the face.

"Tell me I can handle the truth" Obasanjo said

"They are your immediate family members and they are fight over your properties," the correction officer said.

The Nigerian Press reported Gen. Obasanjo wept profusely. It was probably the only time one would read of the uncompromising Obasanjo weeping in Nigeria history. It was probably the time he wrote his book *The Power of Prayers*. He became a born-again Christian and started preaching the kingdom of God through Jesus Christ to other inmates.

When all the two difficult actors to the actualization of the June 12 mandate had died and Gen. Obasanjo was released from jail, and to assure his boss of his love and winning the same draft game of politics Babangida joined hands with others to rehabilitate him with a 140 million naira check after his visit to Abeokuta to see a tired Obasanjo who was released with visible weight loss, he looked just like Awolowo was, when he too came out of jail in 1967, tired and unhappy with the result of how Nigeria treated them after giving everything to the country they love so much, Gen. Obasanjo had to reflect on what the future had for him.

Earlier in history, late Abacha had tried every method like IBB to elongate himself in office, all oppositions had been jailed including his deputy, Gen. Diya from Odogbolu a few kilometers from Ikenne the home place of late Awolowo. All the five political parties out of fear had adopted the maximum dictator, as the their Presidential candidate, but his sudden death led to a power struggle that sidelined both Gen. Usenni and Major Al Mustapha with the emergence of Gen Abubarkar Abdul Salam as the new Head of State.

Under Sanni Abacha, the Yoruba tribe in South West of Nigeria suffered lots of victimization as he became a confused Head of State with lack of trust and he was also paranoid to any development around him and in all his five years as Head of State, Gen. Babangida kept his distance from the maximum dictator, the only noticeable contact between Abacha and IBB was when Col. Mepaida, his onetime ADC, as Chief of Army Staff was roped into an abortive coup and he had to vouch for him to be released other than that, he did nothing to check or advise Abacha on how to manage the affairs of the country.

Furthermore when Gen. Abacha deposed Dansuki the Sultan of Sokoto, which he IBB installed, he never altered a word, he knew Abacha was looking for an excuse to get rid of him like he did with Yar Adua, Gen. Obasanjo and others. IBB knew the rule of the game, see no evil, and talk no evil.

Gen. Sanni Abacha had no regard for any line of authority other than his own; he sent packing the most respected Sultan of Sokoto Alhaji Dansuki over the protection of his brother–in-law Col. Bello of the Nigerian Army to escape the fang of his government over a purported military coup.

It was the first time in history of Nigeria, that the authority of any Sultan of Sokoto would be challenged since the British destroyed the Caliphate in 1903, most of Nigerian leaders either military of civilian had to pay homage to the authority of the Sultan of Sokoto before any authority in Nigeria, but that of Sanni Abacha was different. He also caged Gen. Shehu Yar'Adua a onetime deputy to Gen. Obasanjo in 1976-1979 and when the five political parties he created to return to civilian government saw the direction of detentions and killings going on in the country, all of them out of fear adopted him as the Presidential candidate.

Uncle Bola Ige one of the Yoruba leaders who had refused to participate in the transition processes of Abacha with his *Sidon look* slogan described the five parties as five fingers of a leper, he was warned by other Yoruba leaders to stay away from Abacha dirty hands otherwise, the tribe might be deprived of elders like him. He listened.

However on 8th June 1998 Gen. Sanni Abacha died, of an unconfirmed source, some said, he was having a nice time with some Indian prostitutes, some attributed it to the tea poison and since General Jerry Usenni was the last military officer to see him, he was a suspect. Gen. Usenni recalled that late Yasser Arafat PLO was in Abuja to see General Abacha he was part of the meeting and when Arafat left he was with the Head of State till two am and three hours later when he was sleeping, he was summoned again to Abuja before he was told Abacha had died and Abubarkar Salam had been appointed the new Head of State despite his seniority over every officer. He was the assumed suspect in the death of Sanni Abacha.

Abacha's' death was a relief to the country. People came out in thousands to rejoice over his death, a sharp deference to the time Muritala Mohammed was killed in 1976. However, as MKO Abiola was getting too blissful for a possible release to reclaim his June 12 mandate he too died in the presence of Americans ambassadors that visited him in jail.

Ambassador Susan Rice representative of President Bill Clinton and US Ambassador in Nigeria Pickering both had visited MKO Abiola in jail as soon as Sanni Abacha died and the likelihood of his release from prison was eminent, they offered him tea without the presence of his guardian, after one or two sip from the tea, he developed a cardiac arrest, shortly he died including the dream of the June 12 mandate.

Was he poison? Could his death also be linked with that of his friend Gen. Muritala Mohamed who was purported killed by American government sponsored coup in 1976? Was it just a coincidence? Could his death be, as a result of his demand for reparation for African Americans in the United States and Africa itself due to years of slavery in the same way the Jews benefited from Holocaust from the years of Adolf Hitler in the Second World War?

Despite the so called noise of the United States over human rights abuse of General Sanni Abacha, secretly and shamefully some of the America politicians became supporters of a man who did not believe in democracy or human rights, Senator James Inhofe (OK) and Senator Carol Mosley Braum (IL) spoke very Highly of a man who locked away the winner of the June 12 election in Nigeria.

Rev. Jesse Jackson, who was President Clinton's special adviser on Africa, said Abacha knew what he was doing and with time the world would see how right he was. Minister Louis Farrakhan saw it through his own Islamic faith and years of slavery in America, to spite his country. Gen. Abacha named Eleke Crescent Louis Farrakhan Crescent, which was the street on which American Embassy was situated in Lagos because Farrakhan hated American hypocrisy to African-America rights; the street had since been reverted to its previous name after Abacha died. As if the

United States of America also wanted to play the Abacha game, the street in New York on which Nigeria Consular office was situated was renamed after the assassinated wife of the June 12 winner, late Kudirat Abiola.

Over five billion pounds was reported stolen from the government treasury by Gen. Sanni Abacha and it was secretly transferred to various banks all over the world. His brutality led to the death of Ken Saro Wiwa of the Ogoni tribe. Wole Soyinka, who started a Kudirat Radio to explain more to the outside world the happenings in Nigeria, was tried for treasonable felony in absentia, many of us left the country including this writer in 1996.

Why did President Clinton fail to intervene at a time democracy in Nigeria particularly NADECCO was begging the world for support?

Separately, Gen. Obasanjo was released from jail by the new Head of State Gen. Abdul Salam who was his ADC in 1979. The political transition stage was set for Gen. Obasanjo to return to office as President to correct the mistakes of Gen Babangida for not trusting Gen. Obasanjo enough for picking Ernest Shonekan as Head of interim government over Gen. Obasanjo who was capable of getting the trust of Army as against Ernest Shonekan, the former Managing Director of UAC in 1993. The

Presidential election in 1997 that followed was determined.

A conservative is someone who makes no changes and consults his grandmother when in doubts.
~Woodrow Wilson

Nigeria oil deals has never been an open business to average Nigerian. Oil deals are done in secrecy and what MKO Abiola was asking for during the presidential debate could not be tolerated.

MKO Abiola's death was a big blow to NADECO and in particular Senator Bola Tinubu who later became the arrowhead and youthful leader of NADECO from the aging group of Chief Anthony Enahoro who could not understand the direction of the country. He stood up as the youngest Parliamentarian under the Action Group a political party of Chief Awolowo that asked the

British to grant the country her independence in 1952 or so, and other deflated progressive groups. It was like not getting an answer to one of the variable solutions to a simultaneous equation problem.

Abiola's death was the end of hope for Nigeria on June 12 election or the mandate, the largest concentration of Black race on earth had problems with justice and each time the country was on the verge of getting it right, the hands of enemies were stronger than the goodwill of the people, in the end, what the country got was always cosmetic solution, not the real solution itself, MKO's death was an injustice to fate or natural justice.

It was also a complete turnaround from potential goodness to the policy of manipulations and frustrations from a progressive route that had been reduced from a national issue to Yoruba affair, since all his friends, had deserted him, he should have listened and relinquished the mandate was the general consensus of the people even among his own people, just like the tragic end of Okonkwo in the book *Things Fall Apart* by Chinua Achebe, it was like a suicide mission in the end. Nigeria's journey towards true democracy had been taken over by those who destroyed it in the first place.

Nigeria political journey from 1960 was a bundle of intricacies. Every day in the life of the nation, was like a game of soccer and just as if the opposing team, was about to score the winning goal after the player had dribbled all the players and the goalkeeper, the referee decided to blow the whistle for a foul committed fifteen minutes earlier, that was not seen or noticed by the spectators in the whole stadium or the camera men, then the game was repeated all over again and again, or like wrestling game in which unseen hands usually come to destroy the hope of the winner, that was how politics was played south of Sahara, Africa largest concentration of black people in the last fifty- three years of independence.

It was obvious from the nature of the deaths of the two leaders MKO Abiola and Gen. Sanni Abacha, they were eliminated by unseen hands of the military class for Nigeria of their own dream to move forward, it was not the wish of the ordinary men on the street or regular Army officers, it was indeed the planned handiwork of the military Generals, Emirs, Obas and Obis including politicians.

Indeed, all of them were united by the oil deals that have been the problem of Nigeria since 1956 when the crude oil was discovered at Oloibiri, which a potential MKO Abiola's presidency had questioned in one of the Presidential debates in a question asked by the NRC Chairman Tom Ikimi.

Nigerians at home and diaspora were confused and worried. Those who thought MKO Abiola would be like a Nelson Mandela were deflated, with his death, attention was switched to the calculated enemies of true democracy on how to bring the godfather of the military from jail from his temporary abdication of his position as the Head of the military political class to the presidency, which had been tactically allocated to the Yoruba, and the locomotive train for the return of Gen. Obasanjo as President of Nigeria was set in motion.

Gen. Obasanjo met all the political calculations of those who destroyed the June 12 mandate of MKO Abiola for the following reasons, he was not a fan of Abiola and his mandate, he was loyal to the North and Nigeria Army, since 1979 handover of government to President Shagari, and he was a man, the military could trust.

The need to get Obasanjo out of jail to appease the West of Nigeria was actually the main reason why Gen. Jerry Usenni the most senior military officer was not allowed to succeed the late Gen. Abacha before Gen. Abdul Salam was appointed as the new Head of State. Gen. Usenni would have created a different transition program that would not be in favor of Gen. Obasanjo.

Gen. Jeremiah Usenni joined the Army as a kid at fourteen years. They called him Jerry boy. His military works could be traced to his role in 1967 and 1976 coups that installed General Gowon and Gen. Muritala Mohammed, his performances in all the coups in Nigeria could be legendary, behind late Yar'Adua, IBB and Sanni Abacha, General Usenni had no match, his inability to grab the Head of State position after the death of Abacha was a slap on him, if he could only he be trusted to release OBJ, he would have been appointed the Head of State for the one year transition plan, and he could not pass the lie test. Besides, it was rumored he knew what killed the General because he was with him till 2:00 a.m. on the day he died. Years later in an interview, he tried to clear his hands off the death of General Abacha, but his excuse could not turn back the hands of the clock.

In exchange for the release and presidency, General Obasanjo was given some no go areas, and every attempt by the Press and public for Obasanjo and his presidency to upturn the secret pact were all cleverly rejected.

The deaths of Abiola and Abacha would not be probed.

The disappearance of the three billion dollars in the foreign reserves, which was shared by the political class as a compensation would be over looked

IBB mistakes, past and immediate past would be over looked including the death of Dele Giwa and the annulment of the June 12, 1993, election.

Gen. Obasanjo was to be given 140 million naira for immediate rehabilitation fee to take off as soon as he comes out of jail, which IBB was to spearhead.

The AD political party with Olu Falae as it Presidential candidate the group in the South West, would be frustrated by the Gen. Abdul Salam Abubakar' military government from smelling presidency.

As the political activities were going on all over the country towards the return to civilian government by unsuspected citizens with the believe that they had seen the end of military regime in Nigeria, the military knew from day one, that it would only hand over the government to a man they could trust, to a person who will protect the interest of all the Generals in and out of office, the oil deals, and support of the Emirs, Obas and Obis; that person was Gen. Obasanjo, who was flat broke with a porous personality ready for redemption.

When the election was finally over and Gen. Obasanjo who came out of jail in 1998 to be Nigeria's President, based on the Constitution signed into law by Gen. Abdul Salam Abubakar without referendum from Nigerians. It was a mission accomplished by the haters of the June 12 and the military's dream and that of Gen. Obasanjo became the dreams of Nigeria, like he said later in life, his wish was to live in the life of ignorance in his village, the whole country was ignorance of the dirty deal behind closed doors. *O ma she o!!!*

For the same reason, we failed to get it right, we were too afraid to find justice, and when we came very close to it, we threw it away, not even the justice itself, but the dignity of everything and the love of the nation was turned to jokes and we continue to celebrate ignorance in the twenty-first century.

~ Zents Sowunmi

Chief Awolowo was a man who created a level ground for the common man in the Western Region, that part of Nigeria he was privileged to govern as the Premier between 1952 to 1959, and his legacies on education, health care, rural development and industrial revolution of the Western Nigeria was admired by the British and in most cases drew tears from eyes of an average Yoruba man on the street. They wondered if such a man would walk the same land again in their lifetime, they could not see the same doctrines or ideas in General Obasanjo.

Could the achievements of Gen. Obasanjo draw any tears or sympathy from the Yoruba or Nigerians? The Oracle says No. however, President Obasanjo was indeed a lucky man, in a medieval period, it would be appropriate to say, his destiny was programmed for him by the gods, which must have been secured on top of *Iroko* tree far away from the hands of his enemies in his village at Ibogun, a small village outside Ifo in Ogun State.

Remi Obasanjo his first wife had described him, as a loving husband, until he came out of the civil war, in 1970 when his social and marital life changed. The love he had for his wife Remi changed, at one time, it was reported by the news media that he had her beaten up by his cousin in Lagos but the discussion here was not even about his marital life, which was complicated like that of his school mate MKO Abiola. By the time he became the new President in 1999, he had gone through three wives, and lots of concubines, unlike his friend Abiola who married them.

Gen. Obasanjo. was a one-step woman at a time husband, and each of the wives was on the waiting line prompt to replace the other, and that calculated system itself kept his women in check and all of them strived to win his love. Behind his tiny

Chinese looking eyes, no one could see any sign of love but a man mocking the system, which he created himself.

If Gen. Obasanjo was affected with an untreated PTSD as result of the civil war in 1970, he must have been affected by another dose of it in 1998 from the years Gen. Sanni Abacha kept him in Jail, and Nigerians who expected him to be the Messiah were disappointed, but he did his best for the nation that had nothing in treasury when he took office, a nation hunted with over 35 billion dollars mounting foreign debts, which all the past leaders had not been able to tackle.

In 1988, the Post graduate students of the University of Ibadan in the Department of Economics invited Gen. Obasanjo to deliver a lecture on foreign debt. When he was asked on what Nigeria could do to solve the looming debt.

Gen. Obasanjo said, "Ignore it."

When he became the President almost ten years after, it was probably the policy he implemented after arm twisting the London and Paris Clubs, through his Minister of Finance Ngozi Iweala he appointed from World Bank, he paid off the Principal of the national debt, which made the London and Paris Clubs to write the interest off and the country became debt free like 7th President Andrew Jefferson did for the United States of

America between 1829 to 1837 who also left the nation and presidency with countless enemies.

President Obasanjo restructured the Army and the security system of Nigeria, it was not the first time, as a military Head of State in 1976, after the death of Gen. Muritala Mohamed, Gen. Obasanjo created the security platform for Nigeria, like State Security Service (SSS), and Federal secret prison yards in snake Island.

The establishment of EFCC was one of the finest legacies of President Gen. Obasanjo, and he could have been classified as the Abraham Lincoln of Nigeria, if he had destroyed the ambition of the Zamfara State Governor Yerima who first introduced of Sharia law in the North of Nigeria, if he had insisted that all other religions and businesses were protected, in any State with Sharia maybe things would have been different, his option for political solution led to the resurgence of what became Boko Haram ten years later.

Boko Haram did not just spring up overnight like Professor Wole Soyinka wrote on Newsweek magazine of recent titled " The nation of Butchers ." The 1986 Nobel Award winner in Literature the custodian of African comparative literature, said. It was a religious intolerance that finally became a monster for the country to contend with. The soul of the nation is twisted between surrendering the constitution of the people to the supremacy of Quran in a nation with multi-religious group. This is one of the areas Gen. Obasanjo failed Nigeria, he concluded.

How much of Chief Awolowo was in Gen. Obasanjo? Or how much of Gen. Obasanjo was in IBB or other Generals? More than anyone could imagine. This writer analyzed it in the past that the emergence of Gen. Obasanjo into political arena was the end of Chief Awolowo active political career, and when Gen. Obasanjo came into Gowon's administration it was obvious the man from Abeokuta intended to wipe away the legacies of Awolowo, and his so called progressives and his victory signs.

What made Gen. Yakubu Gowon to appoint Gen. Obasanjo as a member of his cabinet as Federal Commissioner of Works when Chief Awolowo resigned from his government in 1971? Was it to compensate him for his services to the nation as the last Commanding officer who ended the civil war? Or was it to fill in the gap created with the departure of Chief Awolowo from his government to satisfy the Yoruba nation within the Nigeria body politics? Might even be more, of the ambition developed by Gen. Obasanjo along the way or luck and being in the right place at the right?

That will be areas of research for those interested in political history of Nigeria, however, Gen. Obasanjo was hunted by the legacies of Awolowo in the South West of Nigeria, the platform, which Chief Awolowo started his career as a Labor Secretary in the 1940s was first restructured in 1977 by Gen. Obasanjo as a military Head of State with a new Nigeria Labor Congress, and as a civilian President twenty years later, it was the same Labor Union he tried to destroy with a new Labor law.

Somehow, Chief Awolowo despite his legacy knew the game was over for him before his death in 1987, he knew between Gen. Obasanjo and MKO Abiola one of them would destroy him politically and sadly both of them did.

MKO Abiola used his newspapers Concord Press in Lagos, to tear down the wall of innocence of Awolowo, which portrayed the astute politician as a crook hiding under social welfare programs with 370 plots of Maroko land grab in Lagos, while Gen. Obasanjo used the military might to shrink the influence of Awolowo. To the Yoruba nation alone, both of them left him as unfulfilled politician, ironically both were classmate in BBHS in Abeokuta, was it a mission planted into them as student of the school in the fifties by a teacher who had something to do with Awolowo who was also a student of

BBHS himself as reported in the autobiographies of MKO Abiola by pointblank publication online?

Who was the government or civics teachers of General Obasanjo and Moshood Abiola back in their days in the college, was he a friend or a foe of Chief Obafemi Awolowo? Maybe the teacher was even a class mate of Chief Obafemi Awolowo who had something in his days against Papa Awolowo how did two ex-students of the same school hated Awolowo one even benefited from his free education program. But Nigeria was yet to develop room for research that will uproot all the questions of the Oracle. May be in future, the Oracle says maybe.

If only for one day to be President of Nigeria was all Awolowo asked from a country his party Action Group first demanded for its independent from the British in 1952. He was denied. It was sad and the curse of iniquity and directionless of the failure to have him as President never left the shore of Nigeria as the nation continued to be governed by those with no love for the future of black race in the twenty-first century.

President Gen. Obasanjo was a man at war with everything he wrestled his hand with. He was at war with his own government and the people he sworn the constitution to govern, and by the time he left office he had destroyed his own legacies like IBB did with the annulment of the June 12 election in 1993, Gen. Obasanjo legacies, would have been protected, if he had followed the steps of Chief Awolowo who was people oriented, but Gen. Obasanjo's style was militant.

In his eight years presidency, his government went through three Senate Presidents, three Speakers of the House and those who escaped his style never came up politically, six months suspension of Governor of Benue State, his problems with Christian Association of Nigeria he openly abused, and the uncharitable death of his Minister of Justice Bola Ige will forever remain a stain on his doorstep. Late Dr. Chuba Okadigbo was a Senate President who was chased by Obasanjo's government to his home town to secure the mace of office; both had a history of misunderstanding before he became the Senate President.

Dr Chuba Okadigbo was given a large sum of money to perform some unknown business for Obasanjo in the East of Nigeria, he kept the money and when there was no result Obasanjo was mad at him. He asked for forgiveness from Obasanjo, but was never comfortable with the President for staring at him for a long time, until a day he could not take it anymore, he walked to Obasanjo's office in the midst of his political associates to ask for the reason the President was making him uncomfortable with a continuous stare and occasionally winking his eyes at him.

General Obasanjo looked at him with his tinny Chinese eyes again and shook his head with a smile that resembled that of hyena in the savannah. He told Okadigbo, each time he looked at him, on his forehead, all he could see was the amount he took from him for the failed job in the East. If he wanted forgiveness the money must be returned. Okadigbo was later removed as President of the Senate and he died few years after.

However, late Chief Awolowo was a man who lived in the hearts of his admirers or his so called Awoists, to the Yoruba and progressives he was their own Nelson Mandela, his name alone still draw tears in the eyes of those who benefited from his legacies, that could not be said of President Obasanjo despite his commitment and sacrifices, his connection to the average Nigerians will forever be missing in a man who gave it all to his country and will still not be appreciated by the ordinary men and women on the streets until death takes him away.

Will history forgive him? His Oliver Twist mentality for a third term in office as President and how he destroyed the clamor for sovereign National Conference with the one he introduced that sent the group of Anthony Enahoro on a different route; his divide and rule strategies; his unnecessary in-fighting with his vice President Atiku; and his failure to have a sustained Plan B to succeed him.

President Obasanjo failed to sign the Freedom of Information Bill into law, which created the impression that he had a lot to hide.

Furthermore, he turned his eyes away from the establishment of State and City police with amendment to 1999 constitution, which could have solved the internal insecurity of his country, after asking experts on the topic to submit a working paper on it.

However, if the dreams of Gen. Obasanjo had become the temporary dreams of Nigeria, it was never going to be enough dreams of the future of Nigeria in the twenty-first century, even at the so-called Council of State meetings, despite his years out of office in midst of his former boss Gen. Gowon, former President Shagari and other juniors like Generals Babangida, Buhari and Abdul Salam Abubakar, including Chief Shonekan the interim Head of State, Gen. Obasanjo calls the shots, and no doubt, the present Nigeria political and security could be credited to him since 1976. The Oracle will be bold to call him the Godfather of the military control on Nigeria politics.

How long will the House of Cards created by President Obasanjo last? As Nigeria continues to search for a lasting political structure to hold together, the hope and ambition of the coming generations in the twenty-first century, so will those who benefited from his legacy struggle to suppress the demand for an egalitarian society, which Chief Awolowo asked for, or a society, which Mallam Aminu Kano gently asked for in the North of Nigeria; a society where the poor or the Talakawa will have the same opportunity to grow like anyone without fear, the same was the request of Joseph Tarka for the middle Belt..

The Oracle will like to predict that the problem of Nigeria will be over when those who had ruled Nigeria since 1970 are actually taken away by old age or death. From the look of things we have ten more years to go. The only way to fast-track the end of the problem is to adopt the EPS i.e. Expanded Primary system which will remove the hands of the past leaders for a new leadership in Nigeria.

Moreover, when President Obasanjo's eight years in office was over his people, the Yoruba nation, were disappointed in him. They could not see any reasonable development in the West to justify a Yoruba man in office. Their roads were still not tarred, water was still not running like it was during Awolowo, electricity or energy supply was still as bad as it was. Again when they reflected at his eight years in office it was nothing to be proud off, even in his home town, it was just another big village. How he could stay in the beautiful City of Abuja for eight years and return to the dusty cities of Sango Ota and Abeokuta was unimaginable.

They were told OBJ occupied the slot of the Yoruba in his eight years presidency and may never expect the number one position for the next twenty five years, because of rotation on zonal system.

The Yoruba nation and minorities that could trace their political growth to Aminu Kano, Joseph Tarka and other minorities politically went back to what knew better, the comfortable arms of late Chief Awolowo and his legacies, the re-incarnation of Oduduwa, the man who lived in their hearts and who told them to aspire for an egalitarian society.

They voted for AC, which later became APC along with a merger with Gen. Mohamadu Buhari led, CPN, the future to them, will have to be without General Obasanjo and his dreams. It must be based on the re-emergence of the old progressives of the North, few radicals from the East, West and Middle Belt, which was still missing at the time of this book, but it will be the future of politics in Nigeria.

More like a confused man, President Gen. Obasanjo with his dreams of life of ignorance in his village of Ibogun was left behind like a child after his presidency, his own people voted in the Political Party with the values of Awolowo, which was solidly based on middle class development, which was the pivot of the misunderstandings of General Obasanjo on Awolowo doctrines.

What then is the hope for the nation? Perhaps the only Military General in the country, who could look President Obasanjo in eyes and tell him off with his house of cards he created with no room for complete freedom of the people, will be Gen. Buhari who has since been quiet and retired to his village. He could be brought back from retirement to play a major role in freeing Nigeria from the house of cards created by Gen. Obasanjo. (Gen. Buhari came back to politics, as one of the leaders of APC probably the Presidential candidate for 2015 elections)

The country must work for a two party system to bring back Unity and love of the nation, meaning the ACN and CPC must fuss together to combat the political war ahead. (The merger eventually happened as predicted)

Finally, Gen. Obasanjo, despite all his achievements as the last man standing in 1970 at the end of the civil war, the last man standing, in 1979 who handed over to President Shagari, and his second coming in 1999 as President, may end up as an Oriaku instead of Okpataku, if he had been sincere with the way he handled the political future of Nigeria, which to the Oracle, he was not.

However, whatever he is hiding may be uncovered when history will be judging him.

Furthermore, the Oracle would like to ask if he Obasanjo was a disciple of Chief Samuel Ladoke Akintola the assassinated Premier of the Western Region who also advocated for the Yoruba to join the Federal government like Obasanjo did in his role as President of Nigeria.

If MKO Abiola was a poor student and a classmate of Gen. Obasanjo in High School was able to get scholarship under a government controlled by Chief Awolowo to study Accountancy in Glasgow in the United Kingdom, why did Gen Obasanjo fail to apply for the same scholarship before he joined the Nigerian Army at the time it was easier for his generation to get scholarship in Western Region of Nigeria?

Did he apply for it or not? Was he denied? Could that have been one of the remote causes of his problems with Chief Awolowo later in life? Unlike the misconception of many of Awoists on SLA Akintola that he was against Awolowo or Yoruba interest, one of the audio record on him on YouTube in his own voice loafed with deep Yoruba ascents and the use of traditional wisdom, he actually revealed his mind, that he loved his people as much as he loved Nigeria, and all he wanted was for his people to join Federal Government of Nigeria, like other tribes in Nigeria? His views were not better than what Sardauna of Sokoto Ahmadu Bello also expressed about the Igbo and policy of domination.

Could Gen. Obasanjo have been a disciple of Akintola doctrines of integrating the Yoruba at the center, which was what he, Gen. Obasanjo did as President later in life?

When the former Governor of Lagos State, Senator Bola Tinubu was interviewed by the Sun Newspapers on the 03/25/2012, he had the following to say about President Gen. Obasanjo

He was asked, "Can you recall anyone you lost?"

"I think it was the democratization process itself; it's true that I didn't want Gen. Obasanjo to be the President of the Federal Republic of Nigeria and there was no doubt about that. I lost that one; I didn't want him. I didn't want to see him at all from inception."

"Why?"

"Because anybody who has worn the uniform described as a camouflage has learnt the art of deception and that's the way I see Gen. Obasanjo. He had meetings and meetings with MKO Abiola. I was with him, I believe four of us including Dele Alake, and we had amala and vegetable soup with hot pepper in Abiola's house. Everybody was yawning, sweating, and looking for water with MKO

Abiola and Gen. Obasanjo behaving as if it wasn't as hot as we made it seem; behaving as if they had this deep understanding. Then, not up to two weeks after that, Gen. Obasanjo went away to Zimbabwe and announced from there that Abiola was not the messiah," Tinubu said.

Haba! After that, I mistrusted him; I couldn't believe that a man could do that. Stand by some principles, stand by some integrity, stand transparently and honestly on matter of facts as you lead other people to believe you and support you as a key pillar. Then, I start to think whether this man came to Abiola and collected information; information that we had heard that he wanted to be Shonekan; he wanted to be an interim leader and not Shonekan. So, when they presented him that he was going to be the candidate of the other party, I said that Nigeria was in for trouble.

Can I believe this man? No, I cannot trust him. Is that one of the reasons why you have not congratulated him on his seventy-fifth birthday? I didn't even remember his birthday. I opened the newspaper and saw it. There are so many problems confronting us. I won't blame anybody who doesn't read my birthday greetings. I won't blame them if they say they didn't see it, there are so many problems confronting the nation.

There are so many news items that are seriously more newsworthy than to be looking for Gen. Obasanjo's congratulatory messages in the newspaper. A man who had great opportunity to put Nigeria on the right path and failed to do so; failed to do even the Otta road, not Lagos-Ibadan Expressway.

What am I celebrating about him? That is the truth. He deceptively dealt with the country and he handed over to a man who he knew was ill. Gen. Obasanjo is a leader that could not find another successor capable of driving through his vision for the country."

The above will explain why OBJ as President tried everything to destroy Governor Bolaji Tinubu of Lagos State. He used his position to deny Lagos State all Federal Allocation instead of helping to build the most important State in the West, the financial center of the Country. It was a misplaced action from Gen. Obasanjo to his own people. He failed to fully understand Nigeria as he was ridiculed on the pages of newspapers by the same Nigerians from other tribes later in life and no extended arms of his people to console his heart.

Part Five

5

Recommended

Solution

Articles

ARTICLE ONE

The impact of Sokoto Caliphate and Oyo Empire on Nigerian Politics in the Twenty-First Century

The 18th Century witnessed lots of revolutions and spiritual learning curves for the people of South of Sahara in West Africa but the two most important historical events for consideration with hangover effects will be the defunct Oyo Empire and the Sokoto Caliphate. Both are dead, but their doctrines however, still manage to impact the future of the areas they covered in the past as territories in North and South West of Niger River in the present day Nigeria in regards to politics and religions.

In one of my widely circulated articles in 2004, which was first published by Vanguard News of Nigeria in May 2004 titled "Benin and Yoruba kingdoms: The missing gap of history" the article solved the imbroglio of the source of Yoruba and Edo people and how these two cousins could be linked with Oduduwa. I argued with conviction, if the ancient city of Ile Ife remains where the approval of any new king for Benin was given, and the city also where all Heads of any late king of Benin was buried then, Ile Ife must indeed remain without any doubt the spiritual source of both people of Edo and Yoruba and the same town when compared from archeological view point, the City of Ife could still pass the test for the source of both tribes, but that has not been scientifically proved beyond reasonable doubt, as the City of Benin was destroyed by Captain Philip of the British Army when Overameh was Oba of Benin because he Overameh opposed slavery. This undiscovered part of history will be a project for archeologist with DNA to be used to solve in future.

Oyo Empire, which emerged from the linage of Oduduwa through his belligerent son Oranmiyan who had the authority of the great Oduduwa to collect ten percent of any products and service as compensation for the loss of inheritance from Oduduwa that was done in his absence to Benin Kingdom on behalf of the father created the foundation for Yoruba politics that graduated into survival in present day Nigeria.

Oranmiyan the last son of Oduduwa created administrative control in which all his representatives through future Alaafin of Oyo were posted to all the

Yoruba cities to monitor and collect royalties on behalf of the Alaafin (Iku Baba yeye) or Kabiyesi, which in some situations subjected most of the king in most of the Yoruba Cities to ridicules, as some were made to prostrate to the representatives of Alaafin in front of their people before and after the collection of the royalties.

These ugly behaviors of the Alaafin representatives, triggered the revolution that eventually led to the fall of the Oyo Empire, Lisabi who was never a King in Abeokuta emerged to liberate the Egba, Ogedegbe Agbogungboro, of Ilesha, Lagelu of Ibadan, Shou of Ogbomosho, and Afonja of Ilorin whose link with the Alimi of the Sokoto Caliphate finally nailed the coffin of the Oyo Empire that had suffered from over expansionism in the south of Niger as noted by Late Professor Adu Boahen, a Ghanaian and a world class authority on History in his book on West Africa History and Professor Ade Ajayi also in his book on West African tribes.

Above, the River Niger simultaneously, was the Sokoto Caliphate led by Othman Dan Fodio growing after he was expelled by Yunfa from Gobir, which became the umbrella of his Jihad movement and the spread of Islam to every nooks and crannies of the North of Nigeria but was prevented by River

Niger to make a strategic impact in the South of Niger river for logistical reasons.

There was no ferry in those days to move the horses the strength of the Caliphate to capture the cities in the South of Niger in the present West of Nigeria, which must be one of the reasons, it limited the growth of the Islamic Empire of the Caliphate, strictly, to the North of Niger river, spanning across West Africa Sub region.

Also, Oyo Empire, which had a history of ruthlessness and voodoo, which the Caliphate was not sure off until the weakness of the Oyo Empire was exposed to the Caliphate first with crack of Owu war in 1820 and Afonja of Ilorin a deserter of the Oyo Empire in collaboration with Alimi, a Fulani, which became the major and unfortunate reason Ilorin a Yoruba town fell to the Caliphate in religion and political control till today.

Afonja action by extension remained one of the most unfortunate history of Yoruba nation till today, instead of the Yoruba City of Ilorin to have an Oba (King) like other Yoruba Cities, the city is under the control of Emir a representative of the Caliphate and some still wondered if this issue would be addressed in future for political correctness, time will tell.

Somehow, the Sokoto Caliphate was also limited in conviction to overrun Bornu Empire led by the Sheu, which had already accepted Islam before Othman Dan Fodio and his creation of Sokoto Caliphate, yet the rivalry and hidden jealousy could not be openly displayed but it was there. Both were handicapped by Islam to attack each other, however, both treated each other with contempt, which was the reason behind late Gen. Sanni Abacha a Kanuri man from Old Bornu Empire, as Head of State of Nigeria between 1993 to 1998 was able to depose and banned into exile the Sultan of Sokoto Alhaji Dansuki without any sentiment or respect for the history of the Caliphate and divided the North into three regions of North West, North Central and North East to finally weaken the Caliphate without any nostalgic memory of the strength of the Caliphate in the 18-19th Centuries.

The control of the whole Northern Region by the Caliphate has now been limited to North West alone but the institutions of Emirs created by Othman Dan Fodio still remain the remote hands of the Caliphate, which has not been challenged or questioned but it will in future.

Unlike the Oyo Empire, which lost the controlling role of its representatives in most the Yoruba Cities after the revolution and unfinished Yoruba wars before the British colonized Nigeria, the Caliphate kept its hold on the Cities of the North, as the representatives became the Emirs of

most the cities and held their allegiance only to Islam
and Sokoto Caliphate and the Sultan of Sokoto was
regarded as the Spiritual Islamic leader and by
extension, the political power of the North.

The Caliphate adopted the policy of
assimilation in the North as the captured tribes were
forced to learn Hausa/Fulani language in addition,
to Islam, as the only religion thereby destroying the
African religion or culture of the people for the new
found faith.

The Middle Belt of Nigeria, however,
continue to be belligerent to the control of the
North by the leftover of the Caliphate that has now
been eroded with western civilization which was
analyzed by this writer in a published article " "The
Clash of Civilizations Vs. West Africa values" early
last year.

The clash in religion and values could be
traced to the rediscovery of nationality by the people
of Middle Belt and preferences for another religion
other than Islam, which was imposed on them by
the Caliphate, which was assumed settled by the
Caliphate and Islam but it was not, the middle belt
States continue to think and act like the Southerners
to the dismay and chagrins of the core North.

This has made the core north not to accept
middle belt as true Northerners, but unbelievers and

traitors to the goals and interest of the North, and probably one of the reasons for religious crises in Jos

The glaring nationalistic tendencies, of the suppressed tribes of the North by the Caliphate will be the challenges of the twenty-first century as these tribes continue to finds solace in Christianity, even, if it is to challenge the authorities that made them to lose their dignity since the time of Dan Fodio.

Hence, the Junkuns, the Tivs, the Egbira, and Nupes will as events will unfold itself, as Nigeria trudges towards being their own man or continue to ally with the South of Nigeria, which has adopted the western civilization as the yardstick to measure development as against the core north that still invest in Alimonjiri education with disdain for an education that can compete with the South of Nigeria. The cooperation of middle belt and the south was displayed in the last election, a silent war to finish off the Caliphate and its legacy.

However, twenty-first century will witness lots of changes in power control in the North of Nigeria, and recent attack of the Emirs in the North after the last Presidential elections, which Gen. Buhari a favorite of the core North lost, was an eye opener like the powers of the representatives of the Oyo empires were destroyed so will the control of the Emirs over the territories controlled by the Caliphate will be weakened to provide a leverage for the oppressed tribes of the North to catch up with their southern counterparts for them to see democracy as a game of Numbers and a win in one's village does not necessarily translated to national victory for any individuals.

Finally, the sad part of this liberation is that it has taken the North a long time to understand the Sokoto Caliphate had more interest than religion in mind when it captured the cities of the North and destroyed the spiritual and political heritage of these unsuspecting tribes to keep millions of people in bondage and almost 200 years to catch up with the south to free themselves from oppressor and feudal control but it is indeed a welcome development for the future of Democracy in Africa largest concentration of black people and it will not be long before the issue of religion and its benefits between Islam, Christianity and Africa religions will be placed on the table for discussion.

If and when the issue is place on the table, all the dirty linings of the religions will be exposed and no one will be fooled again because the Alimonjiri will abandon the traditional Islamic education for western education to be fully integrated into Nigeria mainstream.

It will be the dreams of everyone to see this great country takes its place among developed nations, and when that happens? It will be difficult to stop the train again with religion, ethnic or tribal politics.

Last week the Oracle asked if the Boko Haram was the last foot soldiers of the defunct Sokoto Caliphate or why will the Sultan of Sokoto asked the government of President Jonathan Ebele Goodluck for amnesty for a group of people whose objective is to remove civilization from the region once controlled by the Caliphate instead of condemnation from the Sultan.

They got sympathy, thereby making a mockery of the deaths of several Nigerians, Muslims, Christians, and non-believers inclusive in a region still and technically loyal and very consistent with belief of Othman Dan Fodio, which was to spread Islam to every nooks and crannies of the Nigeria or to use the language of late Sardauna of Sokoto to spread Islam to the Atlantic ocean. The group was claimed to have originated from Chad or Niger Republic but the truth is simple they are Nigerians sponsored to disorganize the country.

Our dreams or joys can't be attained at the detriment of other people, when we deny others the rights to practice their religion, trade or be who they are, we are no longer human beings, we lose the right to be respected or reckoned with in a civilized world. This is my belief.

Mr. Eric Holder the Attorney Gen. of the United States was asked to defend the rights of citizenship of those who took side with Al Qaida against the people of America, or if an American terrorist should be killed overseas or within the conclave of America society. Eric Holder technically said citizenship rights can be lost whenever you take up arms against your country. So it is with Boko Haram. They have lost the right to be called Nigerians.

In December 2011 the Oracle was in Abuja, and even attended services in some of the Churches in the Federal Capital Territory (FCT) I wrote beautifully on the city of Unity for all Nigerians, and just three weeks after, on the eve of Christmas, innocent Nigerians, women, and children in a Catholic Church were killed by Boko Haram.

The question to ask each other then was why any sane person would ask Nigerians particularly the North to revert to all those objectives that could keep the Region back from meeting the challenges of the twenty-first century? Or why would anyone ask for amnesty for those killers if the person asking for amnesty was not a disciple of the group itself?

The Oracle was made to understand, Boko Haram means no to western education, no to western ways of life, no to Christianity, or Liberal Islam, or African religion, no to LGBT, no to women's rights, acceptance of child abuse and the spread of Alimonjiri as a way of recruiting the spread of it goals and objectives to all corners of the North and in future declare North of Nigeria as Islamic country if all the above objectives can be attainable.

Secondly, some President Jonathan's political opponents, like Gen. Buhari of recent said Boko Haram was indeed the baby of the presidency for his bad leadership. The Oracle jokingly asked for the DNA of this hydra Headed child to know who the father was, which was the reason for the title of that article to be able to trace what could be the motivation of this senseless killers in a society, which the black race still believe will lead them to the promised land.

So let us go back to history, to compare the goals of the defunct Caliphate with that of the modern day Boko Haram, how did the Caliphate in the 19th Century treat those regions or tribes that failed to accept the spread of Islam in the 18th Century? Were they spared with their culture or religion? Or was the policy of assimilation the birth of fundamentalism in Nigeria? What led to the end of the Caliphate? The Oracle is asking too many questions some would say.

Somewhere in Gobir there was an Islamic scholar and teacher, preaching and spreading Islam in his own way, his name was Usman Dan Fodio, but when one of his former students Yunfa became the leader of Gobir he restricted the activities of his former teacher? Why? He had better information of what the teachings of his former teacher could lead to.

A challenge to a system he was to lead in future and as soon as he had the power to be the leader of his community or town he used it on Usman Dan Fodio who left the city with his followers to the city of Gudu on exile, and those who left with him became his foot soldiers to defeat all the vassals cities formerly under Yunfa the leaders of Gobir, between 1804-1808.

Katsina, Daura and Kano were all captured by the Usman Dan Fodio soldiers, in 1807 Dan Fodio defeated Gobir to confirm the fear of Yunfa who knew and had suspected his mission as a student that he Usman Dan Fodio was a man who wanted to use religion to build an empire himself. Was Yunfa right on the long run? Yes he was.

However, between 17th and 18th centuries, Bornu Empire had lost the control of the oasis town of Bilma and other access to the trans-Sahara trade routes as far back as 1759, the loss created room for vassal empires to emerged like Gobir itself, Kebbi and Zamfara, but it never created the freedom they wanted from Bornu empire, they fought each other and sold each other away as slaves including over taxing each other to maintain unending and continuous wars.

The rivalry between these empires created the crack that enabled the empire Usman Dan Fodio was using religion as a weapon to create, and it was not long before his dream became reality and later after the Caliphate became reality, the spine of control was between him and his brother who was situated in Guwandu till 1815, which he ran the Caliphate as Caliph. In the primitive Nigeria society Emir Guwandu was a powerful as Sultan of Sokoto. (Maybe readers will understand why in future Gen. Buhari was powerless in case of fifty-three suit cases)

After the Caliphate had destroyed the Oyo Empire and had been checked mated by the Ibadan soldiers the Caliphate faced decline and it led to administrative cracks and wars in Adamawa and Kano emirates but the first crack that broke the camel's back of the caliphate was when in 1891 when a French explorer Parfait –Louis Monteil visited Sokoto and realized how vulnerable the Caliphate was with the accession of an unpopular Caliph Abdurrahman Dan Abubarkar.

It was his intelligence report the British government used to penetrate the Caliphate in 1902 and the fruitless attempt by Caliph Attahiru (1) to defend the city was defeated and was replaced by Attahiru (two) in 1903 the first Attaihiru was killed when he tried to reclaim his Caliphate and in 1903 the Caliphate was abolished and it was shared between the British, France and Germany in the spirits of the letters of Berlin Conference of 1885.

It was the birth of Northern Protectorate and Lord Luggard became the Governor Gen. with instruction from England. Somehow the ideas of the Caliphate and that of the Usman Dan Fodio never left the ruminants of the empire that was the largest and most powerful in the Sub Sahara until British conquest in 1903.

Somehow those who still believed the Caliphate influence never stopped thinking on how the influence of modern civilization had eroded the unity the North had under the control of the caliphate. Averagely, when the Northern leaders talked of the interest of the North, it is indeed the interest of what the Caliphate stood for, a region under one religion and a liberal Moslem is a negation of the core North ideas.

More like President Putin of Russia still sees the trace of loyalty of the old principles of Socialism of USSR in the twenty-first century despite several decades of changes that has moved his country a little to the left, which is why those who criticized his government or opposed it were killed including the billionaire killed of recent in great Britain. So it is, with those still looking with nostalgia the glorious days of the Caliphate in the modern Nigeria. Those people represent the strength of Boko Haram in the North of Nigeria.

Which is why the North is not bold enough to see the senseless journey the group is leading the North of Nigeria to? Is Boko Haram carrying the dreams of the Caliphate or just a pipe dream of the misguided believers? Why is the North afraid to call a spade a spade? Why is the whole North treating Boko Haram with kid's gloves?

Is the Northern leadership treating Boko Haram like the Republican Party is treating the Tea Party as a Pressure group within conservative's political group in America? Let them do the dirty Laundry of the party and if it works we take the glory and if it fails you are on your own?

Is possible to assume Boko Haram is doing the dirty laundry of two sets of people in Nigeria, the political class that failed to understand the tenets of democracy that when a President dies his Deputy must take over even if the dead President was only in office for two days, equally failing to understand the letters of the constitution and politics as a game of numbers and winning depends on who gets the Highest votes?

Secondly, it must be assumed that who thinks Boko Haram is a continuation of the dreams of Othman Dan Fodio to Islamized Nigeria or that of deadly dreams of Bornu Empire, with conservative Islamic Ideas must the root cause of the problem in Nigeria.

After several decades, the dreams was reactivated by the supporters of Sharia laws in a country with many religions, it was a problem former President Obasanjo used the wrong method to solve by allowing Governor of Zamfara State to get away with the re-opening of principles of Sharia laws that tends to scare the liberal Muslims from reality of seeing Nigeria as a multi religious society, which could be the tips that encouraged the group called Boko Haram to tap into the empire of the Al-Qaida to establish it activities in Nigeria. Like Professor Koura said, Gen. Obasanjo could have asked for Supreme Court to clear the air on the implication of Sharia law, which was one of the greatest mistakes of his administration.

Furthermore, all the governors of the North of Nigeria are now by omission or commission financing the Boko Haram with security votes, as reported of recent, but the most disturbing was the recent assassination attempt on the respected Emir of Kano, Adu Bayero a very good friend of *Ooni of Ife Oba Sijuade Olubushe* and by extension a good friend of the Yoruba or to larger extend a great and complete detribalized Nigerian.

The Oracle took a cursory look at the life styles of Adu Bayero who became Emir of Kano in 1963 who should be eight-two years old by the time of this publication. (*Ado Bayero died early in the month of June 2014*) He became Emir at a time Nigeria was going through social and political changes. He was Nigeria Ambassador to Senegal, a man who embraced western education, as a means of modernizing Nigeria and indeed his people, even though, he had problems with the late Governor Rimi of Kano and was restricted by the military for his overseas travels along with his friend Oba Sijuade. Both of them were great disciple of stock market.

The Emir represented the best of what to expect from an Islamic leader operating in a multi religious society like Nigeria. He was a liberal Islamic leader with western education. Leaders who had seen and been to the mountain top, he knew the purpose of education and development, which must be the reason the fundamentalist, targeted his life and gratefully to God, this good Nigerian was alive until the month of June 2014.

Adu Bayero was a man who believed in Stock market, a business man, and the pride of modern Nigeria. At eighty-two, Ado Bayero until his death he was above all Nigerians from the North in terms of nation building.

Kano State is the arrow Head of change and a better North of Nigeria to expect from all in the twenty-first century, which is why the State is the target of Boko Haram and Nigeria must not allow Kano or any State of the North to be taken over by this evil called Boko Haram. Nigerian must purge the Boko Haram away before we lose the Republic.

Can the Oracle access the current Sultan of Sokoto who is asking the President of Nigeria to grant amnesty to Killers of Nigerian Children, Killers of Nigerian Christians, Killers of Women, killers of liberal Muslims? Does this Sultan have feelings for the dead Nigerians and their families?

Is Boko Haram the child of President Jonathan as claimed by Gen. Buhari and if not who is the baby's father in Nigeria or the father in Sokoto or somewhere in Chad Republic or Niger Republic even in Cameroon?

The Oracle will advise the President not to give in to the amnesty. If he does, it will be unfair to the dead and those who believe in the unity of Nigeria with freedom to all religions and rights of women, children. In fact it will be disservice to the civilized world. Will the amnesty include compensation for those who died, their children, families, and friends?

The Oracle says Amnesty is not the best option; it is even a sign of weakness and the beginning of chains of unfavorable events. The voice of the Liberals in the North of Nigeria is being silenced with constant attacks on Kano the arrow Head of liberalism in the North of Nigeria and some areas of North with liberal tendency by Boko Haram and fundamentalists asking for amnesty. Ummm!! The Fear of Yunfa of Gobir in the 18th Century is now the fear of Nigeria in twenty-first century.

The Oracle says, let my readers go back to history before the entity called Nigeria is destroyed like Gobir was by the Jihadists, because it is coming like the wild winds of the desert. In fact we have less than five years to fight the evil called Boko Haram or we will not have Nigeria again as we now know it.

Late Major Okar saw this problem years ahead of us, far also in history Yunfa of Gobir saw it in the 18th Century. He lived with the fear himself first as a student of Othman Dan Fodio and when he became the leader of his community, he took action which was not enough; if he had killed Othman Dan Fodio the seed might not have been planted. His failure became the nemesis of the Islamic North of Nigeria on what eventually consumed him and his Kingdom.

If we fail today, the same problem will consume Nigeria because the spirit of the Caliphate is still alive in the hearts of the fundamentalist to turn Nigeria or North of Nigeria to an Islamic State and in future, if they succeed the Middle Belt, which now embrace western civilization and freedom of religion, rights of men and women will be hard hit and it will spread down below Niger and Benue rivers.

The Option aside from war against Boko Haram is for President Jonathan to send a copy of the Nigeria constitution for ratification to each of the State in the North to ratify and accept the supremacy of the Constitution over any religious sentiment, which according to Professor Bankole Okuwa was a failure on the part of Obasanjo's government who could have asked for Supreme Court interpretation and implication of the Sharia law when Governor of Zamfara State introduced it about twelve years ago.

President Jonathan can seek the loyalty of the North to the corporate entity called Nigeria with the ratification of the 1979 constitution, right now based on several actions or inactions of the Northern States will rather take the Quran over the Constitution of Nigeria, and this is not acceptable in a secular State like Nigeria with loyalties to several other religions apart from Islam, several tribes, and approach to civilization.

Let the truth be mentioned, we honestly still don't have the complete loyalty of the North to the letters of the Constitution of Nigeria, given the option right now the North prefers the Quran to the Constitution of Nigeria. Am I wrong?

The problem with a topic of this nature in Nigeria indeed in the North of Nigeria is how to separate religion from history. That confusion led many contributors from the North of Nigeria to be skeptical, to the point of being rude, but the Oracle behind the forum asked for readers to be guided with the attitude of polished minds of education, and he reminded them to be guided with the definition of education given by late Professor Fafunwa a Minister of Education in Babangida regime.

Fafunwa defined education as freedom from ignorance, of ideas, of history and events of any sentiment of ones surrounding. This topic is for academic purposes only, which is to give readers and contributors critical thinking on the sources of Nigeria problem, which Pressure groups like Boko Haram, now represents.

With the above in mind, let us go back to the subject of discourse, which the Oracle says Boko Haram is more of the DNA or the last foot soldiers of the Caliphate. If you have not read parts 1 & two please read, otherwise you may be making a fool of yourself, or be lost in the loop, if not, you may be asking questions on issues already trashed out by contributors and we may not have the time to re-address already solved or agreed issues.

Boko Haram as the last foot soldiers of the Caliphate is not an attack on Islam, but on the fundamentalists, the conservative Muslims and those who failed to understand that in a world of seven billion people, or a nation with over 150 million people, a secular society like Nigeria, with history of oppression—from themselves, from the manner they worship God or whatever they believe in—with the control from foreign government from the Berlin conference of 1885 when the partition of the Africa continent was done in a very selfish way without any remote consideration for the feelings, culture and tradition of the affected people, history with critical thinking is the way such a society can address its problem.

Boko Haram is not asking us question on what went wrong. This group of killers of children, women, Christians, and moderate or liberal Muslims of the North of Nigeria, it is probably asking this nation to go back to the past, to be an Islamic State, to believe in the language of force, remove all the gains of the last hundred years, including denying freedom of religion, freedom of women, children and our ability to live with each other without any fear or favor.

In other words, Boko Haram wants to turn back the clock to how the caliphate left it 100 years ago, from intolerance of the religion of Othman Dan

Fodio with the introduction of Caliphate, which destroyed many political and tribal set up, not only in the North but the Old Oyo Empire itself, which suffered from over expansionism and inordinate ambitions of emerging Yoruba empires like the Ilorin through Afonja Ibadan, Egba, Ijebu and finally the Kiriji wars, (*Kiriji Wars: The Unfinished Wars of the Yoruba is a topic the Oracle is writing on which is already into part two for those reading my posting or go to www.kpcPress.wordPress.com*)

To the Liberals of the Islamic society of the twenty-first century, both believed in the language of force, the hatred in the minds of conservative Muslims did not happen in one night, it was planted from generation to generation from the time Othman Dan Fodio destroyed Yunfa and his community Gobir, i.e. to hate non-Muslims or be forced to worship one God.

We will be connecting the dots and pluses of the missing link and how Nigeria became a problem for itself and if the black man is capable of making an egalitarian society for himself in a world now wired together like a global village controlled by western civilization and glory of the past and control of the people though negative forces of religion, or tradition must be jettisoned for the development of the society and the people. The topic here is more or deeper than Islam. It is the future of the nation called Nigeria in the South of Sahara, to require the core north to understand the act of operating in a secular State.

When Gen. Gowon introduced NYSC programs in the early seventies, one of the goals of the programs was to enable Nigerians with a degree from any institution of Higher learning to see Nigeria, understand Nigeria, and think more like Nigerians instead of parochial way the nation was before he became the Head of State?

Did the programs achieve its goal? Yes, it is water down approach on how to remove tribalism, through interstate marriages, friendship, and for Nigerians to go to forbidden or scary part of the nation.

Today, the society has now been assisted with internet and social media like Facebook to bridge the gap of ignorance, which now exposes us to the happenings in other part of the world or country with just a click. Those who believed Boko Haram is not the last foot soldiers of the Caliphate may not have crossed river Nigeria.

They still live with the biased stories handed over to them from generation to generation. They worship the same God that was handed over to them, they will not open their minds to discuss issues in the Quran or Bible, to search for knowledge, to ask questions, to even read the Quran or Bible for the purpose of checking facts and interpret it on their own becomes a problem or be seen as being anti-Islam.

All the disciples of the above somehow, failed to accept the definition of education, as given by Professor Babs Fafunwa as freedom from ignorance instead they listened to die hard mean people with hatred for the unity of Nigeria except if Quran will be seen as being above the Constitution of Nigeria and very unfortunate most of the average Northerners would rather listen to this uninformed, unpatriotic Islamic leaders rather the unity of the country, and those liberals like the Emir of Kano with bigger picture must be eliminated.

We can no longer stand and watch the elimination of those who believe in the unity of Nigeria by this evil and terrorists called Boko haram.

Many of the acceptable issues of the past may not stand the test of twenty-first century, which is to correct and move on which is why the Liberal North, the educated Muslims of the North must stand up and join their Southern brothers and Sisters to condemn the Boko Haram, not just with mouth but by denying the group any root to survive or live in the society called Nigeria and this can be done by cutting all the secret funding of the group, the security votes of the State government must not be used to fund Boko Haram otherwise it is a way of funding the enemy of the nation.

We can go down the memory lane of history on how most religious intolerance from 1903 became the way the North dominated the Nigeria Army, how the secret police of the North became the mobile police of Nigeria, how the East became the victims of religious intolerance and political manipulation, how the man whose party asked the British to grant Nigeria independence was jailed and events that led to the civil war that killed two million Nigerians not Igbo alone but all Nigerians.

We can read and write on Maitasini group, to the beheaded people of Igbo Origin in the North, we can do it, yes we can, but it will not change anything, unless we remove the seed of ignorance, and fear of searching for knowledge, from the Bible, Quran, and religion left to us by our forefathers.

When Yunfa the leader of Gobir noticed the problem Othman Dan Fodio was going to plant in his community, he failed to do ultimate, he sent his former teacher out of his community, which became the group that started Jihad in the North of Nigeria in the eighteenth century. His approach was cosmetic; Yunfa was consumed just like the revolution consumed Louis XVI of France, which led to French revolution in 1789.

In the same way President Obasanjo failed to do the ultimate by not removing the seed of Sharia when Zamfara State introduced it about twelve years ago. According to Professor Bankole Okuwa, he said the former President Obasanjo should have asked for Supreme Court interpretation on the Zamfara action. The Oracle said, Obasanjo could have taken the same route of President Abraham Lincoln of the United States by sending soldiers to protect the rights of the minority religions in the State of Zamfara. President Obasanjo's failure to take action became the tentacles, which the former seed of Caliphate was re-planted or renewed.

The Oracle says if we fail to remove the seed of Boko Haram now, and if we don't stand together as a nation with the fear of God and respect for human dignity, freedom of religion, respect for women and Children, right to trade, and live in any part of the nation freely without someone breathing at the back of your neck with local religious police or preachers of hatred in the mosques and churches, we are by omission or commission asking Boko Haram to change us to what we are not.

Finally, if we continue to fund Boko Haram through our tactical support or through our inactions or if we fail to separate history from religion in analyzing issues affecting the unity of Nigeria we may not have a Nigeria as we now know it in the next five to ten years. Oracle says, Boko Haram or the doctrines of the Caliphate in any form is not the best option for Nigeria in the twenty-first century. A liberal society for all must be based on freedom of religion, respect for women, children and a conducive society, which leadership can be asked question and a society that will place everything on the table for discussion including our religion and tradition. This is the only acceptable way to move Nigeria forward from a mere geographical expression in the twenty-first century.

ARTICLE TWO

Mayoral System of Government

In 1886, Thomas Hardy wrote the book, The Mayor of Casterbridge a classic masterpiece novel and one of the books my generation had to read in the early seventies, it was the story of a young man who was drunk and without thinking, auctioned away his wife and baby daughter. When he came back to his senses, it was too late; he vowed never to touch alcohol again. Somehow, he became rich and became the Mayor of the city of Casterbridge, his story ended with his reunion with his wife and daughter almost seventeen years later. He had lived a secretive life from the people who had thought by implication, he was a widower and expected him to re-marry a young and beautiful lady he was seeing, but he could not because legally he was still married to his auctioned wife. When he remarry his ugly old wife the people said, "He waited too long to achieve very little."

The first known legal backing for a mayoral system of Administration could be found in the Municipal Corporation Act of 1882 section 15 of Great Britain. It explained the formation and procedure for the mayoral system of administration in towns and cities in Great Britain, in this law, it was a one year term, and he may appoint a deputy in case of illness or incapacity that will be less than two months else he loses his mayoral responsibilities.

Until the law was abolished a woman if elected or appointed as mayor would be addressed as Mayoress.

Mayoral system could be classified as weak or strong system in the administration of towns and municipal cities. Both could be influenced by the personality of the holder of the office of mayor or the law that established the system, meaning, a weak Mayor can still make a mockery of a strong mayoral system or a strong mayor can also make the best out of a weak system. Everything is embodied in the personality of any office holder. For example, Gen. Obasanjo as President was different from that of late President Yar'Adua or current President Ebele Azikiwe Jonathan even though they were elected into the office with the same constitution.

In a weak Mayoral System, the Mayor lacks the veto power over the Council votes. He or she cannot appoint, or remove officials without the approval of the council. Strictly, the system is based on Jacksonian Democracy, meaning a weak Mayor or politician is a harmless one.

In a strong mayoral system, the mayor forms the executive branch of the government for the town or city, he can appoints and fires the city manager and any departmental Heads, he is the chief law officer of the city, he can appoint the city police chief, he is only responsible to the electorates of the town and his actions also can only be challenge in any court of the city. An example of this, could found in most Cities in America like Dallas, Chicago, and New York. A mayor is as strong and as powerful as the Governor of the State.

Most towns with over 25,000 citizens may qualify to run this type of administration but there is no yardstick for determining the population criteria since a town with 31 citizens like Emelle, Alabama by 2000 census has a current Roy Willingham as the mayor of the town. The town is known to be the largest hazardous wastes landfill in the United States.

In the United States, with strong mayoral system, a mayor is the leader in the city or town. He is first among equals on the city council, which also acts as the legislative body, and somehow, the Mayor appoints the city Manager to run the day to day administration who acts as the CEO of the City. The city Manager must be a man or woman with a master's Degree in Public administration with MBA for him or her to understand the actual job of managing people.

With the above understanding of what Mayoral System is, it will be just fine to see how this can be of help to Nigeria and probably put an end to un ending demand for States agitation when in actual fact all the people are asking for, by omission or commission is the closeness of the government to the grassroots, all, which can be solved with the establishment of strong Mayoral system.

Can this system work in Nigeria if we try it all? Will President Jonathan and the National Assembly take a look at this idea or like the rest of the suggestions given to him in past on State and city Police be thrown overboard?

The Oracle will survey this method of solving the states agitation with the benefits of Strong Mayoral system in principal Cities and State Capitals to start with, until the rest of the nation can feel the impact, the question is, what will be the role of the Obas and Emirs and Obis in the new dispensation? Somehow we have practiced Mayoral system in the sixties in Nigeria and how would it be applied to the rural situation and what would be the difference from the LGA system that is currently in place one of my readers asked and many more will be addressed.

The first part of this article could be just an ice tip on what to understand about the Mayoral system of government, with some offered suggestions, particularly the role expected of our Obas, Obis and Emirs. Regrettably, the greatest Obstacle to the implementation of this solution to unending demand for States creation may in fact be this mentioned traditional institution. But the Oracle says, there is a way out of this perceived notion if we can break down the various mayoral systems applicable and each State or city should be encouraged to select, which of the systems that suits its environment.

When this program was first introduced in America, just like Nigeria, it was purely rural communities with the exception of three cities, like Boston, New York, and Philadelphia, meaning, Nigeria can take a look at the rural community of each State before implementation of this grassroots oriented administration.

For a city to be recognized it must be incorporated like a Business. It must operate with a city charter or article of incorporation which will be similar to the State constitution. In it, must be stated the powers and limitations of the structured government, which will include the election and appointment procedures.

Readers here must understand that mayoral system could be operated with any of the four types of city articles of Incorporation as mentioned below.

Home Rule: The is probably the most popular and easy to implement because all the people of the city or the locality involved are participants in the formation of Home Rule to form its incorporation which allows the citizens or residents to draft the city articles, which must be placed before the voters for approval and voters must approve, any amendment to the city articles.

The Home rule charter can be granted by the State constitution, or legislation, with a provision that if there is any conflict in future the State law or constitution is above all sentiments, and the State legislature will have the power to revoke the powers of any Home Rule process. The system does not give any power to the State Governor, only the State legislature can fix and unfix the short comings of any Home Rule system.

Gen. Charter: The second method is very flexible, because cities and towns are classified according to population size. The system recognizes the resources and control of the society, and the abilities of the people just like the Home Rule procedures. All powers to amend and accept the charter or the law of incorporation belongs to the voters and again only the State legislature can revoke the method with alternative method. The powers do not reside with any Governor.

Optional Charter: Surprisingly, Optional Charter seems to be the best option, because residents of the locality are able to vote on several areas of the laws they do not want or they want in their community, for example, in a city like Kano or Kaduna, some areas that a Christian controlled can be allowed to do their business or even sell alcohol or grand fathered because that was their ways of life before Sharia became the law of the State.

The above system gives a direct input from every strata of the society into the formation and process of the mayoral control of the cities or towns for them to shape the type of government that is fine with them more like management by objectives.

Special Charter: This is the oldest of all the four, and the power here belongs solely to the State legislature, which may be granted as the condition of the city improves, meaning a city that witnessed a sporadic development can attract special Charter by the State legislature. For example, the population of a White dominated community (Floyd, Texas) was only four hundred according to 2000 U.S. Census. The city does not have any charter.

However by 2005-2013 an all Blacks Nigerian Church, Redeemed Christian Church of God bought almost 700 acres of land for the development of its North America expansion programs like school and yearly conventions.

The first convention attracted over 10,000 Africans, which the conservative community never witnessed before. If the church applies to the State of Texas for the charter because of the population size of its members, if they choose to reside in the community, they will have the power to have their own police, mayor and many more that can change the life style of the white community, and the Special Charter is being consider for the protection of the original land owners.

The same can be applied to the original owners of land in most of our rural community of the country including Abuja and new areas of development to preserve the originality of the society from encroachment from land speculators and culture of the people.

As soon as a city or town is incorporated it must decide, whichever one is workable for the community, from the three known system mentioned below.

1. Mayoral Council System
2. Council Member System
3. Commission system

Mayoral Council System

Here, the Mayor and Unicameral city council must be elected on individual basis, not by political party affiliation, more like independent candidates, the council will have the power to vote or legislate on the running's of the city and the Mayor here, is usually powerful with the ability to veto some of the decisions of the uni-camera council. The bucks stops on the table of the Mayor

Furthermore, he has the power to fire or appoint any of the departmental Heads in the city and like it was first mentioned in part one the mayor is the Chief Law officer of the city. He appoints the city Police, he can also fire the chief of Police even the whole police system.

In the city of Corinth, in Texas in 2006 or so, the city Police was notorious for making the city uncomfortable with funny citations to road users on High Way 35 the major road to the heart of America from Texas. The new Mayor fired the entire police force, and borrowed police officers from the city of Dallas and Lewisville in Texas to run the city until new policemen and women were hired.

The Mayoral Council system, due to Nigeria love of power, is advisable for most our big cities and towns of over 25,000 population size. The

Mayor here can be removed by a two-thirds majority with the approval of the people of the city.

Council Manager System

Here the mayor is weak, ceremonial and the control and running of the city belongs to the appointed city manager, this method could be used in most of our rural community and this where the Obas, emirs, or obis could be used as they will play only ceremonial role.

Commissioned System

A Mayor is chosen among the elected independent commissioners. There will be no political party affiliations. Mayoral leadership here can be rotational, more like the present council of Obas or emirs in most of the States of the Federation. This method gives sense of belonging to every strata of the society, this method is economical. The weakness of this method is too much control or powers with the commissioners as soon as they are elected. Only the State legislature can dissolve these commissioners if petitioned by the people and the process of dissolution is usually cumbersome.

How can this new system affect the present local government structure? Will it gradually fade away the local government structures to a weak local government of commissioners, which will become a part time job? Will this weak local government be the much needed place to keep our Obas, emir, and obis busy? Can the mayoral system work without city police? Can a mayoral system work without the political will of the State of the nation itself? Details will be analyzed in part three.

ARTICLE

THREE

Expanded Primary System EPS

The purpose of an expanded primary system (EPS) is to expand the opportunity of getting all interested candidates to have a fair shot at the presidency notwithstanding sex, race or religion as long as he or she can convince the electorates to vote for him or her. A prospective candidate must meet the requirement of each of the State's electoral Board or INEC requirement in case of non-availability of State requirement like we have now, each State political party must set up a guideline on how a candidate can meet the party requirement.

The Oracle is suggesting the format below. However, the details and finesse of it can be worked out by the experts with the support from INEC to conduct the primary election. It would have been okay if all the parties can do it at the same time, PDP, APC, Labor Party, SDP and others.

To be on the ballot box to run for the office of presidency, a candidate must qualify to be on the approved register list of each State. How can a candidate get the approval? He or she must obtain at least 5000 or designated signatures of party members in the State of those in good standing with the law and a deposit of any reasonable amount to be determined by each State, a police clearance, and proof of tax payment and list of asset declaration that will be published in State or regional circulated newspapers.

The candidate must disclose all his or her financial contributors in the zone to the INEC including monthly contribution on State and national level. This is to prevent the system from being taken over by money bags. Since Nigeria is tentatively divided into six zones—West, North West, North East, South South, East and Middle Belt—the primary election will have to be conducted at the same time in all the States within each zone, while other zone will have to wait. For example, if the East of Nigeria is alphabetically taken as the first zone all the States in the region, like Anambra, Imo, Abia and Enugu must conduct the primary election on the same day.

Other months will be selected for the primaries in the West, North West, North East, South-South, and Middle Belt, meaning we can rotate between North and South until we have been able to conclude the EPS

Each of the candidates would have campaigned in all the States in the region including holding town hall meetings with at least two debates that will involve all the candidates to sell their dreams and plans for Nigerians, for example if Gen. Buhari, Tinubu or Okorocha want to run for presidency, all of them must register their interest with all the party offices in all the States in the East of Nigeria, they must obtain at least 5000 or designated figures from registered voters in the each State of the region to be on the ballot box.

What happen if any of them can't get the 5000 or designated number of signatures of voters in such a State? It is simple. The affected person will not be on the approved list of those to contest in such a State in the primary, and miss the delegates from such State, but it will not stop him for being on the national list if he wins the party ticket on the long run. Winning must be based on the approved delegates. The more States you can win, the more the delegates you will have to get the final nomination of the Party to be ratified at the National Convention.

The above will help to reduce proliferation of political parties in Nigeria and very soon two party systems will become an established institution, not a party structure based on individuals or godfather mentality but a lasting legacy, the same procedure will be followed by the next zone, since East had been taken as the first division for the extended primary EPS, another region presumably in the North will be taken as the next, meaning Buhari, Tinubu or Okorocha would have the same method used in the East to win delegates in the North East, and so on, until all the six zones must have participated in choosing the candidate that will represent the party at the national Presidential election.

In all, we are looking at minimum of 12 debates involving all the candidates and all the citizens would have had the opportunities of asking and knowing the quality of candidates that will be running for the office of president.

Some candidates would have dropped along the way if they are unable to gather enough delegates from one or two zones or after their lack of preparedness must have been detected by the Press and the electorates in the way they answer questions or if their past revealed negative or unpatriotic attitude, this is the beauty of expanded primary system, where the electorates get to know or understand their candidates as the primary goes on.

The National Convention of the party is just a formality that will just be to ratify the results of all the zones of the federation. Can this system work in Nigeria if PDP decides not to go through the same route? This is the questions in the minds of the readers. Yes.

The Oracle says if APC can do this, it will give it a legitimate ground to lay a solid foundation for winning, when the party must have gone through a process of getting sharper and better candidates that will emerge and Nigerians will be properly educated on the what it takes to be a leader of 160 million people and PDP will have no choice, than to follow suit, if PDP fails to adopt similar method it will provide a better opportunity for the electorates to leave the party like bad habit and vote for APC since they plan to be relevant, the party will have to adopt EPS.

Again, the Oracles says the details of EPS is within the political parties and INEC to add flesh to this proposal and if the INEC decides to adopt this expanded primary system EPS, it will help our Democracy a lot. However it will be just okay to give brief benefits of what to expect from this silent political revolution called EPS. With EPS we can solve Nigeria political problems by more than fifty-five percent.

We will be able to eliminate aimless candidates from running for office in Nigeria again. We will be able to re-elect politicians based on performance. Religion will take the back seat, so it is with tribalism, result and performance will be the yardstick for winning, and godfathers may have to find another job. Our Press will become the voice and opinions of the people and those with skeletons in the closets will run away from politics.

The positive effect of it will rob more on our judiciary. They will be too afraid to pervert justice. All our institutions will witness positive change. EPS is the silent revolution of the masses for a better society, based on accountability and result. When we want State and city police for security of our society it will not be stopped. When we ask for mayoral system to develop our towns and cities it will not be challenged by those who don't have anything to offer. Nigeria's train of progress will never be stopped again as all enemies of development will run away and our children and coming generation will be happy to call themselves Nigerians again in any part of the world as a pride to the black race. It will be a revolution that will spread to all the fifty-five countries in Africa.

ARTICLE
FOUR

Is It Possible to Rebuild Nigeria?

When then Senator Obama was running for President of the United States, President Barak Obama gave a speech called "Toward a Perfect Union" on the issue on race, which is available on YouTube.com. The speech has since been ranked among the greatest like that of Martin Luther King's "I Have a Dream." But Barak Obama on race will be the one that is applicable to Nigeria in this very period.

A few weeks ago I visited Philadelphia, the City where the America Constitution was negotiated and signed. In the city of Philly was also the Liberty Bell, which, which several thousands of people lined up to see and at the end of the visit it dawned on me that it was only a white man's history forced on a nation that made the speech of Barak Obama unique and a need for Nigeria to borrow from the expectations of the forty-five minute epistle that, which has since been viewed by more than seven million people to date.

Barak Obama mentioned how the constitution at the time of its creation did not totally address the hopes and anxiety of women, African-Americans, and other minorities. It did however; allow coming generations to perfect the document through amendments, which eventually paved way to free slaves from the strong grip of the southern States, which during the Civil War under President Abraham Lincoln.

There is nowhere in the Bible where slavery is condemned; in fact, the southern States used the Bible to justify keeping slaves as a lucrative business because the Holy Book says, "Slaves obey your master."

Later in American history President Lyndon Johnson from Texas, who succeeded John F Kennedy, signed the law that gave African-Americans the right to participate in United States' political arena. The effect of the law led to the gradual demise of the Democratic Party's dominance in southern States and the actual deaths of many including Martin Luther King and the Kennedy brothers as well as events that paved way for Obama's presidency. As he said in one of his statements, "I ride on the shoulders of giants."

Nigeria at the time of incubation from Herbert Macaulay groups in Lagos, which later included Awolowo, Azikiwe, Saudana of Sokoto Balewa and other medieval generations of Nigeria State agitators did not address the issue of minorities, the hopes of children, religion, and social security for all. It was only based on the need to preserve the hopes and control of Hausa/Fulani, which was a continuation of the Sokoto Caliphate hegemony. In the West among the Yoruba's, it was to protect the relics of the collapsed Oyo Empire and the myth of Oduduwa. And the East is a region always in search of its origin either as a lost tribe of Israel or as a destroyed tribe of Igbo chased out of Ile Ife when Moremi was used to penetrate the myth of the Igbo nation today. Unlike other tribes in Nigeria, no one can say where this vibrant and selfish tribe actually came from, however it spreads from Asaba in the Delta State across the Niger River into the heartland of the Imo River.

Nigeria's first constitutional attempts—from various white men like Sir John Stuart MacPherson to the Rotimi Constitution of 1979 with only "forty-nine wise men" because Awolowo declined to participate under Rotimi—which failed to address the social responsibility of protecting and advancing the hopes of women, children, and minorities as well as the goals of Nigeria within the comity of nations.

Instead, it continued with the status quo of protecting the control of the North, East, and West over the nation with more than 250 tribes betrayed by all the constitutions to date.

The constitution which was written by the military under Gen. Abubarkar, the last military Head of State, is still a relic of the past and a continuation of the same oligarchy and feudal system that, which keeps most progressive minds under bondage and once a progressive mind is able to cross the Rubicon he is forced to keep others in chains without the leans to advance, hence, it has always been difficult to have Leaders or Presidents that will take the nation across the river of progress and remain focused without moving back.

The above could be attributed to the failure of the twice lucky former President Aremu Obasanjo and his failure to sign into laws the most progressive ideas from the last congress or parliament, like the Freedom of Information Act, dissolution of the Federal Police system for State and city police, complete removal of funny looking traditional leaders like Obas, obis, and emirs whose, which dress code does not conform to twenty-first century needs, and who in my opinion which ought to have been replaced with mayors in each city of the nations. Obas, emirs, and obis represent nothing but blood lines of feudal control.

The last administration under Aremu OBJ had all it needed to cross the Rubicon of progressive minds but it failed because it was not intellectually equipped to see beyond the tip of its nose. No wonder its leadership was still in search of the missing link in his academic deficiency after he left office just like Gen. Yakubu Gowon, the Nigerian leader from 1967 to 1975 did after he was kicked out of power.

Can we say academic qualification is a panacea for successful leadership in a nation still in search of its identity? The answer is no and yes. No, because failure and truth are not automatic. When Commodore Lawal, a naval officer with Masters in Business Administration, became the governor of Ogun State when IBB was military President, Ogun State recorded the worst shoplifting in history of governance. He stole rugs, carpets, and conspired to steal and reduced the dual carriage road to a singled way at Idi Aba Abeokuta. When the people of Kwara State elected him as a governor later in the civilian government I said to myself, "Kwara State, bless your hearts."

Yes, it is better to have an educated and focus leadership than to have a President with an unprogressive mind to champion the hopes of millions in the twenty-first century. The rightful place of Nigeria must not be left in the hands of criminals, or the hopes and future of our children with a Congress without any result after two years in office, the present parliament, House or Congress is lazy, corrupt, and lacks focus. This presidency is also lazy, weak, and probably too sick to see the injury its weaknesses and shortcomings are inflicting on the nation.

The Constitution of Nigeria is also very weak in its foundation and goals and it will be difficult to get either a good President out of it or a progressive nation.

Lord Dennings, the Chief Justice of Great Britain, once said, "You cannot put something on nothing."

United States Supreme Court Justice Thurgood Marshall once said, "Illegality cannot stand the test of time."

Nigeria's constitution is a fraud, which does not represent the wishes of the people. It was designed to suppress the hopes of the minority and maintain the status quo.

To rebuild Nigeria, the constitution must be amended quickly by all, not just by few men chosen by the same forces holding back the country. The new constitution must eliminate the Obas, emirs, and obis from the face of governance; it must remove religion in any form from government and once in government leaders must not be addressed as Chief or Alhaji in any form. The new constitution must dissolve and decentralize Nigeria Police with only a reformed EFCC at the Federal level to perform a similar role as the FBI. We have to establish State and city police that, which will replace all the activities of area boys or OPC or Egbesu boys. Furthermore, we need to create a social security system of administration; pay workers per hours or as needed or per diem; let each State or city grow according to its resources; and freedom of information laws must be included to remove all secrecy in governance.

Lastly, the Council of State membership must be abolished in the constitution because the presidency must be freed from any past leadership, which that presently subjects his authority to verifications by past and corrupt leaders. Let us enshrine in the constitution a country operating on a two party system with room only for Independent candidates, if we are to rebuild this nation. If not, we may go the way Austria and Hungary did during the unification of Germany's thirty-nine States during the time of Otto Von Bismarck, move out of the Union and see more of the bombing of oil wells and gas locations all over the Niger Delta. Maybe we can open our eyes to the fraud of the leadership and fake constitution that is keeping us from achieving our potential.

ARTICLE FIVE

Towards Productivity Nigerian Workers Must Be Paid By Hours (May 5ᵗʰ 2005)

Nigerians are by far one of the most resourceful people in the world with little to show for it due to the system of remuneration the country is presently adopting. This article will focus on workers compensation as an effective management tool in a fast developing economy such as Nigeria and it will look into various ways of dealing the shortcomings of the nation's employer's inability to compensate workers efficiently in a very diverse economy which should be the main focus of development in the whole of Africa.

This article was written with an open mind that the country (government and private sectors inclusive) was only paying its staff by salary and commission or commission only with the hope, a new approach will be looked into to increase productivity of the industries and government activity in the present day economy. I will expect constructive positive and negative response after reading this article.

It will be meaningless to place emphasis of salaries as an effective way of compensating workers without looking at the other surrounding factors that facilitate the effectiveness of salaries as one of the ways towards compensation including differential payment, which depends on the time and period of which a worker service is needed, it will be an added advantage i.e. if you work nights or later in the day, you should get paid differently and you even get more if you work on weekends on Saturdays and ever better paid on Sundays which is what differential payment is partly involved.

Although base salary, fringe benefits, productivity and other salient issues that can give workers sense of belonging are one of the ways workers can be part of the decision making body. Individuals must be allowed to negotiate pay rate on hourly basis, subject to a national standard, this gives the opportunity for growth and the negotiation, which must be confidential and non-disclosure, a breach of this agreement on the part of the employer can lead to civil damages, while it can lead to separation of service on the part of the employee, meaning your employer can never disclose your pay to anybody except at the request of the government which must have court order, not even your wife or husband.

Payment per Hour

Again, the only reference this writer could point to was in the sixties and part of the seventies at the time workers were paid twice a month but it is not what payment per hour is out to achieve. Hourly paid workers can put more efforts in the production of activity in any organization more than salary or monthly paid workers. This new procedure will bring the best in them; it decreases the issue of labor organization power and focuses more on performance rather than unimportant issues that labor management sometimes represent. No work, no pay method is one of the objectives of hourly paid system.

The idea of going on strikes and be paid for a job not done does not exist in the payment by hour, meaning, if do not swap your card, you do not get paid. All companies and government agencies must introduce card-punching method of clocking in and out the most current one in the market is the

Kronox System. It does all the calculations for the organization.

Method and Procedure

For continuity and accountability purposes, only management staff i.e. the head of department should only be placed on salary whiles the rest of the workers both in the public and private sectors on hourly payment system. The functional Head of a Department will have his performance measured through results at the end of the day, if he meets the goal of the Board of Directors or that of the group he keeps his job if not he gets fired.

This procedure will keep him or her under constant Pressure to attain his primary goal. He will sleep dreaming of result and wake up thinking the same. The rest of the staff on the other hand will know they are on hourly paid method, they will to work every hour to justify their pay. If they are absent from work they know they will miss the day's pay.

They cannot afford to be lazy or unnecessary absent, meaning, the head of Department or the manager who is constantly under stress will keep his eyes a focus on any shortcoming any anything less than result will lead to termination from the company or organization. The issue of absentee or ghost workers is completely eliminated through clocking in and clocking out most likely through a bio-metric system and control of labor cost is total as this will help the management to keep to budget.

At the end of a work week, the employer must print out the hours worked which must be attached to the paycheck of each worker. All workers must be paid by check or through direct deposit to the employee's banks because direct cash payment can lead to fraud on both parts and is even dangerous as workers' pay may be stolen or robbed, the employer on the other hand must be able to guarantee between 32–40 hours' work per week to keep a staff as full time anything short of this will be regarded as part time, while any hour in the excess of 40 hours is considered overtime depending when the hours are worked a time and half must be paid

Differentials in Payment

The method of differential payment in workers compensation method is perhaps the best for the economy on how Nigeria can move forward in the 21st century. It is an indication that performance is recognized on the employee and employer relationship. If you work nights you get paid differently, if you Saturdays you get paid better and even more if you work Sundays. In this case, it will be possible to keep a ten hours shift of four days and also have the time to have another job.

Pay Negotiation and Attitude.

Applicant must conduct a very deep research on the employer before the date of interview or pay negotiation, the more you know, the better for you and your future. Learn if you can grow in your career with the organization, otherwise, you may be looking for a new job as soon as you join the new company or organization, sometimes it better to look at the faces of the staff. Do they look happy? Or they just hang in there? If you can, visit the company a day before the negotiation for pay, learn to ask question from the staff, visit the company cafeteria, observe the kind of food they are served and the environment, this will indicate if you will be dealing with a stingy and energy sapping management. Again it is your future and that of your family that you hold in your hands.

During negotiation, learn to win favor and respect through smiles and positive attitude. Make yourself a better product. Look your new employer straight in the eyes; maintain eye contact, it shows confidence and it you do join the organization never stopped improving yourself. Keep abreast with the latest information in your profession, and take classes on self-development. Note all vacant positions within six months of joining the organization, ready to move up.

Let your employer know your goal is beyond your present level and if you work for two and half years all roads towards growth are not there move on. Never allow sentiment to becloud your sense of reasoning, not it is your career and future never toy with it. It may be too late to make move in future.

CONCLUSION

In the light of the above, the Nigerian economy will be solely for those who plan to work there, there will be no room for lazy and unproductive workers. The productivity of the Nigerian workers will be improved and recognized tremendously. The present system of remuneration is out dated and cannot move us forward; both the employers and employees including the government tend to gain from this new approach. The Nigeria labor department and Federal government must look into elimination of unproductive legislation for review to keep the nation afloat it is the only way forward for the country to grow in the 21st century.

Index/Words

Abeokuta Club: A social Mother Club to seniors in Egba lands

Abeokuta Elites: A social Club in Abeokuta

Abeokuta: The Capital of Ogun State Nigeria. The tradition home of the Egba

Abeti Aja: Traditional Yoruba Cap

Abiola, MKO: Winner of annulled 1993 Presidential election in

Abuja: The Federal Capital of Nigeria since 1990

Adenekan Yomi: Engineer and director of works in Ogun State

Agbada: Big tradition full regalia dress

Agbongbo Akala: The title given to Lisabi by his people, the Egba

Agemo: The outcome of Alagemo more like masquerade

AGGS: Abeokuta Girls Grammar School

AGS: Abeokuta Grammar School

Ajoke Mohammed: Wife of late Head of State of Nigeria

Akarigbo: The traditional title for the King of Remo in Ogun State

Akintode Col: A military Administrator of Ogun State in Nigeria

Alaafin: The traditional title of Oyo King from Old Oyo Empire

Alaafin: The Traditional title of the King of Oyo

Alaaren: A traditional way to greet the Ijebu people

Alagemo: Traditional Ijebu fetish club

Alake: The paramount ruler of Egbaland

    Also called Sagamu among the Yoruba

Amosun, Ibikunle, the Governor of Ogun State from 2011.

Angola: A country in Central Africa, very rich in crude oil

ArticleBased.com: A news blog for articles

Aselite: Abeokuta Social Elite Club

Asero: Area within Abeokuta City

Awolowo, Obafemi: Leader of Yoruba race

Awori: A sub ethnic group in Ogun State very closes to Lagos

Awujale: The paramount ruler of Ijebuland

Azikiwe: The first President of Nigeria

Balogun, Ayodele Col.: The first Military Governor of Ogun State in

BBHS: Baptist Boys High School Abeokuta

Caliphate: Sokoto Caliphate was a powerful Muslim Empire established by Othman Dan Fodio

CBN: Central Bank of Nigeria commissioned in 1968

Cooper & Lybrand: An Accounting Firm in Lagos

Ebora Owu: The unpredictable one of his Owu ethnic group

EFCC: Nigeria equivalence of FBI

Egba: The people of Abeokuta and its surrounding villages and

Egbado now called Yewa: A sub ethnic group in Ogun State part of old Abeokuta provinces now named after Yewa River.

Eghagha Col: The last military Governor of Ogun State before 1979

Egun: A sub ethnic group in Lagos and Ogun State Empire

Esu Laa Lu: Satan.

Gangan: Yoruba local talking Drums

GPC: Gateway Pharmaceutical Company Ijebu Ode

Guwandu: Second most powerful Emirate after Sokoto in Nigeria

Hoover dam: A dam in Boulder County Nevada in the United States

Ibadan: The capital city of Old Western Region/State and Oyo State

Ijebu Ode: The City Headquarters of the Ijebu people in Ogun State

Ijebu: The people of Ijebu towns

Ikere: The ear of Idowu comes naturally or can be implanted

Irukere: Made from Horse tail. A symbol of authority held by Yoruba

Iya Ilu: The Big talking Drums

Juju: Voodoo assumed to have been discovered in Nigeria among the Yoruba.

Kainji: Hydroelectricity dam across Niger River built in 1964 and

Kano: A powerful City in the North of Nigeria

Kiriji: The internal Yoruba wars before the British colonization in 1914

KpcPress.com: A news Blog of Korloki Publishing company

Kuto: An area within Abeokuta City

Lagos: Former Capital of Nigeria and Seat of government of Lagos

LGS: Lisabi Grammar School Abeokuta

Lipede, Oyebade: The Alake of the Egbaland between

Lisabi Elite: A social club in Abeokuta

Lisabi: The first known Hero of the Egba who freed them from Oyo

Macaulay, Herbert: Founder and father of Nigeria Nationalism

Mohamed, Muritala: Nigeria Assassinated Head of State in 1976 mount ruler

Neto, Augustinho: First President of Angola

Nigeria in 1976 Nigeria.

O ma her o: What a pity

OAU: See Unife, Obafemi Awolowo University

Oba: Yoruba name for the King

Obantoko: An area within Abeokuta City

Obasanjo, General: Twice elected Nigeria President and Military

Obatala: The god of creation according to the Yoruba tribe in Africa

Of America

Ogun Poly: Ogun State Polytechnic now called MAPOLY

Ogun River: The source of this river is Kishi in the Kwara State

Ogun State: A State carved out of Western States in Nigeria in 1976

Ogun: The god of Iron usual worship by motor drivers and hunters

Ojude Oba: A popular Ijebu festival

Ojukwu: Leader of Biafra between 1967 to1970

Olumo Rock

Ondo State: A State carved out of Western States in Nigeria in 1976

Opeke: A damsel or young lady

Oranmiyan: The last born of Oduduwa the progenitor of the Yoruba

Oriaku: Igbo word for consumer of wealth

Orunmila: The god of divinity according to the Yoruba tribe in Africa

Oshun State: A State carved out of Oyo States in Nigeria in 1991

Owambe: Easy going and party loving group

Owode: A city in Owode Egba local government

Oyo Empire: Defunct Empire of the Yoruba people

Oyo State: A State carved out of Western States in Nigeria in 1976

Oyo: New Oyo town that emerged after the destruction of Old Oyo people

Sagamu: The City Headquarters of the Remo people in Ogun State

Shekere: Percussion in Yoruba music

Top Beer: Brand for a local beer in the Nigeria in the seventies
          Towns

U.I: University of Ibadan established in 1948

Unife: University of Ife now Obafemi Awolowo University

Unilag: University of Lagos

Wahala: Yoruba word for problem

Werepe: A skin scratching powder from wild leaves

Whydah: The unverified source of the Ijebu by Awujale the paramount ruler of Ijebuland

Yewa: Formerly called Egbado

Bibliography

Ajayi, Ade, & Smith, Robert 1964 PhD   *Yoruba Warfare in the 19ᵗʰ Century* Cambridge Press

Arinze, Francis, PH.D. 1970. *Sacrifice in Igbo Religion* Ibadan University Press Nigeria

Boahen, Adu. PhD 1965 *Topics in West African History Longman* Press United Kingdom

Olabintan, Afolabi Ph.D. 1994 *"The graces, the grasses and the gains"* Nigeria

Sowunmi Zents MBA. 2011 "W*hat happened to our Democracy*?" Korloki Publishers NY USA

Sowunmi, Zents MBA. 2011" *Before the journey became Home"* Korloki Publishers NY USA

Bibliography

http://www.wisegeek.com/what-does-dog-eat-dog-mean.htm

GUARDING RULES

- ❖ Keep the smile on, it is good for the heart, besides it is free.

- ❖ Never allow the devil to take your joy away.

- ❖ Learn to understand we operate in the world of demons and angels.

- ❖ Give hope to the needy

- ❖ Encourage not discourage

- ❖ Find Humor in everything

- ❖ Learn to laugh at your own mistakes

- ❖ Keep going, if you stop you are done with.

- ❖ Don't take all your advice from failures you might be one yourself.

The Oracle with Pat ILO @ Brighton Beach Brooklyn New York 2013

With Late Zig Ziglar and Della Faye in Dallas Texas 2008

Inside the Basilica Rome Italy 2013

New Release Books from Korloki Publishing Company

New Release Books from Korloki
Publishing Company

Other Books from this Author

Zents Kunle Sowunmi is the President/CEO of the Allzents Groups Inc. a Business Consulting, Staffing/Training and Publishing Corporation with offices in Dallas Texas and Brooklyn New York. Zents Kunle Sowunmi was a staff of US Army Warrior Transition Battalion Fort Bliss, Texas until February 2011.

He holds an MBA and several certifications. He is the author of *Before the Journey Became Home, President Obama: Hero or Villain of Capitalism? Ogun State Policy of Manipulation since 1976 and the Covenant Breakers,* he is also working on several other publications.

Fondly called **The Oracle** by his admirers, Zents Sowunmi lives in Brooklyn, New York, USA. He enjoys walking by the Brighton Beach for relaxation.